A Good Life

by

Ali Zentner

DORRANCE PUBLISHING. CO., INC.
PITTSBURGH, PENNSYLVANIA 15222

ISBN # 0-8059-5906-8
Printed in the United States of America

First Printing

For information or to order additional books, please write:
Dorrance Publishing Co., Inc.
701 Smithfield Street
Third Floor
Pittsburgh, Pennsylvania 15222
U.S.A.
1-800-788-7654
Or visit our web site and on-line catalog at www.dorrancepublishing.com

For my parents—who wanted a doctor not a writer and got both.
And for Jay, who makes life good.

Foreword

Call it a good life

No one would shun her strong will or independence.

They would not scorn her for her mastering

Of language and thought.

Nor would they damn her for her control

Of heart and self.

So, call it a good life.

They would praise her,

As they rightfully should,

For her constant smile and serene eyes.

Yet when they looked past the faces and facades,

Would they be ever so disappointed

At the living, breathing, feeling

Woman that lies therein?

Chapter 1

Monday, 2:00 A.M.

It is very difficult to be spiritual in these times as I stand here at Joe's bedside, holding a pale turquoise bin. My eyes meet his every so often as I wipe the blood from his chin and nose. And as the life slips away from him, I stand there, watching, as though I can see his very being washing out from under him. My heart is racing and my mind won't stop. All my years of training, studying, and "making the difference" come down to this helpless moment. Three degrees, thousands of dollars, and I am left to hold a basin so that this beautiful soul can vomit his life and his entire body's blood into it. It's all very neat and clean despite the insanity of it all. Here where crimson red sits against a turquoise sky with the smell of nitrogen, oxygen, and fear. I catch each drop of blood lest it fall to the floor, like some typical overachiever doing my job as "best as possible." Joe lies there with his eyes fading. All he can mutter between the pain and the puke as he grabs my eyes with his own, "Please, Doc, don't let me die."

I can count on one hand the number of times such a sentence has been spoken to me. Yet each face I look at, each life I walk upon, becomes the speaker of those words, regardless of the context. They have now all become my mother or father in this never-ending journey for a sense of self worth. And in my moments of sheer exhaustion amid the pain and perversion, I am struck each day with the losses and gains and the knowledge that life was never meant to be *this intense*. I am thirty years old with a forty-year-old back and sixty-year-old eyes that have grown bitter. I am embittered having grown up in a profession that makes many excuses but accepts none. I stand there with Joe. The Kleenex box runs dry and his mother's tears continue even when he can no longer vomit. It is days such as these when I hate my job, and the mere thought of spirituality makes me angry and thirsty for alcohol.

Don't get me wrong, this is not an ode to the "hell of life". I am not one of those people who find themselves in a never ending stream of lunch dates saying, "No, I really do *love* my life." It's just that much of the shit that goes on behind these hospital doors is so often slapped with enough lipstick and testosterone that the stories fail to come clean. I mean everyone has a voice these days. So why can't I have mine? I've given this profession ten years so far and grown several gray hairs. I am still not sure what it all is for. I mean why does one's life have to have so much meaning attached to it, that after ten minutes of thought you get sick to your stomach? And why is there this insane pursuit of happiness that seems to end with a man twice my age in some white coat cloaked in judgment? Some "supervisor/staff man," who, as I hold this plastic puke bin, is at home in bed next to the wife he stopped fucking years ago. He's tucked away in a life I can sickly look forward to leading some day. While here I sit with Joe. His eyes are begging me for something that is so way out of my hands I can't bring myself to tell him. We are both condemned to death. Joe in the next few hours if he's lucky, me in this lifetime. Joe will die of D.I.C. "disseminated intravascular coagulopathy", a fancy way of saying every vessel in his body has decided to clot all at once, and he no longer has a hope in hell of stopping the bleeding. Ironic isn't it? He's clotting and bleeding to death all in the same moment. Me, I'm doomed to die that comfortable death reserved for the man in the white coat. The same man who now lays in his bed next to his frigid wife...who incidentally is more in love with being a doctor's wife than she is with her husband. I am condemned to a life "more ordinary", filled with white coats and drug dinners.

Okay, so I sound bitter, angry, pissed off. I am at times, and besides I'm tired. The world always looks shitty when you're alone at 2 A.M. under fluorescent lighting. As for me it's 3 A.M. the lighting is crap, and I am playing catch with Joe's bodily fluids while pondering my own inadequacies as a human. I can handle being a shitty life coper; I can even handle being a shitty doctor.... It's the shitty person that I have such difficulty with. Blah, blah... the bitterness wages on.... But in a few hours I will put my head to a pillow and all of this will be the dream. So bare with me as I "rage against the machine." As I spend the next five years stamping out a place for myself in this hierarchal nightmare. As I fight like mad not to become another white coat in another cold bed. My father always compares success to a track and its participant to a train. All we have to do is stay on track and we are set. I'm not so sure I buy into this fatalist philosophy. But if it's true.... I want a different track—not a new one, a different one. The plans I see laid before me are little to my liking.

I must contain my existential thought to a minimum... everything in moderation. I must not give in to the so-called human condition. For I am a woman. Put the world on my shoulders and I am a doctor with the world at her feet. Who believes this bullshit, let alone thinks of it?

There are times in life I would like to sit down with the "rule makers," the "they" everyone refers to (you know, when asking a question of, when did they decide.... Or the statement, "They said so..." followed by the ever powerful "Did you hear they have a new....") and find out what it is "they" were thinking? Were "they" just having a bad day, or did "they" intentionally mean to make life less understandable? Is that what it is all about? Is the daily frustration and incomprehensibility of my existence merely a part of the master plan, or is it a plot by "them" to sell more self-help books than imaginable?

On that note, I would like to say that it is my experience that most physicians, me included, hate self-help books. I don't think it's because we feel we're supposed to be the one providing the help and not some twenty dollar purchase from Chapters. Perhaps some doctors feel that way. More of us, however, feel threatened on a deeper level by these paperback promises. It's all about weakness you see. If you stand in front of the diet section at the bookstore, well you must be fat, in front of the art section you must be deep; in front of the occult section are the freaks. Well, the weak-minded quick-fix junkies tend to congregate in front of the self-help section. They don't teach you that in Medical School, it's a collective unconscious you tend to reach on your own that further advances your personality as a judgmental asshole.

Who the hell do I think I am? I'm human. I'm some marginally well-adjusted, desperately affected individual who, for no other reason than "family pressure" walked into the medical world some years ago. Amidst the pain and the pressures and the madness of the healers and the sick, I have been trying to make sense of it all. This is not the life my father would have wanted for his prodigal daughter. I know this because every time he is enraged at his own physician over a cancer Dad is powerless to heal, he lets me know how we "doctors" are all incompetent shmucks who don't know the first thing about life. I don't have the heart, as his daughter, to tell him that he is right, myself included. How can he expect a thirty-eight-year-old who grew up in a hospital, to grasp, and what is more, respect the essence of a sixty year old man's life?

And here lies Joe, and there goes his soul, and here my life goes on. The amount of blood brings me back to his bedside and I am now overtaken in the moment, this moment when the battle begins. His eyes roll back in his head and he vomits blood, more than I can measure. It is everywhere—on my hands, on my arms, in his lap. My white coat turns crimson and his heart monitor now shows nothing. The sounds overtake the room. Joe's mother screams, the monitor screams, and I stand there with the words of my attending echoing in my head, "They never bleed out, Eve, never."

Never has come, and the code blue begins. To my right is Terry, the nurse's aide, commencing CPR. At the foot of the bed stands Scottie, bagging the already intubated patient. Laurie begins flipping the caps of the drugs whose names I have already called for. Denise will hang the blood, plasma, and platelets and this terrible ritual will ensue. Joe's mother is now in the waiting room and for the next thirty-five minutes the blood flows, and I am useless to make it stop. Joe will die tonight, and I stand at his bedside watching myself call out orders in the hopes that I will run an organized code. We play in vain with the miracles of modern medicine, and Joe's soul slips out of reach. The monitor does not change its tune, the drugs show no effect. Denise hangs the last six units of platelets left in the hospital and looks to me for guidance. "Enough, Eve, call it." She dare not say it, but her eyes do. They all do, and their experience, far beyond mine, is right.

"Let's call it," I hear myself say, "time of death 03:08."

And that is all.

3:12 A.M.

Joe had a strange form of leukemia (cancer of the blood). To the medical world he was a strange fascination; one for the casebooks. To all it was devastation. His diagnosis was a terrible journey over several months, pained with every invasive procedure possible. It culminated in a removal of his spleen and his dignity. I remember the first time we met. He came to the hospital with a fever and progressive weakness. I sat on the edge of his bed, fearful of another HIV diagnosis, taking a detailed sexual history. He was seventeen, had one girlfriend and was a virgin. It only served to magnify his innocence and my shame at the unfairness of the situation. Somehow I felt terribly responsible, as I think many physicians do. It was not the old adage of a special relationship between patient and physician. Joe represented my mortality and with him was my own selfishness. I admit to this openly now as I recall how completely self-centered I was about his death. Even in this recollection I notice how much more my name frequents the pages. We often reflect on how difficult certain situations are but the empathy comes from our ability to see ourselves in another's place. The fear therein lies when that place is a threat to our own safety. I lost Joe. It was simple. I had failed, I had suffered, and I had survived to be haunted. Like most people, and especially most physicians, it was about me.

Frankly it is not much different now. The change has come in my acknowledgement of that fact.

As for my peers, many will never reach such a realization. Of course it will still be about their own safety, their own egos and their own self-worth. But they will blanket themselves in denial and self-righteousness as insulation from the truth.

Phillip was such an individual. Billed as a genuinely "nice guy", Phillip had trained in the same program I was now in. He finished his "tour of duty" five years prior and was off to the National Institute of Health for further training. There, in addition to his Ph.D. in epidemiology, he earned an invitation to return to his place of birth. And so five years after his departure, Dr. Philip Mackintosh returned to his humble beginnings without a trace of humility left. Phil was a decent fellow. He was brilliant and motivated and truly talented in the area of academia. The problem was, Phil not only knew this, he worshipped at his own temple. It was pitiful. Phil relished in being the "bright new way" and was threatened by anyone who succeeded. He did not want to share any spotlight—he was the spotlight. As such, this "golden boy" never cut any of us any slack.

"Phil," I made the dreaded call. He needed to come in to sign the death certificate. I could hold the bin, catch the blood, run the code, pronounce the patient, but I needed his signature to release the body to the morgue "Joe Campden just coded."

"Did you bring him back?"

"No, we coded him for forty-five minutes; he was exsanguinating the entire time."

"He couldn't have DIC. The leukemia he had does not predispose a patient to DIC."

"Well, he did, Phil. I need you to sign the death certificate."

"Eve, I don't think he had DIC. You must be mistaken."

"Okay, Phil, but could you come in and sign the death certificate?"

"You know, Eve, this is not DIC. But it does bring up a good teaching point...."

I shut off. It was 3 am. All I wanted was a signature. I'd even wait until morning. Had this man forgotten what it was like? I was exhausted and past my tolerance point...in dangerous waters and on the verge of profanity. I put down the phone for a moment and Phil continued to talk on the other end. I lifted the receiver seconds later and Phil continued.

"Phil, I have to go, a patient is crashing," I lied. "The death certificate can wait until morning. Thanks for your help."

"Sure, Eve. That's why I'm here."

"Yah."

"Oh Eve," paused perhaps hesitation, "make sure you don't put cause of death as DIC."

3:22 A.M.

It constantly amazes me what we do for love. The heights people will go to for approval, recognition, or even that proverbial "pat on the back" puts me in a permanent state of disbelief. What is it that makes an intelligent individual abandon all logic for the sake of a brief moment of affection? What power does a gesture of approval possess that it will bring an independent woman to her knees? I could blame this on my parents, as seems to be the trend these days. But I'm quite certain there is more to the insanity.

I'm four years old, it's Halloween, and I go into the kitchen to show my grandfather my new costume. Understand that this man, my mother's father, thinks that I am a God and I haven't even learned to spell yet. Somehow I've attained divine status before the first grade and I know it. Not only do I love the attention, I'm milking it for all it's worth. My older sister is a shit in this man's eyes and I finally have the upper hand. So in I prance to show off my costume and get some advance candy and a hug. The man takes one look at me and falls over. Literally. He has a coronary arrest on our kitchen floor. My mother is hysterical and all I can think is.... What about my costume?

There it begins. With one stopping of a heartbeat, the rest of my life becomes a never-ending battle for the perfect costume.

I've often said that I went into Medicine for my father; a fact he is now quite proud of. This brings me back to the whole "what I did for love" drama. He wanted to be a physician but never had the drive. I never had the vision but had enough drive and a desire to please to go the distance for both of us. Ironically he is now dying of cancer and I want to sit on my ass more days than not. But here we are. I find myself painfully thrust into a world that abides by different rules. Here I sit in this existential sandbox having a difficult time playing well with others. And it's going to take more than a plastic shovel to dig myself out of this one....

I don't blame my father, don't get me wrong. This is my doing. Despite the fact that I am one of those people who takes full credit for her achievements and points the finger when all hell brakes loose (self-preservation instinct, I suppose), I willingly play along. And yes today, I am a doctor. Well, I am a resident, but nonetheless a doctor. Yes I am $125,000 in debt (and still growing). I am in terrible physical health and my mood swings are intolerable. I have almost forgotten what got me into this in the first place. I can barely recall why I am here as I find new answers and new justifications daily. But amidst this pathetic display, I am not alone. Medicine, the institution, recruits exactly this type. It must. For this attitude can be the only thing that would permit any sane person to choose such a life. We are a group of sane, exemplary, highly motivated individuals who are looking for love in all the wrong places. This is a profession where its prototype would cut off his arm if someone said, "Hey man, that stump looks good on you."

What else can it be? Where else did the foundation of a profession rest upon young graduate students injecting themselves with every pathogen under the sun in order to prove a point? Let's take Werner Forseman, a twenty-five-year-old Berliner, who in 1929 was in the equivalent of a surgical residency in Eberswalde, Germany. Purely to prove it could be done,

Werner passed a catheter sixty-five centimeters through a vein in his arm into the right side of his heart. He then climbed two flights of stairs to the x-ray department where he had a chest x-ray performed in order to document the whole process on film. He received bitter criticism from his peers over this but nonetheless, won the Nobel Prize in Medicine, in 1956. Stories such as this one are told all the time. Brave young men and Marie Curie sacrificed their health, safety, and sanity in order to advance a cause. I say Marie Curie because she is the archetypal woman in Medicine. She spent years in a basement struggling for an answer, shared the glory with her husband and died as a result of radiation poisoning, a "side effect" of her work. Marie was just as love-struck as the other members of the Boys Club. The only difference is, she can add the, "it's a man's world" clause to her epitaph.

The point is we're in a profession whose history is based on the lives of poor souls who, under the guise of a scientific advancement, put their own beings at risk. With this said, how in the hell can anyone ever expect to get another good night's sleep? How can I expect to put myself, my family, my soul first when Werner is cathing his own fucking heart? Nobel Prize or not, I still stand by the position that he, like many before and many after, did it for love.

4:07 A.M.

Phillip walked into the Intensive Care Unit about an hour later. He was clean-shaven, smelled wonderful and man-like, which only served to worsen my self-loathing. I smelled of blood and exhaustion. My greens were stained and my head hurt. Phillip was fresh and perfect. In that moment I wanted to disappear. Regardless of what he said, he now had the upper hand and he knew it.

"Did you tell the family?" he asked.

"His mother is in with him now," I said, taking one last whiff of his cologne. It was "Eternity". I kid you not, and the irony was everywhere. He turned to the unit clerk and asked for the death certificate. Incidentally I had placed "leukemia" as cause of death, which, in Phillip's defense, was the real reason Joe died. We need not mention DIC anywhere in the death certificate; it was just Phillip's attitude toward me making a diagnosis before him that infuriated me.

Phillip pulled out his Mont Blanc pen and signed. This pen is truly a status symbol in the medical community. Firstly the pen costs no less than $200. This means that either you can afford spending that kind of money on a writing utensil, or you got one hell of a graduation present. Moreover, if you are going to spend a resident's weekly salary on a pen you are truly responsible enough not to lose it. This black and gold stick with the white star on the end was a scepter of honor. You had cash and you were holding on tight. Welcome to the kingdom, my son, sign right here.

I walked over to Joe's bedside. His pale frame was draped in his mother's anguish. She lay across him, almost like a sculpture, crying softly into the sheets. I stood at the doorway not wanting to disturb her precious moment with my helplessness. She looked up for a moment and saw me there. The tears began to well in my own eyes as my exhaustion permitted a loss of control. In the early hours of the morning, Ruth Campden walked over to me and put her motherly arms around me. Her son had just died and she knew it was the leukemia and not the doctor that had killed him. I began to cry in her arms, not from a sense of failure, for I knew like Ruth that Medicine and the people in it could only do so much. I cried not from failure, but from loss. Ruth had lost her son; I had lost my innocence. Neither of our lives would be the same again.

"It will be okay, Dr. Solomon. Joe will be okay" she whispered.

Joe would be fine. His soul and the memory of his short life would live on to inspire. Mrs. Campden would heal as much as any mother could. Joe's death, as with all physicians would be about me. It would start me on a whirlwind of questions. It would be the start of many deaths, many sleepless nights. Joe's death would stand to symbolize my contempt for the system and my self-doubt. Then it would bring hope and fulfillment. It would stand as a catalyst of my redemption. It would catapult me into a place of peace, where all would be forgiven once all was lost.

But first I would go home, put my head to the pillow and let the nightmares begin.

Wednesday, 2:00 P.M.

I am dying inside. I can feel this negative force in me eating everything in its path and it really pisses me off. I feel as though my whole life is under a microscope and I'm powerless to make a change. Yet in spite of it I do feel as though I am a being worthy of salvation. I loathe the drama and the self-pity, but it is integral to my being. It forces my humility and pronounces my virtue. I want more. I want to hope again. I want to bathe in that supernatural vice that will carry me to freedom.

I'm sitting in a church, staring at Joe's coffin covered in flowers. Most residents have never been to their patient's funerals. Lately I find myself at many. I used to think it was because it gave me closure. I needed the finality of what I had done. I also needed the praise of the mourning family to know that I hadn't completely fucked up. There was always the ritual of a family member introducing me to others as "So and so's doctor" followed by the, "Thank you so much for all you did". It's sick, but it's honest. Some docs drink after they lose patients. I got drunk on empty gratitude in a church or temple or mosque somewhere. Same effect—bad for the brain, but at least my liver is healthy.

Now I'm not even sure why I'm here. But I am sure it has nothing to do with the deceased and everything to do with me. It's definitely still the praise that keeps me coming. I hide this in a self-righteous package of needing to know whom it is that my actions affect. But the truth behind these rituals still evades me and yet compels me to attend.

I really should stop. It's getting out of hand already. Since I began my Intensive Care rotation, I've been going to a funeral a week and it no longer has the same effect on me. Besides I think certain families not only don't expect me there, they don't want me there.

Joe is different in that I was his primary doctor. A fact I kept reminding myself as the smell of incense becomes overpowering. A young man walks to the front of the church and stands beside Joe's coffin. His face is pale, almost albino. His blond hair is shoulder length and the light from the stained windows reflects on his skin, giving him an angelic look.

"Joe loved life," he speaks. His voice is steady, eloquent, focused. "Joe taught us all how to love life in some way. He was diagnosed with cancer four years ago and I never once heard him complain or ask, 'Why me?'" He pauses, takes a sip of water, and continues, "It was Joe's thinking that even though his life had just begun he would continue things as usual. He always said that even if he died, his life had gone according to plan. All he wanted before he died was a huge party. So I thought the only way to say goodbye to my friend Joe would be to show you what that party was like. Joe, wherever you are, buddy, it was one hell of a party! We love you, man."

The lights dim and a slide show begins. Joe's face flashes across the screen. He looks normal and healthy. He is laughing. I don't know why I went to other funerals, but I knew why I was here. In that moment I found Joe the person, not Joe the patient. And in that moment, I found me. The doctor was gone and the woman remained. It was beautiful.

Chapter 2

Tuesday, 6:30 A.M.

The day started as it usually does. My alarm began screaming at 6 A.M. and the never ending pounding of the "snooze" button began. Between hits I rationalized the debate. *Maybe I can call in sick. I could really use a day off to get things done. Yeah, I'm calling in.*

This was followed by the promises. *I could wake up, make Jack breakfast, drink coffee all morning, go for a run and then study all afternoon. It will be really productive. I'll do laundry.*

Finally the strategy. *If I call now and tell them I have the stomach flu it will give me the whole day. Medically speaking they'll believe me. It's a twenty-four hour thing. That or food poisoning. Something where I'm vomiting beyond reproach but promise to be well by tomorrow.*

By the fourth alarm my conscience has kicked in and I am fully awake, no longer able to enjoy a day off. I hear Jack in the shower and go to join him.

"Hey, sweetie," he chirps through the water. His thick black hair is full of soap and he's smiling. Jack is one of those people who truly loves his job. He is one of those rare individuals, the subject of many myths, who wakes with a spring in his step and a sense of purpose. Jack works in computer animation. He's brilliant, beautiful, and a genuinely decent person. Moreover, Jack, the love of my life, worships me. No matter what I have done, I am safe with him. I haven't quite grasped this concept yet, despite our four years of marriage. I still find myself striving for his approval in the strangest of ways. Call it a need to please or a subconscious search for parental approval. I think it's just me.

"Going to work?" he asks.

I immediately take this the wrong way. He asks an innocent question and I think he's questioning my work ethic. See how fucked up being a grown-up can be? It's pathetic. "Of course I'm going to work, babe," I respond half asleep and nauseous. I begin the ritual of the morning and wash the sleep from my eyes and hair.

"How'd you sleep, sweetie?"

Jack loves to talk in the morning. He loves to talk in the shower. I am a talker but mornings are not my best work. I remember reading a poem about a woman who loved a man and every time she asked him how he slept it meant, "I love you." I smile at Jack and kiss his wet cheek and begin to shampoo my hair. Jack also loves to fuck in the shower. I love to fuck, but again, the shower is not my best work. It gets too hot and steamy and I'm always unsure of my footing. Besides I really prefer to screw in a more horizontal position. I mean I understand the passion factor of doing it standing up but frankly it's lost on me. Make love to me on top, on bottom, from the side. As long as I can have more than a foot on a solid surface, I'm happy.

I finished brushing my teeth and left my love to enjoy the steam. Drying off, I wandered into our bedroom to make the bed and put on a robe. The coffeemaker in the kitchen had taken cue from its timer (one of the best wedding presents we received), and I could smell the brew as I entered the main room. We live in a loft. I love this place for so many reasons. Firstly it is the coolest home I will ever own. Secondly it has an air of fabulous about it that is nothing like the home I grew up in. Why this is important to me, I will never know.

I pour two cups of coffee and begin to doctor them (excuse the pun). Four artificial sweeteners and cream for me, just cream for Jack. I have a very strong opinion about coffee as I think many people do. I think it has to do with the fact that it is the only legalized stimulant on the market. Furthermore it is an expression of one's self. It's a personal beverage and one that all drinkers have a definite claim to. Even the most indecisive people know exactly how they take their coffee. Give me sugar instead of the pink stuff and I'm just not as fulfilled. Milk is fine, but cream is better. I hate dark roast and love milder blends. Ironically, I am the type of woman who has to lay out her clothes the night before because the indecision of "what to wear" guarantees a twenty minute delay each morning.

I also firmly believe that if you love someone, you know how he or she takes his or her coffee. Forget middle names and high school achievements. These are trivial pieces of information which bear nothing on a relationship's success. The details of love are in the coffee. Enough said.

Jack is by far the best thing that ever happened to me. This sounds trite but it is true more now that ever. He is "the prince of peace" in an often-chaotic world. He has a beauty about him that I am convinced will be the key to my soul's salvation. All of this information was of course a mystery to me when we married, let alone met. Life has a funny way of happening as one might have exactly planned, without all the clever foresight involved. Things happen (hopefully for the best) and we take credit for them in a manner suggesting far too much anticipatory genius on our parts.

Jack began as all my relationships had in the past. He was beautiful and new, and like a shiny new toy I had to have him. With all the gusto of an overachiever, I pursued him and found myself in bed with him within a week. It was while lying next to his warm post-coital frame still fresh from the smell of lovemaking, that I found truth. He turned to me, brushed the sweat from my brow and something in his gaze asked to be considered not just as another conquest. In the backwards impulsiveness many women suffer from, we dated thereafter. Within six months I bought him a ring and asked him to become my doctor's wife. We spent three years courting a long distance romance while I went to Medical School. This only served to cultivate our ignorance about one another.

Distance has the ideal advantage of fostering a mythical interpretation of reality. There are brief rendezvous filled with passion, which preclude the ability for arguments. These moments are interspersed with telephone calls, which catch you on your best behavior. After all, if you are in a terrible mood, you don't pick up the phone. Furthermore there isn't enough time to fight. There is an unspoken agreement that time is a precious commodity which will not be tainted with conflict and harsh words. Four years of this strange situation and we emerged triumphant. I had become a doctor and a wife all within three weeks in May.

We moved here two weeks later so that I could start my residency. Jack took a job at a computer animation company. They fell in love with his skill and creative vision. It was hard not to fall in love with Jack. He forces you to look at a world filled with promise. He convinces you that all could be made real. He is a realist who creates a reality in his mind and then goes about giving it life. I adore him with an unprecedented fervor. He worships me in the manner to which I have become very accustomed. It is, as they say, "a perfect match."

Jack enters the main room smelling of soap and promise. He is awake, and refreshed. He reaches for his coffee and my cheek. A sip and a kiss later and he asks, "Late day today, sweets?"

"I should be home around seven. It depends what time we get through with sign out rounds." I say between sips of coffee.

"Want to study at the coffee shop tonight?" A usual request as we typically go to the corner coffee shop after work. I read my medical journals and Jack devours computer magazines. It's actually a very civilized way of studying while still staying close.

I am a fiercely independent woman but there are certain things, and I think most of us suffer from this, which I hate to do alone. Moreover it is a majority of these tasks that I find such joy in when I do them with Jack. Despite what anyone may say, *that*, my friends, is love.

7:30 *A.M.*

The resident parking lot for the Princess Margaret Hospital (a mammoth center of disease and health, the size of a small city) is a fifteen-minute walk from the main building. This is a good thing as it allows me a quarter of an hour walk in the sunshine before I begin twelve hours under fluorescent lighting. However, being eternally late for everything means I must allow myself the extra time for the "trek" to work. There are days, I must admit, where I will park in staff parking, risking the $30 fine, only to be on time. The things we will do for love....

I park my piece of shit car and gather my bag from the back seat. The car was, of course. a gift from my parents for being accepted to Medical School. At the time, the 1972 Plymouth Valiant had character. It is now a car which is older than my spouse and in desperate need of permanent retirement. Ironically the car, which is one year my junior, must last another two years in this parking lot. The same goes for its owner. We are both waiting for our turn at redemption.

The sunlight reflects off the windows of the hospital on the hill. It truly is a giant monstrosity. Its height only adds to the intimidation factor. I used to hate hospitals many years ago. I think many people do. After all they aren't the happiest of places. Realistically, the only joyous time spent in a hospital is when you are born. Who remembers that, other than the woman who endured the agony of your birth and the man who tried desperately not to faint at the sight of it all, while capturing the moment on video? I have, however, grown to call this place my second home as most of us do. Its walls have born witness to my best and my worst moments. I have experienced every human emotion behind these doors, and its corridors have raised me with the best of intentions.

Medicine is a strange place to raise a child. We enter eighteen years old and hopeful. We are fresh and naïve and truly unaware of what lies ahead. Twelve or so years later we emerge confused and disenchanted. Our youth has been taken from us, our innocence lost. We were captivated by an idea that never reached fruition. There were no advance warnings, nor could there have been. We spent our twenties staring in a mirror, under a microscope, asking the eternal question, "Who the hell do I think I am?" Yet if asked, we *would* do it all over again. For this is all we have known, and after all, when it is good, it is gold.

7:50 *A.M.*

I hang my coat in the doctors' lounge and go over to the café to indulge in my second coffee of the day. I'm convinced when all this is over I will have severe osteoporosis from the amount of caffeine I consume. Yes, coffee causes bone loss, warn your daughters now. An arm wraps around my shoulder and a friendly voice is in my ear, "Hi, Boo."

I turn to face Katarina and she kisses both my cheeks. Katarina Vlahov is one of my old classmates, my best friend, and an incredible woman. She is by far one of the smartest people I know, as well as one of the most beautiful women ever made. She finished her Family Medicine Residency two years ago and now runs a practice downtown. She is frighteningly real and her own boss. She is also very well respected and the reason I made it through medical school. Interestingly she also attributes her completion of our medical training to me. As such we have an unusual bond, particularly for our profession. And she is the only woman I would ever leave Jack for.

"Coffee first, then we talk." I mutter as I order us each a latte.

"I had a disaster of a night on call; get me a doughnut as well." The woman looks too good to have been up all night. But again I love her too much to loathe her perfection and am somehow able to take pride in it.

"How is it that you were up all night and look like that," I wave at her perfect black suit and knee-high boots as I hand her the chocolate glazed, "and I got sleep only to resemble this?"

"I'm Russian, sweetie. We thrive on adversity." She laughs and sips her coffee.

"So why was your night so bad?" I ask, a sincere ear awaiting her tales of battle. Katarina's practice has seven doctors who share the in-patient responsibilities. As such she is on call three to four times per month.

"Our group has twenty-two inpatients right now. It's insane and the administration doesn't give a shit. I was here all night admitting people no other service would take." It is the usual story and everyone is feeling it right now. The hospital is always full and services are overworked. Family Medicine tends to be the "dumping ground" for anyone with a nonspecific diagnosis. I feel Katarina's frustration.

"I'm sorry, my sweet. Why don't you come for dinner tonight? Jack misses you." Jack loves Katarina as most men do. Jack, who is usually untrustworthy of many of my friends and colleagues (I am a terrible judge of character), finds Katarina very worthy. He is also grateful to her for my safekeeping in Medical School.

"Can't, Eve. Nico is taking me to the opera. I have to go. My first patient is at 8:30. I will call you this week. Okay?"

"Sure."

And she is off in a brilliant puff.

Katarina was the first of her family to be raised outside of Russia. Her parents emigrated here in the late 1970s when Katarina was fourteen. In Russia, her father was an engineer and her mother a doctor. When they left Russia, their wealth and positions remained in the motherland. Here, her father drove a taxi and her mother was a waitress. It put food on the table and Katarina and her brother, Misha, did not ask questions.

She spent nights in the bathtub, with her head submerged in the water up to her ears practicing English to erase her Slavic accent. At seventeen she graduated high school and left for university on full scholarship. Her motivation was not shame, it was pure desire.

Katarina's father died the week before her Medical School interview. We rarely spoke of him and I often wondered what affect this had on her opinion of her medical brethren. Occasionally I would pause and ask, "Do you miss him?"

"Sometimes," she would respond, knowing her relationship with this man had been anything but straightforward. From her viewpoint he had been a strict man with a vision for his family. Katarina was as stubborn as he and with a vision for herself. The two were neither complementary nor compatible. Katarina was to be the great capitalist hope. Her heritage told her to marry young and breed early. She defined success by a grander scale. Hers would be a life filled with a great deal of money, a trail of lovers, and no children. She would have success in her career, her closet, and her bed. The only commitment she wished to make was to herself. She often said it was a good thing her father never lived to see her dreams realized, as it would have killed him all the same.

The production of a person is a process, which continues to fascinate me. How Communist Russia produced a woman like Katarina was a mystery. I suppose her wanting came from a life of misbegotten. She had seen what equality had to offer and she vowed to emerge on top.

Katarina wanted to be a doctor for as long as she could remember. This had nothing to do with her mother and her forced change in careers. Katarina had foresight and she wanted this for herself. It wasn't until Medical School that the lines began to blur.

I remember one night sitting in the living room of her one bedroom apartment. She was the only student I knew who had both a living room and dining room set. Her apartment was painted pale green and all of its furniture came assembled. It was a mystery to me. She looked up from her pathology book and said to me out of the blue, "I'm not really sure I want to do this anymore. Was it supposed to be like this?"

"What?" I asked, thinking she was talking pathology and failing to see the philosophical picture she was painting.

"In undergrad I was so focused. I wanted to be a doctor so badly and I knew I could do it. Now that it's here I'm not sure I want it." She was stating that which had been before me my whole life. The difference was I had only convinced myself I wanted to be a doctor and now the façade was beginning to show its wear. With Katarina the argument was real.

"Kat, we usually want what we don't have and have what we don't want."

"Don't be trite with me, Eve. That's bullshit talk. This is not about a conquest; it is the rest of my life."

She was right and I had no answer. We stared at each other in silence for what seemed like an eternity. Then she sighed, took a sip of her wine and returned to her pathology textbook.

Many a night was spent in the same manner. The conversation usually focused on the "why" rather than the "what" of life. We became each other's lifeline during those years. Our love was that of true sisters and it has been unfailing ever since.

I put three artificial sweeteners in my coffee, added a lid, and left the doctors lounge to begin rounds in the Intensive Care Unit. The day had begun regardless of my wishes and I was powerless to do anything but play along. I straightened my white coat and reapplied my lipstick. With coffee in one hand and proverbial sword in the other, I walked into the fluorescent daylight.

Chapter 3

Rounds were continuing even though I had lost my focus hours ago. I found it difficult to pay attention to anything for longer than an hour and we were well past that point. Dr. Leonard was the staff person in the Intensive Care Unit along with Phillip McKintosh. Leonard had started talking at 8:45 and was still going strong. It was a nightmare. All I could do to maintain composure was to excuse myself politely every so often to go to the washroom. It was a pathetic attempt at a break from the monotony, but at this point it was all I could do to keep my sanity. I tried daydreaming but that only made me sleepy. Since falling asleep in front of the great Dr. Leonard was not an option, I chose the artificial washroom drill. By 1:00 P.M. rounds had concluded, Leonard was hoarse, and I had the staff thinking I was pregnant from all my trips to the ladies room.

It is interesting the clauses that exist for women in this profession. We march our way into the next millennium and there is this grand misconception that all is forgotten. In many ways it's worse than before. I'm not tooting the feminist horn and making a case for discrimination, so relax. I'm just stating the obvious. It's no secret that to be a physician you have to forgo many of life's benefits. For men such sacrifices come with a sense of forgiveness. When Dr. Bob stays late at work to help a patient and misses little Jimmy's Christmas concert, it's understood that a heart surgeon's life isn't an easy one, and well, Jimmy, Daddy had to save that man's life. When that same Dr. Bob cancels his clinic to stay at home with little Jimmy, now sick with the flu, what a father! That man has his priorities in order.

Somehow I don't see women afforded the same treatment.

Evelyn Jacobs was one of the best cardiac surgeons in the country. Ten years ago, during the last year of her training she began an affair with Dr. Adam Everson, the head of the Department of Medicine. As with any secret in a hospital, this was made quite public when one night, the resident on call for Internal Medicine called Dr. Everson to discuss a case and a sleepy Evelyn picked up the phone. The following year, Evelyn went to Michigan to complete a fellowship in valve surgery. When she returned, Adam had divorced his wife and he and Evelyn were married. Two years later she was pregnant and the great divide went into action. Evelyn operated until two days before her due date. She gave birth to a healthy baby girl and took four weeks maternity leave. She returned to the silent understanding that now that her priorities had changed, she would never be department head. She returned to the disapproval of most women, who felt she hadn't enough time off with her daughter. Because Evelyn dared to want it all, she couldn't win. Men saw her as weak and women sat in judgment. What a great place to work.

Adam, on the other hand, was somehow excused for sleeping with a resident while still married. He remained department head and in fact the department even bought him a box of cigars when his daughter Hanna was born. I'm not complaining. I knew this was a club for boys when I applied for membership. Anyone who tells you differently is fooling himself.

"Dr. Solomon?" I was being summoned.

"Yes, Dr. Leonard?"

"Could you tell us what is the evidence for use of thrombolytics versus angioplasty in the Acute Coronary setting?" Being the senior resident on the team he looked to me to answer his questions. Being the loudmouth on the team he asked me difficult questions in the hopes that he could silence me with humiliation. It had not worked thus far. I still answered his questions and went about my business. Only now I thought he was a mean little prick with a Napoleon complex.

At that instant my code pager went off and over the loud speaker I heard "Code Blue, Unit 102."

I turned to Leonard quickly and said, "Sorry, sir, it will have to wait." I turned and ran down the hall to the doors of the unit and headed towards the elevator. If I made it to the elevator with the crash cart I would not have to run up ten flights of stairs. There was no way in hell I was running up ten flights of stairs. In the elevator I turned to David Auerbach, a first year Orthopedics resident. His face was pale and he looked scared. This would be the first code where he would be in charge and I could smell his fear.

"David, you want to run it? I'll be right behind you."

"Thanks, Eve." I asked Maggie, the nurse on the team, for a pair of gloves for me and for David. We put on our latex, the elevator doors opened, and off we went.

"David, put your hand on the femoral pulse and watch the monitor. Tell everyone else what do to. Okay?" I said as we ran up the hail to Unit 102.

The room was already full of people. The patient was lying on the bed; he was motionless and blue. One of the nurses had already started CPR. David walked in before me and as per protocol, announced he was running the code. He put one hand on the femoral pulse and watched the monitor.

"Jeremy, can you intubate?" Jeremy grabbed a number eight endotracheal tube from the cart and prepared to insert it in the patient's airway. "Eve, I'll need a central line, please." He winked at me.

David was doing just fine. The chaos had become controlled and he knew it. He was in charge. These were the moments that were perfect. Things were happening because of you. The rhythm was set and it was amazing. He asked the ward nurse to read him the history and ordered the appropriate drugs. Within ten minutes the patient had an airway and a central intravenous access. CPR continued and his rhythm screamed flat line.

I turned to look at the patient, thin and naked, splayed out on the bed before me. He was eighty-five-years-old and the hospital for a bowel resection for cancer. There were tumors throughout his liver and lungs. The operation was more of a palliative measure. His family had refused to let him die. Unfortunately, he had other plans, which was why we were here. I looked over at Mary who had both knees on the bed. Her fists were at his sternum engaging in chest compressions. I could hear another rib crack as she put her weight into it. The scene began to blur into so many like it and I knew this was no way to die.

When you become a health care professional your visions of death alter. There begins to exist the proper way to die. When you stand in rooms like these over the years, resuscitating patients who by all logical and spiritual parameters should be dead, you learn a different understanding. God does not exist in that room. He/she left the premises hours ago. It's you and a body and a mirror as big as your head. The patient is dead but you've got a list of self-assessments as long as the hallway and everyone looks to you for the next drug. The room is filled with critics and it no longer is about a life saved, it's about saving your face. Run a good code and it doesn't matter the outcome. Fuck up and the patient died because of you. And when it is all over, you will die at home in your bed with your loved ones around you and a "Do Not Resuscitate" sign above your bed.

The rhythmic beats of the man's heartbeat returned on the monitor after forty-five minutes and three broken ribs. The rate was fast and irregular, suggesting atrial fibrillation. I knew that he had thrown a clot to his lung.

"Maggie, could you call the unit and tell them we're on our way, please?" David was charged with energy. He'd just lost his virginity and there was no turning back. I moved the monitor onto Mr. Tobias Burnow's bed (I looked at the chart to discover his name) and the team began to push the bed towards the elevators. It was a crazy dance around the bed to control the intravenous poles, the oxygen bag, and the endotracheal tube while maneuvering the bed all at the same time. The room was left in a shambles. Empty packaging was strewn on the floor, and Mr. Tobias Burnow's teeth and flowers were knocked over in the initial commotion. As I ran back to grab his chart I took one last look at the battlefield only to notice a crayon drawing of a sun pasted over his bed which read, "I love you, Grandpa". I thought of the chaos that had transpired under such a promise. I mourned for Tobias Burnow and his unrequited death.

We were back in the Intensive Care and Mr. Burnow was now on a ventilator. Dr. Leonard was at the bedside adjusting the settings when he turned to me and asked, "Well, Eve, what's your diagnosis?"

"I think he had a pulmonary embolus, sir. Also in the differential is a cerebral bleed or massive stroke with aspiration, but I think given his metastatic disease we have to rule out a hypercoagulable state." I was having a good day as far as diagnoses went.

"What's your next move?" he asked.

"I think a spiral CT is in order. He's day two post op so I'd be hesitant to empirically start Heparin and thrombolytics are out of the question. I think given the extent of his cancer we should meet with the family right away to discuss how aggressive we should be." It was a reasonable plan of action. This man had two months to live at most and he had suffered enough. There was little that could be done for him now. Although it was not only my decision to make, he needed to be allowed to die.

"Good work, Eve."

Praise does not come easy in this place. Shit, on the other hand, flies like crazy. You take it when it comes and swallow it whole.

"Thank you, sir. I should say, David ran his first code and did an excellent job." He had and he did. David deserved a piece of the pie.

"Good job, David. We'll make an Intensivist out of you yet." Leonard chuckled and left the bedside. David turned to me, his eyes shining as he wrapped his arm around me and pulled me to him.

"I'll book the family meeting for two o'clock. Okay with you?" I asked getting ready to move.

"Just stay here a second, Eve," he said, his arm still around me. I understood that praise had not come easily to David and he wanted a moment bask in the glory. He had done a good job and he wanted to savor it for a moment before he faced the world again. Either that or he was hitting on me. I preferred the former interpretation and stood at his side. Moments later my pager went of and I pulled myself away to answer the call.

2:45 P.M.

Dr. Leonard emerged from the family conference room and I could see the rest of the Burnow family seated in the pale green couches. They were expectedly tearful and Allan, the Unit Social Worker, was speaking words of comfort that I could not make out from my position in the hallway. Leonard waited until he was out of ear-shot and turned to the head nurse Jena and said, "We'll give the family time to say their goodbye and then we can extubate Mr. Burnow. How many beds do we have for tonight?"

"That will make four beds. If we transfer bed seven, we'll have five." I did not envy Jena's job.

"Eve, are you on call tonight?" he turned to notice me standing at the desk finishing my notes for the day.

"No, it's David Auerbach and Alex Connor tonight." Alex was a second year Family Medicine resident with attitude to spare. He came from a long line of doctors with the impression that this was his destiny. Alex took unnecessary risks and engaged in invasive procedures without good reason. He was overconfident and therefore dangerous. Moreover he was a mean little shit and it made him unappealing to all who were around him. When Alex spoke you could see the condescension. He belittled nurses and laughed at other residents' mistakes. Alex brought out the worst in people. I couldn't wait for him to screw himself over.

"Was Connor at the code?" Dr. Leonard wasn't the nicest of men, but if you did your work he was fair. Slack off and he made your life hell.

"No," I said, almost happy that Alex was digging his own grave.

I am not a bitch. I am, however, very black and white. I love or I hate, there is no middle ground. The only way to get to the hate list is to piss me off severely or screw me over. Alex had succeeded in doing both several times during the first week of our rotation. Simply put, I wanted blood and I was in a position to get it. At times like this I felt I was personally responsible for Dr. Connor's lesson in humility.

As I watched Dr. Leonard walk off in search of Alex Connor, I recalled how only last week, Alex had caught me in the call room, crying over Joe's death. It was later that day that I overheard him telling David and Jake that, "The bitch must be getting her period. Man, these chicks as doctors, they cry at everything."

Leonard found Alex at the computer station and they passed me on their way into the staff-doctor's office. Alex refused to meet anyone's gaze and Leonard looked fuming. The door closed behind the tiger and his prey and I caught my reflection in the glass.

I was smiling for the first time that day.

4:00 P.M.

"Want to grab a bite to eat?" It was David standing behind me at the sink. I had just finished putting a chest tube into a patient and had removed my gloves to clean the latex powder from my hands. I realized it was now well past noon and I had not eaten lunch.

"Sure, David, just give me a minute."

David was one of those genuinely nice people we all went to high school with. His beauty and his kindness had not faded with his youth. David was born and raised in Australia. He had moved here to do a Ph.D. in Kinesiology and to be with the love of his life. Two weeks before his thesis was to be defended, he caught the woman in bed with another. Apparently she could hide being a lesbian no longer. He stayed. A post doctorate as well as several affairs mended his broken heart. I had no doubt that David did well in both areas. He was very bright and a hard worker. He was also very gorgeous and an Australian accent did not hurt his pursuits. He had a "thing" for nurses and was known to sleep around. This would be fun for some time, but I was sure such a habit would catch up to him. As women, we enjoy a good lover, but it's a known fact, we hate to share. I only hoped David would not learn this from experience. David's latest fling was an Emergency nurse named Leanne. They had met at the gym, of course, and had been together for almost a month.

Leanne joined us for lunch in the cafeteria. Someone should have told Leanne that this was a mistake. There was an unspoken rule somewhere that when a nurse sleeps with a doctor, they best keep it outside the hospital. The next time Leanne got one of David's drug orders wrong in ER, he would silently ask himself why he was sleeping with an idiot. By the same token, the next time David screwed up in Emergency and was the topic of conversation at a staff dinner, Leanne would wonder where this relationship was going. The best way to avoid these encounters was to keep their social interaction out of the hospital. It was bad enough the entire staff knew they were fucking. What made it worse was the reality of this illusion every time they were seen drinking coffee together.

Leanne was a nice person and very attractive. Unfortunately she was a mediocre nurse and quite dumb. I could see David's boredom on the horizon.

"How was your day, sweetie?" *Mistake number two.* She was referring to him by a pet name in front of another colleague. I knew it was Leanne's way of marking her territory but this was not the place. The poor girl was already on her way out and she was blind to the signs.

She leaned over to kiss his cheek and he pulled away before she could reach. *Had no one shown this woman the manual?*

I said hello and then excused myself to go to the bank machine. When I had returned, David was alone, big surprise, and standing in line at the sandwich counter. I poured myself a bowl of soup and found a table for us.

"Leanne had to go back to work," he remarked, putting his tray down on the table and taking off his white coat before sitting down.

Interesting how if you stay silent long enough, most people will start talking. This is a trick I learned in communications class in Medical School and it has served me well in exactly these situations.

"What's your story, Eve?" he asked. Usually people talk about themselves rather than ask questions. David caught me off guard.

"Sorry?"

"You know, tell me about yourself."

"Not much to tell, David," I laughed almost nervously, "what you see is what you get." It was trite but it was so true with me. I couldn't put on a front if I tried. It was my worst flaw and my greatest strength.

"Are you seeing anyone?" he asked, standard question.

"I've been married for almost four years."

"I didn't know that. What does he do?" I was surprised. Everyone knows everyone's business in this place.

"Jack's a computer animator." I smiled. The mere mention of his name softened my mood.

"You really love him," David said. You could see it on my face. "I envy you that, you know."

I looked up at David. His underbelly was showing. Beneath the sex machine was a man in search of love. That or he was hitting on me again. I chose the former interpretation once more and smiled at him.

"It happens to us all, David." I looked back down at my meet his gaze.

"I hope you're right, Eve."

We ate the rest of our meals in silence.

Chapter 4

Sign out rounds finished late as usual and I began the walk down the hill to my car with the sun beginning to set. A day can easily be spent without seeing the sun if one has the drive. I stopped at the grocery store on the way home to get some fresh fruits and vegetables and phoned Jack from the car to let him know I was on my way.

"How was your day, sweetie?" he asked, a smile in his voice.

"Busy but good, Love. You?"

"I have some new footage to show you. The project we're doing is really coming along." Jack was an artist with the computer. I tried to share his excitement over his work but I think the appreciation for some of the techniques was lost on me.

"I'll be home in twenty minutes. Will you start the pasta for me?" Jack's culinary skills consisted of coffee, which I had taught him how to make, and tuna melts. He could heat soup and barbecued hot dogs, but anything more intricate and he was a mess. At times this was maddening, but most often it was one of his endearing traits.

I put a soundtrack into the CD player and began to sing along. I have a weakness for singing show tunes in the car. Which is why my stereo system cost more than my automobile. It is definitely my escape as I speed towards home imagining my Hollywood debut as the next musical diva. Jazz and Pop are as good as show tunes, it just so happens that today it's *The First Wives Club* and I *am* Bette Midler.

I park the car in its usual spot underground and grab the groceries. Jack is standing at the elevator door with a funny look on his face and I immediately know something's wrong.

"Call your mother," he said. I can feel a steel rod poke through me as I think of my father.

"What happened to my dad?" I asked and handed him the groceries.

"Nothing, he's fine."

I feel relief and walk with him towards the loft, "Why'd she call?"

"Your sister was arrested."

"Oh, shit."

My sister is another story entirely.

8:00 P.M.

"Hi, Ma. Jack gave me the message. What's going on?" My mother is chain smoking on the other end and blowing the puffs in the other direction of the phone in the hopes I won't suspect that she has taken up the habit again.

"Well," she takes a big drag, disguising it as a pause, "Penny was picked up by the police for questioning." She exhales.

"Why? What did she do?" With Penny it could be a number of things.

"Nothing, really. It has to do with Elliott," she said, inhaling again. Elliot was my sister's ex-husband who would not fully relinquish himself to her past. Elliot was a cocaine addict and an asshole. They lived in a warehouse and had been married while I was in high school. Elliot made a career out of being unemployed and my parents were happy to support the two as long as they got a grandchild out of the deal. My parents bought Penny a car for her thirtieth birthday, her husband sold it to pay off his dealer. Elliot stayed home and frequented the young male prostitutes down the street while Penny worked nights as a nurse at a geriatric hospital. After ten years and several teenage men later, Penny, with much coaching from my father (Get rid of the prick already!), kicked Elliot out. The divorce became final almost a year to the day. By that time, the lovely couple had a three-year-old daughter, Ahava, and Penny was on her second car. Periodically Elliot would get arrested for possession and list his ex-wife as his next of kin. My sister was stupid. When the police came to question her she would oblige rather than tell her ex-husband where to go. I'm convinced they were still sleeping together. My sister would do just about anything for a good fuck.

"Well, Ma, what would you like me to do?"

"Call your sister, sweetie. She's at home now. Maybe you can talk some sense into her." This was laughable. My sister and I hated each other. There wasn't even the "I love you because you are my sister, but I don't like you" clause in our relationship. Furthermore we had not spoken more than ten sentences to one another since she decided to pull out of my wedding.

However, I had long ago given up placing my pride ahead of my mother's happiness where Penny was concerned.

"Okay, I'll speak to you after I talk to her." This would be in a few minutes, because I knew Penny would hang up on me the minute she heard my voice. It was simple, Penny was shit and I was the golden child. She hated me and I gave her good reason. Moreover Penny had mental issues far beyond any of our capabilities and she refused to seek help.

I dialed the phone and she answered. I knew this meant they had disconnected her call display.

"Hello." She sounded her usual. The world was falling down around her and Penny seemed just fine.

"Hi, Penny. It's Eve."

"Oh." She exhaled. A habit she blamed on our mother. Penny never took responsibility for any of her actions.

"How are you?" I asked, trying to sound easygoing.

"I'll bet you damn well know how I am. Called to check up on me, eh bitch?" The phone went dead.

This was no surprise to me. I was actually taken by the fact that the conversation lasted as long as it did and with only minimal profanity. Jack sat at the kitchen table shaking his head at the whole scene. He had long ago learned to stay out of my family politics.

I called my mother back to let her know what had happened and to warn her that Penny would be phoning at any moment to give her shit. On some level she deserved it. Penny needed to be left to learn to take care of herself. The problem was she would never be left alone and she would never learn. I think on some level she loved the power she had in creating a situation where the lives of several centered on her own. As dysfunctional as it was, Penny called the shots in this family and she loved it.

"Well, darling, thanks for trying," my mother said between puffs.

"Ma, you've got to quit smoking." I had to get it in.

"Darling, I just had one. You know, to take the edge off."

Lying was our family's greatest strength. I hung up the phone and started dinner.

9:45 P.M.

We finished dinner in silence. I was too tired to talk and Jack had spent the last half-hour enthralling me with tales of his latest project. His excitement served to take my mind of the events of the evening.

"Too late for coffee, isn't it?"

"Hmmm. I'll just study here," I said, walking towards the den with him behind me.

The day had taken everything from me but it had been a typical day. I had at least an hour of reading to do and the night was already well under way. I settled into my favorite chair and opened the *ICU Book.* There would be another slew of questions tomorrow from Dr. Leonard and it would be less painful if I knew at least some of the answers.

I often envied other professionals. Their day at the office began with coffee at the water cooler and ended with drinks at the bar before home to bed. My day of diseases began with putting a central line in a cancer patient and ended with reading about more of the same. The studying never stopped. I remember one of my advisors in school telling me, "Medicine is as big as the oceans, and the human brain is as large as a pea." I think what he was saying was that I was screwed from the start. At the time I thought it was just a ploy to get me to work harder. In any case, I would study every night and still be ignorant to a vast amount of knowledge. It was an existentialist's wet dream.

Jack worked on the computer while I read a chapter on Swan Gantz Catheters. I would periodically look up from my book to catch him staring at me. This was a game we began in university and it had endured. We would sit in the library across from each other studying. We had only been together for a few weeks and I would look up from my books to catch him staring at me, studying me. He would look deep into my eyes and hold my gaze for a very long time.

"What?" I would say, still meeting his gaze.

"Nothing. Just looking." He would smile, eyes still fixed on me.

This often ended with me returning to my books or with him taking my hand and walking with me to the back of the book stacks. It was dark and secluded and no one ever went there. He would kiss me passionately amid the smell of old leather and worn paper. Beneath the protection of the shadows we made love with our clothes on and he would return me to my place in the library afterwards. There he would sit across from me, smelling of leather and worn paper, of sex and mischief. He would smile at me with his red cheeks and misplaced hair and watch me while I worked.

Tonight he watched while I struggled to make it through the chapter. Half way through I could barely keep my eyes open.

11:30 PM

I put the news on in the bedroom while I washed my face and brushed my teeth. Another Concorde plane had crashed somewhere in Europe and CNN was buzzing. I crawled into the sheets next to Jack, feeling his warmth against my cold feet. He was naked beneath the covers and I found myself surprisingly aroused after such a long day. He shut off the television and I shut off the light. I could feel his kiss on my neck and his hand on my breast. His other hand slipped between my legs and in that moment I had forgotten trials of the past twenty-four hours. A wave of pleasure washed over me and I closed my eyes and enjoyed the beautiful ride. I could stay in the book stacks forever.

Chapter 5

Thursday, 6:30 P.M.
We were in the middle of sign out rounds when I was called to Emergency to see a patient in respiratory distress. The patient had a blood oxygen level of 40% (normal is 90 and above) on room air and three other services had already been consulted. All had declined to take the patient for fear that he was too sick and his condition was now worsening. The Emergency physician felt he may need a ventilator and the diagnosis was still up in the air. These are the challenges I love. The diagnosis is a mystery and I have the advantage of being the last one on the scene. All of the previous questions have been asked and answered, all of the lab work done. Anything I contribute is gravy. In a sense, if anyone will make the diagnosis at this point it will be me, purely because of the fact that I now have the benefit of eight peoples' brainpower working for me.

I excused myself from sign out rounds, motioning to Ethan Baker, the Surgery Resident who was on call with me, that he could brief me on what I had missed. Entering the bright light of Emergency, I proceeded straight to the monitored area where the sicker patients are. I grabbed the patient's chart and proceeded to his bedside. His name was Randy Adler and he was twenty-seven years old. Randy lay in the Emergency bed looking surprisingly comfortable. His blood oxygen level was now 88% on a 100% non-rebreather mask and he was reading a magazine when I arrived. I must admit, based on his numbers I expected Randy near coma.

"Mr. Adler?" I walked towards him to introduce myself.

"Call me Randy." He muffled from behind the plastic mask. His breathing was only slightly labored. I knew something was up.

"Randy, I'm Dr. Solomon, from the Intensive Care Unit."

"Hi." He shook my outstretched hand.

"Randy, what happened to bring you here today?" I began my history, knowing that he was stable enough that I could gather some information from him.

"Well, two days ago I started coughing a lot and I felt just awful. So I went to the doctor today to get my shot cause I'm two weeks late. He sent me here."

"What shot is that?"

"My Depo." Randy pulled five small vials of Depo-Provera, a female hormone, from his pocket. He picked the lint off the vials and handed them to me. "Could you give me my shot? I'm really overdue." He placed the vials in my hand.

"What do you take these for?" I asked, maintaining my composure. Depo-Provera is a common treatment for pedophiles and sex offenders. They receive the female hormone shots every five weeks or so. If they miss a shot, the effect diminishes very quickly.

"I'm a perv." He said through the mask. I looked down at his ankle and noticed a black mechanical bracelet and put the pieces of the puzzle together. Randy had been arrested for pedophilia several times in the past five years. He had been paroled from his last offence six month ago and was now on the Depo program. By day he worked in the flower market, wrapping bunches of roses to be shipped to retail stores. He supplemented his income by working as a prostitute down in the warehouse district. Randy suffered from Paranoid Schizophrenia. He had been in and out of various mental institutions since the age of eighteen. He now self medicated with illicit drugs as many patients with mental illnesses did.

"What other drugs do you take, Randy?"

He began to list for me the antipsychotics and mood stabilizers he was on as I filled a syringe with his Depo and gave him the shot. His oxygen levels remained stable according to the monitor and I continued my questioning.

"What other drugs do you do? Heroin? Cocaine? Marijuana?"

"Well, Doc, I only do Morphine once a month now and I've pretty much stopped everything else." Given Randy's presentation and his numerous risk factors, I put AIDS and Pneumocystis first on my differential as I continued to talk to him. I asked the nurse to draw serology with Randy's permission.

"Why do you do Morphine only once a month?" This seemed odd to me, but I was learning never to assume anything.

"I get a disability check at the end of the month and it pays for the Morphine." This seemed very logical in a strange sort of way.

"Any other drugs, Randy?"

"Well I stopped sniffing a few months ago, but I still do Rush once in a while." He stated calmly, his oxygen saturation now at 89%.

"What's Rush?" I learn as much from my patients as I do from the books.

"It's jet fuel, Doc," he said matter-of-factly.

"What do you do with it?"

"You sniff it," he responded. I could see the pieces coming together and the diagnosis becoming clearer.

"When is the last time you did Rush, Randy?" I almost knew the answer before the question left my mouth.

"Two days ago. And man, I haven't felt good ever since. I've been coughing like crazy. Must have done too much." It was plain; he had chemical pneumonitis until proven otherwise. The jet fuel had caused a massive inflammatory reaction in his lungs and that was why he couldn't breathe.

I continued my history, asking Randy about other symptoms, including his HIV risks and he let me know that he was tested every month by his parole board and was "still negative." Halfway through my physical exam, Randy asked if he could go for a cigarette. He was really quite endearing in a strange way. Here was one of life's fuckups and he had a way of getting out of bed every morning. Randy had mastered the art of adjusting to one's surrounding. Sure it was dysfunctional by all logical standards but there was something so honest about this man. He was just good or bad; criminal or insane, there were no pretenses. On some bizarre level I found him fascinating.

After checking his chest x-ray and going through his lab work, I explained to Randy that I thought the Rush had irritated his lungs and he would need to come into the hospital for a few days to be put on steroids. This would stop the inflammation and make him feel better.

"Sure, Doc. Can I go for a smoke now?"

"No, Randy, you can't smoke for a few days at least. First it can irritate your lungs further and make your condition worse. Second, you are on 100% oxygen. If you light a match anywhere near this, you'll cause an explosion."

"I can take off the mask, Doc, it's okay." He was making a logical argument.

"No, you can't, Randy. You need the oxygen to keep you alive. Can you hold off without a smoke for a while? I can give you something to help take off the edge. Okay?" Legalized drug distribution; I knew he would agree.

"Okay." He sat back and continued to read his magazine while I ordered the steroid and called the unit to tell them we had an admission. I then paged Phillip MacKintosh to give him the story. He seemed quite excited by my story and my diagnosis and wanted to meet me in Emergency to discuss it. Phillip was the first to offer praise when you were right or were doing a good job. He also loved to teach and was enthused by any opportunity. These were some of his endearing qualities and I knew my night was off to a good start.

8:45 P.M.

I started Randy on high dose intravenous Steroids and gave him a small dose of Morphine to take away his sense of breathlessness. He never felt breathless but I was scared he'd leave for a cigarette at any time and I'd have to intubate him on the front steps of the hospital. The Morphine would hold things until I could get him to Intensive Care. I sat down at the desk to finish my note when Phillip walked into the department and waved at me. I put down my pen and got up to go over the case with him.

"I'll see the patient first, Eve, finish your note." He waved at me.

Phillip returned to the desk just as I was signing my name to the admission note. "Quite the character," he remarked.

"Fascinating case" I said, agreeing with him.

"I agree with you, Eve, this is definitely chemical pneumonitis. Did you send off HIV serology, just to be safe?"

"Yes, I also gave him a full dose of Septra in case this may be confused with Pneumocystis." I replied.

"What's your next plan, Eve?" The teaching had begun.

"Would Bronchoscopy with washings add anything further?" I answered in the form of a question.

"Yeah, I think that's a good plan. We'll get him to the unit and we can do the Bronchoscopy there. Does the unit know he's coming?" he asked.

"Yes, and I've entered all his orders. We can go at any time." I turned to the nurse and asked her to get ready to transport Randy to the ICU. I then explained to Randy what we were going to do. He asked again for a cigarette and I declined. Within ten minutes we were on our way down the hall to the ICU. Randy continued to ask for a cigarette in usual intervals along the way.

9:16 P.M.

It is safe to say that Randy did not want a Bronchoscopy once the procedure was explained to him. I can't imagine anyone wanting a tube put into his or her lungs with a camera on the end of it. Tell this to a Paranoid Schizophrenic and you will be hard pressed to find him in agreement. However, when Randy was told that he would be given drugs before the procedure (he wanted to know which ones and if he had a choice, he preferred Seconal) he quickly came on board. Surprisingly he tolerated the whole procedure well and I was shocked that he didn't need to be intubated after it was over. I grabbed a quick supper in the ICU staff room and changed a central line on a patient before Phillip called me and Ethan to go around and "put the patients to bed". This was a routine for the on-call house staff to go around with the staff person and discuss any problems that might arise in the night. It was now near midnight and with a stable unit, Phillip would be safe to go home for the night unless something drastic happened. We passed by Randy's bedside. He was sitting up with a mask on his face still reading his magazine. I had promised him he could keep his clothes on if he promised he would not go for a cigarette. It was a good deal, which Randy periodically forgot and would repeatedly ask his nurse for a smoke.

"He's driving me mad," Betty whispered in my ear when we were at the bedside.

"Doc, can I go for a smoke now?" Apparently this was repeated every three minutes or so.

"Sorry, Randy, not now," I answered and glanced at the monitor. His oxygen saturation was steady at 90% and we had confirmed this with a blood gas reading after the Bronchoscopy.

We finished walking around the unit and made note that there were six empty beds. "No need to fill them, guys," Phillip joked as he walked out of the unit.

"I'll take the next admission, Ethan, since you took the last. Okay?"

"Sure, Eve, have a good night," he said. We walked into our respective call rooms to change into hospital greens and hopefully catch a short nap if we were lucky. In Medicine, you eat when you can, sleep when you can, and pee when you can. It's a primitive existence, but it works.

2:45 A.M.

My pager woke me with a start. I had fallen asleep on top of the covers with my shoes still on. The unit was paging me and I lifted the phone and dialed their number. Vicki, the night unit clerk, answered the phone, "Eve, you better get down here quick. You will not believe this."

I hung up the phone and grabbed my white coat and ran down the hall to the front desk. Vicki directed me to bed eight where Randy had been admitted earlier that night. I was not prepared for what I was to find there.

Randy sat in his bed, face covered in soot. The smell of burnt flesh was in the air as I examined my patient before me. His hands were burnt red with pieces of skin missing. His left eyebrow was singed beyond recognition, and beneath an oxygen mask that was half melted to his face laid the remnants of facial hair and a smile. He saw me approach and yelled from the bed, "Doc, I swear, I didn't do it."

I looked down at the floor and there lay the evidence of a burning cigarette and his matches. Yes, Randy could not resist the nicotine temptation and when his nurse had gone to get him an extra blanket he lit up, literally, like a roman candle. Randy had mixed fire with oxygen and had almost burned down the unit in the process.

"You're lucky you didn't blow yourself up, Randy." I looked at his monitor and to my shock his oxygen saturations were 88%. I turned to Betty, his night nurse, who had a look of disbelief on her face. She was in the process of fitting another mask to his face over the now melted one.

"Betty, cover his hands with flamazine and gauze for now. Vicki," I called from the bedside, "could you page plastic surgery for me right away?" I turned to my patient, who had been muttering sentences of denial since my arrival and said, "Randy, you're busted. Let me see your face. Betty, could you give him five milligrams of Morphine?" I put on a pair of gloves and took some sterile scissors and forceps from the dressing tray. I proceeded to cut away the free pieces of the melted mask, leaving only the parts that were melted into his skin. I then cleaned the area with sterile water. By this time the Plastics Resident was on the phone and security had arrived at the bedside.

"Should we call a Code Red?" The beefcake from "protection services" asked. A Code Red is the hospital language for a fire.

"There is no fire. He tried to have a cigarette and was on oxygen. Can you just grab a chair and sit at the foot of the bed? If he tries to smoke, grab the cigarette." I looked at him blankly, taking off my gloves and moving out of the way so Betty could attend to Randy's hands.

I took the phone from Vicki and tried to maintain my composure. Quite frankly, I was in shock. I'd never had a patient explode before and I was now convinced I'd seen everything.

"Hi, it's Eve Solomon, who's this?" I asked with the phone to my ear.

"Eve! It's Salim. What can I do for you, my dear?" Salim had been my Junior Resident on the Medical Teaching Unit. He was brilliant and an excellent clinician. He was also a sweetheart.

"Salim, you are not going to believe this. I have a patient in ICU who tried to have a cigarette while on 100% oxygen."

"Shit. Is he okay?" Salim couldn't help but laugh on the other end of the phone.

"Well he has a mask melted to his face and likely second degree burns on his hands. I've cleaned the wound as best I can, but I need your help." I went on to explain why Randy had been admitted in the first place and Salim assured me he would be right down to assess things.

I returned to Randy's bedside. The security guard sat at the foot of the bed reading a magazine and trying not to faint while Betty cleaned and dressed Randy's hands.

"How do you feel?" I asked Randy. He continued to smile underneath the melted mask. I couldn't help but chuckle, "What's so funny, Randy. Why are you smiling?"

"It was a pretty cool explosion, Doc," he said frankly.

"Randy, you could have blown up the unit," I scolded, feeling more like his mother and less like a doctor.

"Sorry, Doc, I won't do it again."

"Dr. Solomon," Vicki's voice came over the bedside speaker, "Dr. MacKintosh is on the phone."

"Shit. Randy, I asked a Plastic Surgeon to come see you about your burns; he should be here any moment. Does he have anything flammable on him?" I turned towards Betty.

"All taken care of," she said.

I walked towards Vicki's desk to answer the call from Phillip, unsure of what kind of reception I would face. As I picked up the phone Salim entered the unit and I waved to him and motioned to Randy's bedside while speaking into the receiver.

"Hi, Phillip."

"Eve, is everything okay?" he sounded concerned.

"It's under control, Phillip. It seems that Mr. Adler tried to have a cigarette and almost blew himself up."

"WHAT?" Phillip was as shocked as could be expected.

"Yeh. Anyway he has second-degree burns on his hands and the oxygen mask is melted to his face. I've asked Plastics to see him and they are assessing him now," I reported.

"Is he okay?"

"Surprisingly well. The unit is in a state of shock but the patient is as stable as can be," I said.

"I'll be there right away. Thanks, Eve." Phillip hung up the phone and I sat at the desk for a moment, put my head in my hands, and burst into laughter. It was at least five minutes later before I gathered my composure, washed my face in the nearby sink, and went back to Randy's bedside.

3:45 A.M.

Within the hour Phillip had arrived and surveyed the damage. The nurses had set up fans at Randy's bedside to get rid of the stench and the security guard hadn't moved from his position. Salim had finished his consult and Randy was booked for surgery in the next fifteen minutes. The anesthetist on call was also at the bedside explaining to Phillip that he would keep the patient intubated for at least twenty-four hours after surgery, given his underlying problem and the swelling around his face post operatively. I walked over to Randy and explained to him what the plan was. Randy agreed as long as he could have some Morphine to tie him over. I asked Betty to give him another five milligrams and the operating room called to say they were ready for the patient.

High on Morphine and smelling of his burns, Randy was wheeled smiling down the hall. Phillip turned to me and laughed, "So anything else exciting?"

I shared in his laughter and responded, "That's as exciting as it gets around here."

7:30 A.M.

The rest of my night had been relatively uneventful. Randy returned from the operating room at around 6:30 with grafts to his third degree facial burns. He was safely sedated and on a ventilator and was a delight to take care of for the rest of my night. At about 5:00 the morning I admitted an elderly man with pneumonia and the case was relatively straightforward. The sun had risen and I was on my way to the doctors' lounge for a coffee. The sleepless night was hitting me as my adrenaline levels had faded several hours ago. I grabbed my usual latte and returned to the ICU. If I could see all my patients before sign in rounds and finish my notes, I might well be home by noon. I passed Dr. Leonard in the hallway and he nodded.

"How was your night, Dr. Solomon?" he inquired.

"Eventful, Dr. Leonard," I responded, taking a sip of my coffee and smiling at the magnitude of my understatement.

Chapter 6

I had managed to finish my notes for the day and got out of the hospital by
a little after noon. The walk to my car was like a march of freedom. The sun
seemed exceptionally bright and I took my time stopping periodically on the
way to close my eyes and face the sky. I felt the warmth and the wind on my
face and celebrated it as though all of this was new to me. As usual I
approached the parking lot and could not remember where I had parked the
Valiant. It is a comical routine many residents undergo. Stand by the
Resident Parkade between 12:00 and 1:00 P.M. every day and you will see a
parade of lost souls half-asleep and looking for the car they parked the day
before. Twenty minutes and individual sweeps of the first three floors and I
was safe in my automobile and on my way.

I stopped at the drug store on the way home to buy bubble bath, oblivious to looks I was getting dressed in my hospital greens. They are nothing
special. They are sanitary green pajamas with DO NOT REMOVE FROM HOSPI-
TAL stamped in black across the front. The cashier at the front was a teenage
girl plagued with too much makeup and bad gum chewing technique. She
rung in my order, surveyed my outfit and then asked, "Are you a nurse?"

"No. I just work at the hospital." I was not in the mood for the usual
conversation that might follow, "Really? You're a doctor? Blah, blah, blah...."

"Oh, do you think you could get me some of those greens? They look
really comfortable." All I wanted was the bubble bath. Funny how this was
not the first time this had happened. Hospital greens were a new fashion
statement in the teen scene. I had even seen them being sold on the street for

$50 a pair. Katarina and I had joked how we could make more money selling the damn pajamas as opposed to wearing them.

"Sorry." I grabbed my bubble bath for dear life and left without waiting for my change.

3:00 P.M.

The loft smelled clean when I arrived shortly after the bubble bath fiasco. I remembered that Lisa, our cleaning lady, had been by earlier that day. Lisa is one of the best things that happened to our marriage. She lives in the loft below us and has a small cleaning business on the side.

Essentially couples fight about three things in a marriage. The first of course is money. Jack and I have given up this argument as there is no money right now and some day there will be. We have agreed, rather, I have convinced him that it is pointless to argue about this, as we are powerless in this regard at the moment.

The second is shared time. There is never enough time. There's no time for sex, there's no time for talk, there's no time spent together. One person's time becomes more important than the other's and it becomes a power struggle. Jack and I have never had this problem for some reason. We've always been saved from this by the fact that we have few friends other than one another. Furthermore this argument often begins when couples have children, a fate we have yet to suffer from.

Finally the marriage partners fight about shared space. Men for the most part are designed to take off their clothes and leave them on the floor. Women by contrast, perhaps because of the whole Barbie influence, hang everything up, or at least put it on a chair. Men leave dishes where they were last used, women load dishwashers. Jack is true to his sex in this respect. Furthermore it takes him forty-five minutes to iron a shirt and it is agony. I hate ironing but would rather do the task than watch him struggle through. This is where Lisa comes in. While we used to fight over unmade beds and dirty dishes, sixty dollars a week buys us two visits from Lisa and peace has been restored in our home. She is our nanny and we are without children. It's perfect. I am convinced that cleaning personnel could make a sincere dent in the nation's divorce rate if given the chance. I really believe Lisa should stand outside marriage counselors' offices and hand out cards. She'd make a killing and a real difference.

I thumb through the mail to the expected realization that it is all bills and head straight for the bathroom. On the mirror is a note from Jack reminding me of a dinner with his boss at eight o'clock tonight. I run the bath and add the bubbles I worked so hard to get. I go into the closet to get a towel and lay out my black suit for tonight.

The warm water hits me as I lower myself in and realize how much my body aches from the night. Furthermore I smell terribly. I lay there for a few moments as a wave of exhaustion washes over me and decide to wash up quickly before I fall asleep and drown. Minutes later I'm wrapped in a towel, the blinds are drawn, and the alarm is set for 7:00 P.M. I put my wet head to the pillow, close my eyes, and continue the sleep from where I left off sixteen hours earlier.

8:15 P.M.

Edo is one of the nicest Japanese restaurants in the city. It takes almost a month to get a reservation but as a frequent customer, Larry Averdow, Jack's boss has a mysterious connection. Throw money at people and they are yours forever. Go figure. I don't know Larry very well. In fact I've only met him at a few Christmas parties but Jack is now their golden boy on a new project and Larry has decided to welcome us into his sacred fold. I'm indifferent either way, as long as my husband is happy. In reality I enjoy playing the coquettish wife once in a while, although my husband tells me it never works out that way. In any case, I love sushi and get to wear something slinky so why complain? Besides this is one of those circles where being a doctor is glamorous and sexy, and I'm willing to play along with the myth for one night.

We are late of course, as my nap went longer than expected and are shown to our table where Larry and his girlfriend Margaret are sitting in what looks like the aftermath of an argument. There are two empty seats remaining and I am told that Larry's other partner will be joining us later. Larry stands and shakes Jack's hand and kisses both my cheeks. I extend my hand to Margaret who is trying to hide a pout behind a smile. I now realize the only way to survive this evening is to drink through it. Jack and Larry begin to talk about business immediately and I am left to amuse Margaret and myself. She begins to tell me of their recent trip to Europe and I am thankful that, given the right questions, I know she will do all the talking. Margaret strikes me as the kind of women who is dying to be heard and I am only too happy to feign an ear tonight.

Two martinis later she is genuinely smiling and I am pleasantly buzzed. Larry has taken the liberty of ordering a chef's sampler for us; the chef is a dear friend of his I am told. Margaret turns to me out of earshot of her beau and matter of factly states, "I'm fucking his partner, you know."

"Really," I smile, convinced I have heard her wrong.

"Yes, Evan Green. He's an animal in bed."

"Oh my." I look over at Jack, trying to catch his gaze, but Larry has him captivated. My evening has just gotten interesting and uncomfortable. Inside I can't help but laugh. On cue the waiter returns and I order another martini. This earns me a look from Jack who read somewhere that a majority of doctors are alcoholics and has been scared ever since. I smile at him and give him a look that tells him that I need this drink more than he knows. Margaret begins to tell me of their trip to a Tuscan vineyard when Evan Green and his wife Nancy arrive at our table.

Evan is in his late forties and an impeccable dresser. He has that look that says he was born in a Hugo Boss suit. His wife Nancy is a fitness queen and I can tell from her face that she's had work done. I shake Nancy's hand and introduce myself as she takes the seat to my right. Evan kisses both my cheeks and sits across from his wife at the now completed circular table. I note that he is strategically placed next to Margaret. This is going to be good. I have Nancy on my right, Margaret on my left, and a perfect view of the playing field. Jack is across from me for visual support and my third martini has arrived. I'm having the time of my life and I've said maybe twenty words in total.

Human behavior fascinates me, as I'm sure it does most people. I watch Margaret and Evan exchange the odd lustful glance while their words to one another sound almost hostile. Larry and Margaret do not speak, do not look at one another, and Nancy is pleasantly hammered. In fact she was drunk when she arrived and is now slurring her words. This earns her the odd look from her spouse and I trade my martini in for a glass of water before Jack has a stroke. An evening that was supposed to have raw fish as its highlight is turning out to be surprisingly entertaining. Nancy orders another vodka on the rocks and Margaret continues her report on her trip to Europe. I began to wonder what Margaret did with the whole Evan thing while she was in Europe.

Evan turns his attention to me. "So Eve, what kind of a doctor are you?' he asks, with a genuine interest. Margaret turns her attention to Nancy as I face the men across from me.

"I'm finishing a fellowship in Intensive Care, Evan" I respond and take a sip of my water.

"How long will that be?" Larry asks.

"I've completed four years and have one more to go."

"How do you like it so far?" asked Evan.

"It's really a challenge. I love it."

People don't want the truth, Well, some people want the truth. But the men who pay my husband far too little money to play with computers do not want truth. They don't want to hear how I have slept four hours since Wednesday. Nor do they care that I've taken it up the ass at least a dozen times this week by the greatest egos mankind has to offer. These men want to know that as a "girl" in "medicine" I'm well adjusted, loving my job and can't wait to have children so that I can proclaim complete fulfillment. Despite the alcoholic freedom I am now benefiting from I know best to give these men exactly what they want. I know best because in addition to the worried look now on my husband's face, I have been in this situation many times before. I have learned that to keep things simple and to lie like a dog in the street makes everyone's evening more enjoyable.

"Yes, Larry," I smile, attempting to be dazzling, "it is such rewarding work. I find that I learn something new every day and I am constantly amazed by the power of the human spirit." This was true but polished. I did find rewards in my work and my patients often amazed me with their will and their humanity. It was the pretense and the ego that could taint things so and it was difficult in these times to find pure enjoyment among the political crap.

The boys were speechless and Jack sat back smiling. I innocently sipped my water as the consultation began.

"Being in the Medical field, what do you think of gene therapy, Eve?" Evan asked.

"Never mind that, what do you think of Viagra, Eve?" Nancy piped in. This was met by a dirty look from her husband and a coughing fit from Larry.

"Gene therapy really isn't my field, Evan, but I think there is no straight answer. It has such amazing potential in the area of medical treatment, but it raises so many ethical issues," I said. It was an interesting interaction. I wasn't sure why I was the focus of this conversation. Was it because I hadn't really spoken to these men before or because the other women at the table to choose from were an adulteress and a drunk? I often found myself at the center of conversation. It didn't bother me. In fact I enjoyed an intellectual exchange. What bothered me about this was that because of my medical degree, I was no longer a participant in the conversation but an authority on gene therapy. I knew less about it than Jack, who had spent many a night watching documentaries on the subject. Jack was fascinated by evolution. The idea that we selected out certain traits based on environmental challenges captivated him. The subject of gene therapy had such an effect on him. I think it was because he saw the human body like a computer he could not master. Genetic engineering was a form of understanding and controlling this life force before him.

"You know, Jack really knows more about this than I do. I'm sure he has more of an informed opinion on it than I could offer." Yes, the conversation could now be shifted back to Jack and I could easily listen to Margaret for another half an hour while my third martini kicked in.

Jack began to discuss one of the recent documentaries he had seen on the subject and I excused myself to go to the ladies room. Of course, true to form, Margaret and Nancy joined me. Why do women insist on going to the washroom together? I really wanted a few moments to myself. It's one thing to go to the washroom with your close girlfriends, it's quite another to urinate with female strangers. I knew these women less than an hour and already they wanted to pee with me. I did not share the camaraderie. Quite honestly this women washroom thing had always been lost on me. I play along but really I'm blind to its appeal. We don't really do anything in there. The conversations had in the ladies room could easily be had in another location. Furthermore, peeing with other women does not foster a great new sense of sisterhood. If it did, we would have gotten our acts together as women long ago. Men think we're holding some kind of meeting in there. Well we're not. We void, wash hands, reapply lipstick and immerse. A majority of times this is done in silence. When we do speak it is an exchange of polite chitchat or a slam basting review of another woman's outfit, behavior, or spouse's sexual exploits.

As per usual, I peed in silence while Nancy reapplied her lipstick and Margaret washed her hands and complimented Nancy on her handbag. I finished my business and walked over to the sinks.

"Jack's a doll, Eve, you're very lucky," Nancy slurred.

"Thank you, we're very happy," I replied, touching up my lip liner. I suddenly became nervous that Margaret may say something to Nancy about her sexual exploits. I hurried to put my liner back and returned to the table.

"The boys are very happy with his work, Eve, he's got partner written all over him," Margaret said. I wasn't sure if she was being honest or charming.

"That's wonderful news, Margaret, I'm glad. Jack loves his work. He's very happy at the company." I could be charming too.

I made my way to the door and the women stayed behind. I wasn't sure what words would fly in my absence. These were two bitter women on their best behavior and I did not want to be there to find out what they really thought of each other. I returned to the table and the first of several courses had arrived. Pieces of fresh sashimi were elegantly laid on a small block of ice with a cilantro and lemon sauce. The men had started eating and I began to do the same, knowing Margaret and Nancy would be a while. The fish melted in my mouth. It was wonderful. I looked across the table and could tell that Jack was equally enjoying his meal. We had long finished our sashimi when the rest of our party returned. It was obvious they had both had a cigarette. Margaret finished less than half of her fish and Nancy had barely touched her plate. These were women who spent every Friday and Saturday night at restaurants like this. I was enjoying my treat and they were bored. I felt like a virgin at the prom surrounded by has-beens.

11:00 PM
The evening continued in much the same vain. The food was extraordinary. Fresh fish mixed with stale relationships breeds hostility. I had enjoyed myself very much but could easily wait some time before a repeat of tonight's performance. We thanked our hosts graciously and Jack drove his still tipsy wife home.

"Did you know Margaret is sleeping with Evan?" I asked Jack, feeling pleasantly buzzed.

"No. How'd you know that?" Jack's mind seemed elsewhere.

"She told me. Right at the table, she leaned over and confessed." I felt quite proud of myself in this moment. I had brought forth this steamy gossip. In a sick way his office life was no longer perfect. In a strange way, I was not the only one with a profession filled with adulterers, alcoholics, and dysfunction. It was some competitive pronouncement that computer geeks could fuck around just as much as doctors could. Jack could worry about my *addictive personality* and *professional hazards* all he liked. I had now evened the score. His picture perfect animation world was one big sex scandal. I could have all the martinis I wanted at this point.

Forty-five minutes and some of the best sex I've had in along time later, and I fell into a much needed, dreamless sleep. My job as wife had been completed and I had been dazzling. How could anything be more satisfying?

Chapter 7

Saturday, 11:45 A.M.
I awoke alone to the sound of the phone ringing. I could hear Jack in the den talking to my mother.

"Yes, Eleanor, she's still sleeping. She was on call the other night and is catching up on her rest." My mother had no concept of what I did for a living. She would often make remarks like, "Well tell them you just can't, dear," when I had a talk to do or had to work an extra night on call. Furthermore my mother thought sleep was a waste of time. I'm sure finding me in bed close to noon was not met with the best reception. I let Jack field the call and snuck into the bathroom.

Jack interrupted my shower with a cup of coffee and a kiss.

"Your mother called," he reported.

"I heard. Is my sister in jail?" I laughed.

"She's been deported," he joked and climbed into the shower with me.

"What should we do today?" I asked.

"We could go for a bike ride and then see an afternoon movie," Jack proposed.

"Sounds great. I have to finalize the arrangements for the New York trip at some point today." I had a conference in New York next month and Jack was taking the time off to join me. We had a week planned together in my favorite city and I couldn't wait. Of course part of it would be spent at a conference but I could stand the educational experience if it came along with an equal amount of glamour. I finished my business and climbed out of the shower.

"Stay," Jack beckoned, "we'll play."

Again he loves sex in the shower. This was one of the few things we just didn't see eye to eye on. Showers were places for cleaning up and moving on. Fornicating in the steam of a five square foot place was just not my thing. Give me a Turkish bath where the area is twelve feet by sixteen feet with a bench and perhaps I would see things differently. In the small confines of my less elaborate clean up space I couldn't get sexy.

I was already out and reaching for a towel when I said, "Get started without me and I'll meet you in the bedroom for the finish." I was laughing at my own joke but Jack just grunted. Now almost fully dry, I grabbed my coffee and went into the bedroom to get dressed for our day out. I knew my love would be at least another half-hour so there was time for leisure. Like the true masochist I am, I picked up the phone and called my mother.

"Hello?" She picked up sounding perfectly well adjusted. My mother was a master of disguise. Rome could be burning and she'd have the perfect phone voice for the occasion. This was a trait that had only marginally rubbed off on me but one Penny possessed with grace.

"Hi, Mom. How are you?" I asked. Getting a real answer out of my mother would be taxing at best.

"Fine sweetie, how are you? Jack tells me you've been working really hard. Are you okay?" She was not smoking, this was a good sign.

"I'm just fine, Mom. We had a really nice dinner last night with Jack's partners and I had a great sleep last night. We're doing just fine, Mom." I was desperately avoiding talk of Penny. If I could move the conversation along quickly enough, I may very well succeed.

"You know who I saw the other day and she said to say, 'hello'?" Thus began the information section of our conversation. I had been saved from talk of my sister by my mother's need to gossip.

"Who?" I played along. We no longer lived in the same city, but I still knew the infinite details of most of the people I went to high school with thanks to my mother's inquiring mind.

"Allison Black. She looks fabulous. She married Les Hyman you know. He's just loaded. They are both so happy." I knew my mother was just being informative but I couldn't help but take this as a shot. Allison Black had been one of my closest friends in junior high. She was a gorgeous teenager, compared to my average looks. Her blonde hair, blue eyes and perfect body were balanced by the fact that she was very dumb. I was Allison's tutor in most subjects and we became friends. Like me, Allison did not come from money. Unlike me, Allison married into it. It had appeared, from my mother's report, that she had married into it again. This was particularly stinging information since Allison and I had a terrible fight just after graduation and had really not spoken since. Allison, to put it mildly, had a vivid imagination. In reality she spouted lies about almost everything. When Allison met a man

45

who had a fondness for wine, it was pure coincidence that her family "owned a vineyard in the south of France". When the man had a degree in Astronomy, she was defending a thesis in the very subject. If Allison's beau was Greek, she was half Greek. If he was Spanish, she was half Spanish. It became difficult as her friend to not only play along with such charades, but to follow them. There were days when I couldn't remember if she was descended from royalty or Russian spies. Combined with her love of a fairy tale was her promiscuity, which made being her friend an exhausting experience. I finally confronted her one day in the cafeteria at university. This was met with a fanatical screaming fit and a vow never to speak to me again. Unfortunately Allison thereafter spoke of me frequently. She would regale anyone who would listen of concocted tales of my emotional torture and financial irresponsibility. When Allison was finished with me, any outsider might have thought I was a suicidal thief. Fortunately her reputation as a liar had spread and there were few who believed her.

Despite our history, the Blacks were very close friends with my parents. This forced me to invite the bitch to my wedding, where she was surprisingly civil. When my father was first diagnosed with cancer Allison sent me one of those "bury the hatchet" letters. I responded with a polite thank you and informed her that our lives had taken different directions and we had best just move on. When Allison's first husband, Eric, a multimillionaire from France (she could barely speak the language) left her for a man I was vengefully overjoyed. She went so far as to phone me for support and I failed to return the call. Allison was dangerous and I hadn't the patience for her. However, I didn't have the courage to tell her to go screw herself either. Now she was married and fabulous all over again. God had a sick sense of humor.

"What is she doing with her life?" I'd play along for my mother's sake.

"Well she says she got into Medical School in Europe but has turned them down. She's going to open a clothing shop in town. She looks wonderful." Medical School my ass, she was really amazing.

"Yeah." I refused to bite and tried to sip my coffee calmly.

"She and her husband are going to the mountains for their honeymoon. She asked me for your number, I'm sure she'll call you." Great. Fabulous. She was worse than an ex-lover.

"Yeah," I was still not biting. "How's Daddy?" Segue into new conversation.

"He's great. You know your father. His blood counts are perfect; the doctor is convinced he'll live forever." I love medical professionals who make false promises to their cancer patients. My father had metastatic end stage terminal cancer. I don't know how more final it could be. He also had an egomaniac for an Oncologist who saw it as a personal failure if my father would succumb to the disease. This, along with my mother's blind optimism, was a danger. My father's only request was that when his time came to die, it would be quick and painless. Fortunately he and I had always had a special connection and he knew he could count on me, among the madness, to put his wish into action.

"Is Daddy around?" I asked, hoping to say hello. It was almost as though she screened his calls. It made me crazy when I lacked the patience to try to understand her ways.

"No, he's gone for lunch with the boys," my mother responded, alluding to my father's time-honored tradition of Saturday morning brunch with his friends. Eight men would sit around a table of bagels and eggs, talking about their prostates and urinary frequency. I had come along with him once, which was fun. But it was a mistake as I only felt more like a consultant for their woes rather than my father's daughter.

"Oh, that's the other line," my mother said with an air of urgency. We could be in the middle of a million-dollar wire transaction over the telephone and my mother would pause to get the other line. Call waiting was not a convenience with her, it was a religious experience. Jack and I made the mistake of calling her from our honeymoon in Europe. At $9.00 a minute she paused half way though hello to get the other line.

"Okay, Ma, I've got to go. We're going to get some lunch. I'll call you later."

"Bye, sweetie." I hung up the phone and took a deep breath and a sip of coffee. I could easily stay in my pajamas all day but I felt obligated to face the day at some point. I put on my biking shorts and tee shirt and went into the den to check my e-mail. Jack had finished his shower and was now dripping dry, seated at the computer with a towel wrapped around his waist.

"Go get dressed, babe, and we'll go," I said, shooing him into the bedroom.

My e-mail of course consisted of six different offers to consolidate my debt and two offers to check out live teenage sex on the Internet. Amidst the junk mail was a message from my dear friend, Theo, a banker in New York. Theo not only had the brass ring in life; he had stocks and bonds in it. He was the ideal capitalist. Theo and I grew up in the same city. He was four years older than me and I was in awe of him all through high school. He then moved to Massachusetts to get a business degree, at Harvard of course, and has been printing money ever since. Socially, Theo is the unluckiest bastard in the world. God certainly divides. Theo's first wife left him six weeks after their wedding, stating she didn't love him. His second wife left him the day of the wedding without a reason. He was now living with his girlfriend in New York. She was costing him a fortune and insisting they have sex only once every two weeks. He was a wonderful friend and I had secretly adopted him as my older brother.

E. V. HELLO FROM FRANCE. THE FIRM SENT ME TO PARIS TO CHARM A GROUP OF POTENTIAL. CLIENTS. THE WORK IS GREAT BUT THE BASTARDS ARE KEEPING ME TOO BUSY. PARIS IS PERFECT, AS

WE LEFT IT. I WENT TO THE LOUVRE TODAY AND THOUGHT OF YOU THE ENTIRE TIME. JENNIFER IS TAKING ME TO MEET HER PARENTS IN OREGON FOR THANKSGIVING. THIS COULD BE SERIOUS. SHE HAS GREAT LEGS AND A DECENT MIND SO I MIGHT AS WELL TAKE A SEMBLANCE OF A PLUNGE. NEED YOUR INSIGHT BADLY. WILL BE BACK FROM PARIS LATER THIS WEEK FOR VERBAL CONSULTATION ON THIS MATTER. MISS YOU MADLY, THEO.

Theo had joined me in Europe after graduation and we had spent a week together in Paris. Knowing he was there took me back to the days when my life was simpler. I had just finished high school and was on top of the world. I was spending my first year of university taking Art History in Paris. The course would give me full credit at my home university and I was on Scholarship. Under these conditions my parents had agreed to my "year off." On paper, I spent that year learning Art and French. In reality I spent it learning the art of Frenchmen. I did get a wonderful education while I was there, but my sexual awakening took priority. My year at private school had gone far to nourish my virginity. What took six years of virtue to build in North America was easily forgotten in one night in Europe.

Theo had come to visit me that year. It was a gift from his parents after his divorce became final. His ex-wife Jackie had gotten the house and its furniture, and he was in much need of a consolation prize. We spent the week at the art galleries where I could show off my new knowledge. I was sleeping with Etien, an acting student who was an amazing lover but it ended there. Theo and I spent many nights over wine and tears, mourning the loss of his promised personal perfection. Perhaps it might have become more than friendship but he was never the man for me and I was definitely not the woman for him. Despite our wonderful bond, we suffered, to this day, of eternal misunderstandings and our life views were paradoxes of one another. Theo, a modern man, still secretly wanted a woman to come home to. He wanted someone he could take care of. He was a giving man in the most self-ish of ways. He needed to be seen as the loving, almost martyred, husband. This gave him the ultimate praise and boost to his self-esteem. I was always too independent for him. I wanted to solve his problems, not create them. We fought like mad, even to this day. If I wanted an argument I need only bring up his personal life and we were off and running.

I elected to respond to Theo's e-mail later as I heard Jack putting on his shoes. I joined him at the door and we went into the garage to get our bikes.

"How's Theo?" I told him I had received the e-mail and Jack felt obliged to ask about my friend.

"He's his usual. He's in Paris on business and he's visiting our old hang-outs." Jack does not like Theo. He thinks Theo's unconventional in a bad way and questions his sense of fidelity. Theo has slept around on every one of his relationships. This is usually because they are so shitty he feels justi-fied. This does not sit well with my husband, who I think fears I may be the next object of Theo's desires. I knew this was bullshit but I was powerless to make him think otherwise.

2:45 P.M.

The sun was perfect on our ride. It was neither too hot nor too cold and we took the path along the river to enjoy the view. We rarely speak on these rides through the city. It is cherished time together when words are unnec-essary. It is in these times when I know I have found my proverbial soul mate. We are rarely of one mind in these moments. It has nothing to do with "reading one another's thoughts" or some bizarre form of celestial commu-nication. Jack is usually thinking about how much more RAM he could potentially acquire on his beloved motherboard, while I wonder whether we should paint the bathrooms dark gray. No, these are the moments in a mar-riage when there is this wondrous celebration of silence. We ride along together in our separate thoughts with the pure pleasure of one another's company. These moments are pure, untainted by his work, my career, the house, the bills, or the parents. It is a man, a woman, their bikes, her can of paint, and his hard drive. For a woman who worships the spoken word, these quiet moments are gifts in my life. I raise my face to the sun and hear the sounds of the river and the wheels and I am free.

Chapter 8

Monday, 6:45 A.M.
Saturday was followed by Sunday, a day spent in a coffee house with several articles and a laptop in preparation for the rounds presentation I was to give on Wednesday. I found myself surprisingly productive and was pleased that almost all of my slides were complete. I was to present a case and then discuss the findings while citing the most recent literature on the topic. I decided given the events of the week, it would be both interesting and educational to present Randy's case. I titled my talk "What a Rush". I was particularly proud of my wit.

Now Monday had come quickly as it always does with the usual promises and exhaustion. As with every Monday, I was convinced I was coming down with something and struggled to the shower in a post weekend haze. Jack was still asleep as Mondays were his late days. This office was the way of the future. They finished at four o'clock on Fridays and started at nine-thirty on Mondays. I was convinced they knew something the rest of the planet did not. The shower didn't help to wake me. I vowed as I did every morning that once I was in my own practice I would start at ten in the morning. Why not? What is it about doctors that make them think a job is better done at the crack of dawn? The logic is lost on me.

I leave the shower, grab a robe and start my morning routine in darkness, whispering through as not to wake the lucky bastard in the bed I just came from. As I pour my second cup of coffee and convince myself this addiction is helping my career, I catch the first signs of morning outside my kitchen window. The sky is red and turning golden as I walk into the bedroom to get dressed. Jack sleeps, undisturbed by my morning ritual. Thirty minutes later I am dressed and presentable. I kiss my husband's warm cheek and head for the door. I'm not quite sure when everything became so difficult.

The route to the hospital is uneventful aside from Nina Simone singing along with me. I have long said that Nina is by far one of the greatest jazz singers but she is under appreciated. Leave it to me to love a woman who is under valued.

I enter the hospital through the door to the Emergency Room. The waiting room is terribly crowded, which signals to me that my day will be busier than usual. I grab my usual coffee and head to the ICU to get started on my morning. There will be a new set of staff men given the new week and I'm curious to see how my patients faired in my absence this weekend.

I long ago gave up the notion that I was the best person for the job. When I first began my training, I spent many a dutiful night in the hospital, double checking things with a neurosis that implied I could not trust anyone else to take care of my patients. After two years and severe exhaustion, this quickly faded. I learned well that I would quickly marry this job and nothing else if this attitude persisted. This is not to say that I don't value my work, quite the opposite. I know I bring something unique to the work but we all do. To hold on to the idea that your patients will die without you is pure ego. It is a fantasy that undermines your colleagues and diminishes your patients as independent individuals. And so, I let go. Sure there are times when something will happen in my absence that I don't agree with, but I'm sure that I've made treatment changes on many nights that have been contrary to someone's practice. Welcome to being a grown up.

The unit is buzzing. There's the Monday morning energy along with seven new patients whose names I don't recognize. One of my patients has been transferred to the regular medical ward and I am left with Mr. Brown, the elderly gentleman with pneumonia who is now in septic shock, and Randy who is still intubated and in full nicotine withdrawal. I grab hold of my coffee and proceed to Mr. Brown's bedside.

Harold Brown is a seventy-five-year-old bull rider who last saw a doctor in 1976. He was admitted several days ago with pneumonia and started on the wrong antibiotic combination by his family doctor. I transferred him to the ICU last week when he was found blue and with a whiff of a blood pressure. He was now on broad-spectrum antibiotics and a ventilator. He has also gone into kidney failure over the weekend and risked being started on continuous dialysis sometime in the near future. This man is sick but innately strong and something in me knows he will be okay. It's strange how you develop an instinct for these things after only a short time in the field. Some call it a sense, others a "gestalt". Regardless of its name, the power to know whether someone will die or be okay is unexplainable and not without fault. People will surprise you without fail. There have been several cases where patients have surprised me just by their ability to live through the horrors of their illnesses. Unfortunately, as you progress in your career, the surprises become infrequent and the predictable losses remain.

At Harold's bedside sits his young wife. I know from the history in the chart that he has had three previous wives and twelve children in total. His present wife is forty-five and a horse trainer.

"Hello, Mrs. Brown. I'm Eve Solomon. I'm one of the physicians looking after your husband. Sorry we did not meet before; I was off over the weekend."

"Hi, Dr. Solomon. Please call me Kathy. How is Harold doing?" she asked softly, shaking my hand.

"Please, Eve is fine. Harold has pneumonia as you already know and it has caused him to go into a shock state. He's very sick, as I'm sure you appreciate, but we know what type of pneumonia this is and we have him on the right antibiotics. He's responding, although slowly, to the treatment but it will take some time." My answer was honest, to the point and without all the fancy medical bullshit. This was what I was best at. I explained to Kathy what all the machines at the bedside were and asked her to move to the other side of the bed while I examined her husband. I began by checking his vital signs on the monitor and reviewing the current drugs he was on. I noted that his blood pressure had dramatically improved over the weekend and he was on minimal medications for this. His lungs actually sounded better than they had on early Friday morning and his ventilator settings had not worsened. The rest of his physical exam was unremarkable and I continued my review by checking in the computer for his labs. His blood counts were stable and I noted that his white count was dropping and was now within normal limits. His electrolytes were all okay except that his kidney function was worsening, but he was still making urine.

I smiled at Kathy and said, "Kathy, everything looks stable for now. All we can continue to do is keep Harold on the current medications and see how he responds. Do you have any questions?"

"No, Eve. Thanks. Oh, is it okay if I sit here for a while longer?"

"Of course. If you need anything, let me know." I picked up his chart and walked to the desk to make a note of my exam and the lab work in the chart. My plan for the day would be simple. Continue physiological support and watch his urine output as well as his kidney function. The note was brief and to the point and I returned the chart to the bedside. I then made my way to Randy's bedside where I found him alone, ventilated, and wide-awake. He had a clipboard with paper in one hand and a pencil in the other. On the paper he had written lines of questions at an attempt to maintain communication. I leaned over him and said hello.

"Hi, Randy. It's Eve. Do you remember me? I was the doctor who admitted you to hospital," I said over the sound of the monitors and ventilator. He waved a sign of recognition and reached for his pencil and scrawled 'hi' in shaky letters. His face was wrapped in bandages that covered his mouth and cheeks. His eyes were open and I could see clearly that he had singed off all of his eyelashes and one eyebrow in entirety. The part of his face which was exposed looked sunburned. This gave him a slightly demonic appearance. Randy had done well over the weekend and would likely be extubated today. The surgeons were successful in grafting skin from his thigh to his mouth area and he could look forward to a lengthy hospital stay with daily bandage changes and physiotherapy for his new skin.

I continued my examination of Randy in the usual fashion and called Jackie, the respiratory technician, to the bedside for a briefing on his ventilator status.

"Holy shit, Eve, he's lucky," Jackie responded grabbing her clipboard from the top of the ventilator.

"How's he doing?" I asked. Randy was a freak. This was clear to all who had heard his story. He was an aberrancy that would be discussed for years to come around cafeteria tables and at parties. I wasn't in the mood to engage in such banter at this time. Besides, as crazy as the whole situation had gotten, something in me wanted to protect this soul. I didn't pity him or feel he was weak. If it was a choice whether to ridicule or defend his dignity, I was choosing the latter.

I listened as Jackie reported to me about his ventilator settings and most recent blood gases. The patient was clearly ready for extubation. Phillip was standing at the front desk looking weary after a weekend on call. I walked over to him.

"Good morning, Dr. MacKintosh."

"Good morning, Eve."

"I think Randy Adler is ready to be extubated. May I do the honors?"

"Go ahead." Phillip's tone was almost a whisper. I could tell he'd had a rough night.

I turned and motioned to Jackie that she could pull the breathing tube. I returned to the bedside to write a note in the chart. Minutes later Randy was off the ventilator and had a mask on his face for oxygen. I went to his bedside and smiled at him. Glancing over at the monitor I could see that his oxygen saturation was 96% and he was breathing comfortably. Sitting up in the bed, he looked over at me and smiled beneath the bandages. He motioned for me to come closer and I leaned forward to listen to him. He put his lips together and in a hoarse tone said but one word, "Smoke?"

"Not on your life," I responded with a chuckle.

11:45 A.M.

Rounds were the usual pace for a Monday morning, given the new patients to see and the new staff people to see them. The staff doctors changed at the start of each week. This had its benefits. When there was a less favorable staff doctor, he would be gone in a week. This could be most unfortunate if the staff man was a nice person and a good teacher. I use the masculine in these descriptions, as there were no female staff physicians in the department of Critical Care. Whether this was an act of chance or a fault of recruitment was not known nor discussed.

Dr. Steven Wong was one of the senior staff men in the ICU. He was in his late forties and one of the smartest men I knew. He was also one of the most descent people around. Steven exuded dignity and honor. He was one of my favorite teachers on staff and was well liked by most residents. I watched him at the bedside numerous times. He had mastered the marriage of art and science. His manner with patients was matched only by his amazing diagnostic ability. I couldn't have been happier for my upcoming week.

In contrast, Dr. David Michaels was a prick. He and I had several unfavorable encounters in the past, which led me to believe he had issues with smart women. On several occasions I was the object of Dr. Michaels' personal attacks and where most would have kept their mouth shut, I talked back, only to worsen the conflict. My last encounter with him was three weeks ago when he was on staff in the ICU for the day, covering for Dr. Leonard. We were standing at a patient's bedside and I was presenting the case. The patient was a seventeen-year-old girl who had taken a drug overdose. I had just begun to tell the story when he spoke up with his usual condescension, "Dr. Solomon, how do you know this is a cocaine overdose?"

I was expecting opposition but not this early in the case. "Well, Dr. Michaels, the patient has a history of—"

"History of abuse doesn't tell the story," he interrupted and went on to tell the rest of us what the physical findings of cocaine addictions were. This was his way of belittling me. Having not slept the previous night and knowing the case fairly well, I didn't feel like playing along. Furthermore I had a mouth on me and was not afraid to use it.

"Dr. Michaels," I interrupted, "the patient does not have a history of cocaine abuse. In fact her history is significant for several suicide attempts, as well as long standing morphine abuse and heroine overdoses. Her last heroin overdose was two weeks ago. This overdose was heroine as well but mixed with cocaine for the first time. The patient was lucid on presentation and was able to give me the history of her drug use. The story goes —"

"Dr. Solomon," he interrupted again.

"Please let me finish giving the history, sir — I'm able to think better that way." Boom. I couldn't help it. He was pissing me off and I would only take it so much. It would have been different if the bastard actually knew what he was talking about, instead he was talking to hear himself speak and on my airtime. I was tired and angry and had lost patience for this bullshit.

My response was met with the dirtiest of looks but I continued to present the case. When I was finished with my treatment plan and summary, Michaels began his gunfire.

"Dr. Solomon, can you list the clinical features of heroine overdose for us? That is if you are able to think now."

I began to answer his question and was met with a wave of his hand and a dismissal, "Yes, all right, I think we've heard enough from you for today."

We moved on to the next bed and when we were out of earshot he pulled me aside and asked me to meet him in "his office" at the end of the day. Of note, Michaels didn't have an office. I reminded him of this and he informed me that the staff doctors' lounge would suffice.

I met Dr. Michaels in the staff doctors' lounge that day and he sat very close to me on a couch. The man weighs at least 270 pounds and has the worst dental hygiene I've ever seen. Sitting right next to me was intimidating and uncomfortable. He loved every minute of it.

"Eve, I'm not just here to make you a better doctor but also to mold you into a better person. You need to be aware that everyone in the department is unhappy with your behavior. Your little display this morning in rounds is just the tip of the iceberg. Now I think you and I should meet on a regular basis to go over your behavior and rectify the situation."

I was shocked and mortified. Firstly I had just received an excellent interim evaluation from the ICU staff and the head of the department, Dr. Lawrence. Secondly this man was way out of line. I wasn't sitting there any longer. I stood up and headed for the door.

"Eve," he grabbed my arm, "we're not finished here."

"Yes we are," I said, fighting back tears of fear. "Please take your hand off me, Dr. Michaels. In the future, if you would like to have any more evaluations of me I would like Drs. Lawrence and Leonard to be present. I find this environment inappropriate and will not meet with you in this way again. Furthermore, if my performance is so upsetting to the staff, then why didn't my evaluation reflect this? "I turned and left the room. From there I stopped by Dr. Lawrence's office and let him know what had just happened. I asked him to keep the incident confidential, as I did not want to make an issue of it; I only wanted him to be aware of it.

I picked up another patient in rounds who had come in over the weekend. Her name was Patricia Maxwell. She was a thirty-three-year-old woman with metastatic breast cancer. She was currently on a chemotherapy regimen and had just started her third cycle of the program. The cancer was not responding and had now spread to her spine, necessitating urgent Neurosurgery for spinal chord decompression. Post operatively she had developed an infection at the surgical site and it had spread to her spinal fluid and her brain. The meningitis and cerebritis had caused septic shock. She was so sick. I was told in report that she had both liver and kidney failure as a result and her immune system was gone from the chemo. I was glad Steven would be overseeing things on this case in particular.

"What do you want to do, Eve?" Steven asked at the bedside.

"For now she needs continuous dialysis for her renal failure, which we should start right away. I need to review her cultures and make sure we haven't missed anything. She's been on antibiotics for twenty-four hours. If in another twelve hours we don't see an improvement I think we should start antifungal treatment given her risk. In the meantime, let's have Infectious Diseases consult here. I need to familiarize myself with her case a little further after rounds before making any other changes. She's so sick but she's stable for now, so I'd like to give myself the opportunity to examine her and go over her labs before any other fine tuning." I took a deep breath and waited.

"Sounds like a plan. I'll order the dialysis now; we can meet back here after rounds. Can you schedule a meeting with her family later this afternoon?"

"Sure, Steve. Thanks."

"Good work," he winked. This was the essence of Steven; kind, appreciative and a gentleman. I adored the man.

I asked Joanne at the desk to schedule a family meeting for Mrs. Maxwell's husband, parents, and sister at 3:30 and returned to rounds. The group had made their way to the last two beds and Alex Connor was presenting a case. David Auerbach came up behind me and whispered in my ear, "I'm on call with you tonight."

"Great. I can take the first admission if you like, David" I said softly. He nodded and we turned our attention back to Alex. Despite the fact that I strongly disliked Alex I was slowly learning to work with him. This had become an occupational hazard of late. This was not a profession, as I'm sure many are, where you could tell your coworkers what you really thought of them. Likes and dislikes fell to the wayside when there was work to be done. The complaining and bad-mouthing came after the day was over and the work was complete. I did not have to like Alex, but I did have to work with him. It was in my best interest to keep my mouth shut when he was talking and to never show my true feelings when he was near.

Alex had been on call last night and was presenting a trauma case of a twenty-four-year-old involved in a motorbike accident. The man's name was Jonathan Steele and his blood alcohol level twenty-four hours after the accident was three times that of the normal limit, He had attempted to drive a friend's motorbike home from the bar and literally hit a wall on the way home. The key issue now was whether or not he could be legally declared brain dead so organ donation could then take place. This I had learned through my years of training was a long and detailed process. First we would wait for the alcohol to run its course through his system and John would have to fail the *apnea test*.

Normally when a healthy brain is cut off from oxygen the body's carbon dioxide levels will rise in the blood. This rise will eventually get to a point where they will stimulate the respiratory centers of the brain to breathe. If one is brain dead, there is nothing to stimulate and no one breathes. So the key to an apnea test is to take a patient off the ventilator and let the carbon dioxide build up in their blood and wait for them to breath. If they don't breathe, they have failed the apnea test and are considered to be brain dead. This is only the first step in the process. Next comes a cerebral perfusion test. This is a nuclear scan to determine if certain parts of the brain are in fact metabolic. When a brain dies, its metabolic properties die with it. Thus the nuclear scan.

Considering he was on call last night, Alex would be leaving after rounds to get some sleep. He turned to me after presenting the case and asked me to follow up on the apnea test and the nuclear scan. Essentially I would be taking over the case since all of this would happen over the course of the day. I immediately said yes without hesitation. This would again be a terrible case and I could see it unfolding in front of me after my words entered the air. I often wondered why I got myself into these situations more often than others. Was it an inability to say no or was I asking for emotional punishment? Part of me knew my eagerness was due to a desire to shine. I was good with families. My strength lay in my ability to bring humanity to the bedside. Like most, I centered on my strength in times of opportunity, rather than focus on a weakness and an occasion to learn and to experience something new. I had forgotten how human we could be within these walls. The vulnerability of the outside world was rearing its head and I was willingly playing along. I grasped my third coffee of the morning and followed the group to the next and last bedside.

Chapter 9

2:34 P.M.

The day raged on in its usual fashion. I stood at Patricia Maxwell's bedside watching her breathing. There was a catheter in her skull and a milky fluid, which could only be puss, was draining slowly from it. Her husband Jason sat at her bedside holding her hand.

"Hello, Mr. Maxwell, I'm Dr. Solomon. I'm one of the residents on call in the unit. I'll be involved in your wife's care while she is in the ICU."

"Hello." His eyes were moist and he shook my hand from his seat at her bedside. "How's she doing?" He looked worn and weary and his battle was far from over.

"She has an infection in her brain and in the fluid surrounding her spine and brain. It is causing her body to go into shock. She is very sick, as I'm sure you already know. But we have her on antibiotics and we're doing all we can. The next few days will be critical." I could feel that my words lacked conviction. This woman would die and I knew it. I was powerless to prevent it and would only prolong it. There she lay, too close to my age wearing her mortality like an albatross. There I stood in the shadow of her husband's love and hope casting darkness, an intrusion upon them both. I asked Mary, the bedside nurse, if she had any concerns. She shook her head and I put my hand on Jason's shoulder.

"I'll see you shortly, Mr. Maxwell. We have a family meeting at 3:30," I said softly.

"It was changed to five o'clock so my in-laws could be there."

"See you then," I smiled. I turned, feeling really shitty and walked over to Jonathan Steele's bedside. His blood alcohol level was now undetectable and we could now start the process. Jackie, the respiratory technician, was already at the bedside waiting for me to begin the apnea test. Jackie unhooked the endotracheal tube from the ventilator and silenced the alarm. I stood at the foot of Jonathan's bed, watching his chest, waiting for movement. I knew he was brain dead. I knew his organ donor card was complete. I was waiting for death to be official. I was welcoming the finality. We stood at the bedside watching his chest with the knowledge that if Jonathan did breathe he would live the rest of his life in a persistent vegetative state. His life would be condemned to diapers and feeding tubes and nothingness. His life would signal the loss of a liver, kidney, heart, or lung for someone in need. His life would be a painful message and his death a release. His death would be a gift to his family that could only be understood with the permission of hindsight and experience. I stood with a silent prayer, an unspoken wish that Jonathan's chest would remain motionless. I ignored the irony that this was one young life I did not want to be saved. I wanted him to die as terrible as this was. My view from the bed was one void of hope and vanity and fear. I stood, empty of tears, watching his rib cage and waiting. Jackie looked at me and I asked her to take the first blood gas sample. Jackie walked over to Jonathan's arm and drew an arterial blood sample of the line in his wrist. She marked the time on her clipboard, 2:46 P.M. and left the unit to run the sample to the lab.

2:59 P.M.

Fifteen minutes and three blood gas samples later and Jonathan's chest remained motionless. I checked the chart for the eighth time in the last twenty-four hours to ensure that he had not received any sedatives or paralytics. His carbon dioxide had risen as expected and the test was complete. Jonathan was brain dead. I asked Jackie to hook up the ventilator again and to start ventilating him with 100% oxygen so as to keep his organs in good condition. I walked over to the desk and asked Joanne to page Dr. David Michaels so I could tell him the news.

"Dr. Michaels," I said into the receiver, "Jonathan Steele has failed the apnea test. Would you like me to proceed with the cerebral perfusion or is that sufficient?" I couldn't judge what I was most upset by, Jonathan's death or the fact that Dr. Michaels would be supervising me on this case.

"Eve, what was his blood alcohol?"

"Undetectable."

"Are you sure?"

"Yes, sir. I checked it twice before the test began."

"Well then, call for an EEG right away and I'll be right there." He hung up the phone.

I called the EEG (electroencephalography) department and told them the situation. They agreed to do the test right away. An EEG would give us an electrical picture of Jonathan's brain. I turned to Sue, Jonathan's nurse, and asked the obvious next question, "Where's his family?"

"There is no family. He has a brother in Australia and a mother in Toronto. The organ donor card was in his wallet and on his license," she said in a toneless voice.

"Has anyone spoken to the mother or brother?" I was shocked.

"Yes, his mother is an alcoholic and refused to come in. He has a stepfather in Toronto who lives with his mother. They asked for the body to be sent to Toronto when we're done. His brother is aware of the situation and can't get a flight out until next week. He doesn't want us to wait. Apparently the brother and Jon had a talk about organ donation. Jon was adamant that this is what he would have wanted." There was no family to talk to. The only conscience to face was my own. I walked up to Jonathan's broken body and held his bloodied, bruised hand.

"Dr. Solomon," Dr. Michaels was now at the bedside. "Where are the blood gas results?" I handed him the patient's chart, complete with my note accounting the entire apnea test and its results. He stood at the bedside, chart in hand, reviewing the case. Moments later the EEG technician arrived wheeling the monstrosity of a machine in front of her. We moved aside and she positioned the machine at the head of the bed. She began to move parts of Jonathan's hair aside with a small comb and place small electrodes on his scalp with adhesive jelly. When she was through, Dr. Michaels had reviewed the chart and Jonathan had multiples of colorful wires coming from his hair. We dimmed the lights above the bed and left the technician to her test.

"We'll wait and see what the EEG shows, Eve. Where's the patient's family?" he asked.

"There isn't any family here. He has a mother in Toronto who we've spoken to and who does not want to be involved. He also has a brother in Australia who it appears is quite close to Jonathan and wants us to proceed with organ donation if we can." I looked at Michaels who was now playing with his beard and surveyed my enemy. His shirt was untucked and he was wearing wool pants in the middle of summer. Strike one. His teeth were their usual brown, and his breath was rank even at this distance. Strike two. The final blow was delivered when I noticed the ketchup stain on his shirt from the lunch I likely called him away from in order to be at this bedside. All my energy now focused on maintaining composure in front of the beast.

"Hmmm. Let's see what the EEG shows and we'll go from there." He turned with the chart and walked towards the staff doctors' lounge to document his interpretation of the situation.

I watched him go and wondered how much of my strength had already been expended with the self-serving task of personal restraint. Why could he get away with such behavior and I had to maintain composure? Was it an issue of power or an issue of gender? Was my silence and composure born out of my extra X chromosome or was it due to the fact that this prick was my senior and part of my job description involved encounters such as this one? Most women in my position might have immediately excused this as a gender issue. Perhaps Michaels himself saw this as such. In fact on closer inspection this had nothing to do with my female persuasion and everything to do with the fact that this man, this person, was a senior staff man and I was not. He had the job I could someday hope to hold and until that time I was to keep my mouth shut, my eyes diverted and above all, behave myself. I hated behaving. It meant that I was to be less of what I was. I remember Katarina telling me that she spent her Family Medicine buried. She awoke every morning, put on face, took a deep breath and held it for two years. Although a severe measure of survival, it had proved successful and I'm sure many of us live our lives in this manner. We get up each morning, put on face and clothes, take a deep breath and submerge for days, months, perhaps even lifetimes. What happens when we tire of this is often either known as a breakdown or a break through. I couldn't bear the thought of a career, nor a life under water. Long ago I had become convinced I was destined to a life less ordinary. Moments must bring with them emotional responses and reactions. Try as I might, I could not be buried; a weakness that should have been a strength and was now leading to my downfall. It was taking everything in me not to yell after this man who had tried to break me, that he was wrong, I was right. My way would triumph. Where many could walk away from this, let it wash over them, I would let this erode slowly at my insides until the next asshole took hold. I had let myself be locked up. In lieu of a burial, I had chosen a cage of self-reflection. I would get up each morning, put on face and clothes and ponder, lament for hours, days, months. Now, holding my breath seemed effortless in comparison.

3:45 P.M.

Jonathan Steele's EEG was now complete and I called the Neurologist on call to have him read it immediately. Dr. Michaels had decided that if the EEG showed definite activity consistent with brain death, we could make the call without a nuclear scan. I paged Dr. Martin, the Neurologist on call, and explained the situation to him.

"We're having a surprisingly slow day, Eve. I'll be right down and we can settle this for you." He was pleasant and accommodating and I welcomed the behavior as my mood was souring and I had a long night before me. I hung up the phone and put my head down for a moment. There was a tap on my back and I looked up to find a coffee cup in front of me.

"Latte, skim milk, three of those pink things." David smiled at me.

"Oh," I was startled by his gift and his knowledge of my coffee tastes, "let me give you some money." Reaching into my coat pocket, he put his hand over mine.

"Eve, my treat. I can see you are having a rough day. I thought you might need a boost." He smiled again and I caught sight of his good looks. David was at least six feet tall, which meant compared to my 5'5" frame I was always looking up at him. He had a strong build, one he obviously worked at. His hair was sandy brown and his eyes were green. He was beautiful by anyone's taste and I stood before him, coffee in hand, naked in the knowledge he knew how I took my coffee.

"Thanks so much. How'd you know I take this shit in my coffee?" I asked, almost nervously.

"I watched you." He smiled and walked away. I was no longer imagining it. He was hitting on me. Holy shit.

Sex is not something that typically enters this workplace. Ninety percent of the nurses are women and ninety percent of the doctors are men. The exchanges that exist between these two parties often have a sexual component to them, particularly among the younger nurses and the male residents. As a female resident, you both embrace being a woman and bear all of the disadvantages this brings, or you join the boys club and sell the farm. The former alternative means you hold close to your feminist ideals while remaining true to your breasts and your brain. You want it all—career, family, sex, good dinners, and fabulous shoes. This meant that at times your breasts would be noticed before your brain both at work and at play. Woman who joined the "boys club" focused their energies on their careers and their success. They were doctors first, mothers later and their shoes were comfortable.

I had chosen the Doctor Diva route long ago and was still shocked when men at work noticed my face first and then the mind behind it. I knew I was a good-looking woman, but in my life I had always pursued men, rather than the reverse. As such, advances from other men would always be minimized. I thought for a moment about the interactions I had with David over the past few weeks. There had always been an endearing tone to them; one I had thought was of a friendly, platonic nature. I had never imagined there might be more to this. I sipped my coffee and thought of my husband. Jack was nothing like David, neither in physical nor in personal form. In contrast to David's strong country looks, Jack was dark. His mother was black, his father white. The result was a beauty that struck me to this day. Jack was almost as tall as David but he was long and lean. His skin was light brown, his hair black and curly. Jack had massive brown eyes and a perfect mouth. Physically he was my ideal. Mentally he was the archetypal intellectual. He was my big love. So why did David's harmless advance make me feel so uncomfortable? Perhaps because it twisted my perceptions beyond my comfort zone. I took a sip of my latte, skim milk, and three sweeteners and smiled as my discomfort over the precious scene disappeared. The coffee was perfect.

4:03 P.M.

I watched Dr. Martin sit at the back desk of the ICU with the pages of Jonathan Steele's EEG before him and a pen in hand. After surveying the test once and again, he stood and walked towards me. His face held an expression of regret and he handed me the sheet he had been writing on.

"He's brain dead, Eve. I've been over it twice. The activity is classic. Sorry."

"Thanks, Dr. Martin. I'll let Dr. Michaels know."

"I can talk to him if you like. I'll just make a copy of the EEG for rounds. We rarely see such a textbook case." He turned and walked to the front desk to page Michaels. I stood at Jonathan's bedside and waited. I knew what would be next. There had to be two physician signatures on the chart to confirm the patient was brain dead, as per hospital policy. Then I would be asked to call in the surgeons to harvest Jonathan's organs and it would be over shortly thereafter. I was grateful and saddened and too busy to be burdened with these familiar feelings at this moment. They would be filed as they usually were and dealt with in time. We all did this. We pack up our emotions in their appropriate cases. When the time is appropriate or convenient or perhaps never at all, we unfold the memories and their correlating feelings and the reactions ensue. At this point in my career I had boxes of the shit. This is baggage and mine was wrapped in designer luggage.

It's not that Jonathan's life was any less valuable than another's. It is not that this soul was less important than my own. I remember the first time I was at a code blue. The patient was pronounced dead after twenty minutes of CPR and it was all very neat and clean and matter of fact. The straightforward nature of death within these walls is what shocked me the most. It was not void of emotion but it was just so honest, plain, void of the ceremony of death. There was life and there was death and there was the simplicity of all of it, which to an outsider seemed so blatantly insensitive. Now many deaths later I understood that what I had seen was in itself a ceremony. This was a ritual of necessity. Many would say it was done for the emotional protection of those involved, others would comment that it had become habitual. I could not explain the nature of this dance to death but only to say that it was not without emotion. I do not sit in defense of myself nor of my colleagues who bury others during the day and come home to dig their own souls out. This is one of those tasks in life that has many interpretations, all in the hopes of finding meaning where there may be none. An artist paints and we spend years explaining the inspiration behind it. A doctor ushers in life and ushers in death and the world wants tears and psychiatric assessments as a means of payment for the opportunity. Jonathan's brain was now officially dead and his remaining organs would soon belong to someone else's life. If I was looking for reason or meaning in this moment I would be lost to find it.

4:15P.M.

"Eve, he's brain dead. We've documented everything. You can call the transplant team in." Dr. Michaels was now at Jonathan's bedside adjusting the ventilator to make sure the oxygen was set to 100%. He did not look up at me as he stated the now obvious. I walked over to the front desk and paged the organ donation team leader. He was expecting my call and answered back immediately.

"Dr. Martins, here, I'm the harvest team leader. What's the story on that young lad of yours?" His accent was British, his tone was direct.

"Dr. Martins, it's Eve Solomon, the ICU fellow. Jonathan Steele has been pronounced brain dead. The apnea test was positive and his EEG confirmed it. There are now two staff signatures on the chart. You can harvest the organs at any time," I said, draining from the ordeal.

"What can we harvest?"

"Everything. His donor card states that you can have all organs, tissue, and bone." People always have a choice what to donate. Jonathan had chosen the whole package.

"We'll be right over. Make sure he's on 100%. Thanks." He hung up the phone.

I returned to the bedside and asked Sue to place saline gauze over Jonathan' s eyes, as they would be taking his cornea as well. I looked at the clock and noted that I had a family meeting in the next half hour. All of my other patients had been seen, my notes written. There was only one thing left to do. I pulled a chair to Jonathan's bedside and sat down. I grasped his broken hand very gently and waited, listening to the sound of his heart monitor, for the team to come and take his organs away.

Chapter 10

5:15 P.M.

We were sitting around the table in the conference room. Dr. Steven Wong, Edith, the ICU social worker, and Leslie, the bedside nurse, and I were seated at one side of the oval. The Maxwell family, husband Jason, parents Ted and Annabelle, and sister Lisa were across from us. Patricia's parents were broken by my initial report of her condition. The next twenty-four hours would be crucial, I had told them and "we were doing all that we could". I watched my words echo in the room and in their faces and it was as though the moment was under water. I could see things so clearly but my fatigue and presumption permitted a moment when I stood outside myself watching this scene. I was as old as the patient herself and here I was issuing what seemed like her death sentence. The irony was this was a typical day.

"What chance does she have of coming out of this? Like what number are we looking at here?" It was her husband Jason's voice filled with concern and anger. People so often needed numbers, percentages. I wasn't sure if this was the television influence or just society itself, but somehow numbers were concrete. A percentage was something to hold on to in a situation when everything was blurred and slippery. The number I had for him was less than 10%. It was a number that was met with anger.

"You know those doctors who operated on her told us she would make it through this surgery just fine. She was doing perfectly well before the surgery and now look at her!" I could see the hurt and the rage in his face and was not about to justify things. Patricia was not perfectly well before the surgery. As her oncologist had documented, she was dying and was on an experimental chemotherapy that was not working. The surgery had been purely palliative. I was not going to correct Jason with this information. This was not the place. The man was losing his wife and he knew it. He had either been in denial or misinformed and it was not my place to correct the situation. I had learned this long ago. The only thing preserved by my correcting this man's perceptions would be my ego. This was a situation where my needs were irrelevant. I met Jason's eyes and searched for the "right words".

"Jason, I can only imagine the nightmare you are in right now. I don't know what has happened in the past, but I can tell you we will do everything we can to help Patricia through this. There may come a time when we have nothing further to offer her. At that point all we are doing is treating ourselves. I don't think we are at that point. I know she is extremely ill and she may die. But at this point we are doing everything we can and will continue to do so. We will keep you informed every step of the way. Okay?" I could feel the tears at the back of my own throat and paused to compose myself.

"Okay. Sorry I yelled, it's just that —"

"You don't need to apologize. This is your wife we're talking about. Your feelings are justified. Just let us know if there is anything we can do for you as well." I put my hand on his.

The meeting ended minutes later and I left Edith, the social worker, with the family. I walked past Jonathan's bedside on my way to Patricia Maxwell's. Jonathan's body was gone. What remained was an empty cubicle and a woman from housekeeping mopping the floor.

Patricia Maxwell continued to be paralyzed and sedated. We had instituted this that morning to give her body the rest it needed to fight the infection. She continued on dialysis and her blood pressure had remained stable throughout the day. She was holding her own but it would be a long road. I made some small adjustments in her paralytic medication and walked over to Randy Adler's bedside to see how he was doing.

Randy was sitting up in bed breathing on his own, with bandages covering half of his face. Pieces of his red hair stuck out from the white gauze on his head. I imagined him smiling underneath the gauze. He was pleasant and on enough Morphine that he was no longer going through nicotine withdrawal.

"Hi, Doc. How are yah?" Yes he was stoned.

"Fine, Randy. How are you feeling?"

"Just fine."

I checked his most recent labs and repeated my physical exam from the morning. He was healing well and could likely be transferred to the burn unit later tomorrow or later tonight if we were stuck for beds.

"Randy, I think we can transfer you to another ward in the morning. It will be the burn unit where they can look after your face. Okay?"

"Okay. When can I go home?" I doubt he understood how lucky he was.

"Not for a while. We have to make sure your burns heal first."

"Okay," he said cheerily and waved a bandaged hand in my direction as I walked away from his bedside.

It was now almost time for sign out rounds and I had not eaten lunch. I told Joanne at the desk that I was going to the cafeteria to grab a sandwich and to page me if I was not back in time for sign out rounds. I turned and walked the hall to the doors to the unit.

6:02 P.M.

Returning to the unit, turkey sandwich in hand, I saw Katarina leaving the hospital and called to her from the lobby.

"Hug me," I said when she was beside me. "I'm very small today."

"What's wrong, my love?" She said arms around me. She smelled great. Her hair was perfect, her lipstick fresh.

"I've had the worst day. The first patient was a twenty-six-year-old kid declared brain dead. The second was a thirty-three-year-old woman with metastatic breast cancer. I hate my job," I said, pulling away from her embrace but still holding on to her.

"Come with me to La Cage tonight. I have a drug dinner there, you can be my date." La Cage was the best French restaurant in the city and at $50 per person I was a fool to say no.

"I can't. I'm on call."

"Well, how about lunch tomorrow after you get off? I don't have a clinic in the afternoon and I miss you. We could go to the gym and then for a bite to eat."

"Sounds perfect." Katarina's gym had a steam room that I would live in if they'd let me. I kissed her goodbye and watched her head off to her drug dinner.

I loved drug dinners. These were one of the great benefits of medicine. Pharmaceutical companies, worth billions of dollars, would rent out a restaurant in the city and hire a speaker to talk about a given topic. After forty-five minutes of a slide presentation preceded by cocktails, an extravagant meal was served. This was the company's way of furthering medical education. Of course the concept was a complete mystery to anyone not in the medical field. How a company could spend severe amounts of money on a dinner was beyond them. It also made the general public question whether this was education or merely a fancy form of bribery. "Eat my steak, buy my drug", was the great misconception. As much as I loved the steak, it rarely changed my practice. Occasionally there were talks that were very educational and I emerged with a greater knowledge base. Occasionally the food was substandard and I just drank my way through the dinner. Usually the dinners were excellent and had now become commonplace.

6:52 P.M.

Sign out rounds went quickly as much of the business of the day had already been sorted out. David had taken the first admission of the day, given the events of my day, and presented the case briefly. The patient was a seventy-year-old woman who came straight from the operating room for a bowel resection and was now septic. Things were under control but she was difficult to extubate and they wanted her in the ICU at least overnight. Our bed situation was growing thin and I suggested we transfer Randy to the burn unit tonight. I finished the orders and arranged for a bed in the unit. As I began the transfer note on Randy's chart, my code pager went off.

"Code blue, patient care unit 42. Code blue, patient care unit 42," sounded the loudspeaker in the unit. I ran to the elevator with David at my heels and the code cart in front of us. This could now be classified as a bad day.

We crammed into the elevator with the cart behind us. Jennifer, the code nurse, dispensed the gloves.

"I'll take this one, David. You can start the central line." He nodded and put on his gloves. The doors to the elevator opened, my heart was racing and we ran down the hall to unit 42. The room was already full of people. It always reminded me of a traffic accident that people would stop at just to see. I headed straight for the bed. On it laid an elderly woman, naked and motionless. The respiratory technician took his position at the head of the bed and put a mask over the patient's face. The dance began. I put my hand on the femoral pulse and announced that I was code team leader.

"Everyone who does not need to be here, please leave," I asked firmly. The leads were already on the patient's chest and the monitor showed ventricular fibrillation.

"Get ready to shock, please. Charge to 200 joules." We charged and completed three serial shocks in sequence with no effect. Harry intubated the patient and I asked David to start the central line. I ordered a milligram of epinephrine and we shocked again. All the while the nurse practitioner performed CPR, breaking ribs between shocks.

The patient was a diabetic with end stage kidney failure and a long-term dialysis patient. She was in the hospital for an above knee amputation and was to go to the operating room tomorrow. My mind raced with the possibilities; *hyperkalemia, hypoglycemia, sepsis, pulmonary embolus, myocardial infarction, pericardial tamponade*. We continued the code working our way down the list of medications with intervals of electricity until the patient flat lined. Forty minutes later and nothing had changed. We were now on our third nurse practitioner and I was out of ideas. We had tried intravenous pacing at the bedside but the heart was failing to capture the electrical impulse. This woman was dead and there was nothing left to do but to state what everyone else already knew.

"Let's call it. Time of death, 8:14 P.M." I left the room, took off my gloves and turned to a ward nurse to ask where the family was.

"There is no family. She was a widow and they had no children."

"Oh." I called Steven Wong and told him about the code and proceeded to write a code summary in the chart. I then phoned the Orthopedic Surgeon under whom this woman had been admitted and told him his patient had died.

"Yeah, thanks. I'll take her off the list for tomorrow."

"Okay, but I need you to come in and sign the death certificate as the patient was under your care when she died."

"I can't. I never met the patient." He hung up the phone and left me to clean up the mess. I paged Steven again and informed him of my recent conversation. He promised to take care of things and asked me for the patient's name and hospital number. I hung up the phone, finished my note, took a deep breath and returned to the ICU. Fear, anger, hate, disappointment, and frustration. I had run the course of an emotional marathon of loathing and the night had only begun.

9.15 P.M..

I stopped at the cafeteria on my way back to the unit. I could feel a wave of exhaustion wash over me and thought another caffeine fix might ward it off for the moment. My pager sounded and I went to the phone to answer an outside call.

"Hi, it's Eve Solomon," I said into the receiver, coffee in hand.

"Hello, my love." It was Jack.

"Hi, sweetie. How was your day?"

"Good. You?"

"Long. Brutal." I had reduced myself to one-word sentences between sips.

"Well, Katarina just called and she wants us to go for dinner tomorrow night. How does that sound?"

"Sure." As I said it I remembered that I had rounds to present the following day and already began to organize my day. If I left the hospital tomorrow at noon, I could finish my presentation by two or three o'clock and have a quick nap before dinner.

"Sweetie, I have to go. I'll call you later, okay?" I knew Jack was bored and wanted to chat, but I really didn't feel much like talking right now and there was always work to do.

"Okay, Eve. I love you."

"I love you too." I hung up the phone and returned to the ICU.

11:15 P.M.

"You know, I had to go up there and sign that death certificate. The surgeon wouldn't come in and do it." Steven was telling me of his recent events on the fourth floor in the aftermath of our code.

"Really?" This was not an unusual occurrence. Patients came in for elective orthopedic surgery and didn't see their surgeons until they were on the table. Rounds were done at six o'clock in the morning with the patients half asleep. If you had a leg removed and didn't remember the man with the knife it was not a surprise.

We finished our final rounds on the patients for the night and were at Patricia Maxwell's bedside. The Infectious Disease team had been by to make recommendations and we had added yet another antibiotic to the cocktail she was already on. Her temperature was still 39.5 degrees Celsius and the shunt in her brain continued to drain puss. A CT scan done just hours ago showed no focal pocket of infection and nothing to drain further. She was dying. I had loaded her on enough Valium and dilating to prevent her from seizing. Eventually with her fever and her infection nothing would help. It was a matter of time.

"Call me if anything happens, Eve. She's our sickest. Hopefully things will turn around in the night. If not I'm staying in the call room downstairs, so page me." Steven checked her chart one last time and left the unit.

David and I ordered morning blood work on all of the patients and divided up the patients amongst us for the night. There was a strange calm in the unit and I was hoping for a quiet night. David had the next admission and I would be wise to get my head to a pillow and try for some asleep while I had my chance.

"Goodnight, David." I smiled, heading to my call room to change into greens.

"Wait, I'll come with you." He looked up from the papers in his hands.

We walked down the hallway to the call room in silence.

"Hopefully, I won't see you until morning," I said with my hand on the door handle.

"Leanne and I broke up." He blurted out. I turned and looked at him. He wanted to talk, I knew it.

"You want to talk about it?" I asked, knowing the answer.

"Sure." He began to follow me into my call room and I stopped him. Rumors would fly and this was the last thing I needed.

"Let me change and I'll meet you here in five minutes. We can go to the doctors' lounge and talk." I smiled and walked into my call room.

I sat down on the bed in my call room, the door closed behind me. I was uncomfortable with David's recent approach. Perhaps it was my own vulnerability that made me over interpret this interaction. David was powerfully beautiful and my intellectual equal. I had no upper hand. Isn't that the way women view things? We need to have a dominant area of some kind in order to feel safe. Control on any level puts us at ease. This usually translates into a need for success in one area or another. Success comes from knowing you are better at something than someone else.

I thought of Jack and his ability to be at ease with himself in almost any situation. I thought of his integrity and his fidelity and how these were areas in which he would always be superior to me. Jack held his principles on high and they were infallible. Perhaps it was my own interpretation of my husband, which allowed him to hold these perfections. Nevertheless I was convinced, whether real or of my own making, that Jack would never put himself into a situation where he would discuss love, sex, and relationships with a six-foot goddess from Australia who exuded sex appeal and would easily jump into bed if only given the invitation. I changed into my greens and deliberately washed my face without reapplying lipstick. I was determined to at least create the appearance that this was nothing. I opened the call room door and there stood David, waiting for me in the hallway.

"Things are quiet in there, we should be fine." He smiled and turned towards the doors to the unit. I followed him knowing that I was taking this to mean more than it was.

Still I knew this was now going to be more than a working relationship. We were going to start a connection and I wasn't prepared for what was to come.

I walked into the doctors' lounge ahead of David and took a seat across from him in one of the comfortable chairs.

"So, I'm listening," I said looking at him, "talk."

"Oh, Eve, I'm so tired of dating. I mean, I want to have fun and all but these women I see get so involved so quickly and I don't even have a chance to get to know them before they are proposing marriage," he said, looking back at me.

"Who are *these women*, David?" *That 's it Eve, keep listening, he'll keep talking and you'll be safe.*

"Well, Leanne and then Barbara before her and well, nurses mostly. I've pretty much been through half the union since Julie left me. Did I tell you about Julie?"

"Is that your girlfriend you came here to be with?" I knew it was. He nodded sadly and I told him I knew of Julie.

"It's just frustrating," he said. "At times I think I want to find someone special and then when I think I do, it goes so quickly that I want out and fast."

He was describing what I think many men feel. They want to be loved, to be embraced by "that someone" but on their own terms. Where women fall in love quickly and fall out of love quickly, men take their time and fall hard. And then it hit me sitting there why David was so promiscuous. He was trying to recover from Julie. He was trying to prove that he was still virile, worthy, attractive. At the same time, he was searching desperately for a replacement.

"David," I said slowly, trying to find the words, "can I tell you what I think?"

"Of course, Eve," he said with a look of desperation. *Man he was beautiful.*

"I think the reason you have dated so many women is because Julie left you for another woman. I think you have some need to prove that you are a sexy, attractive man who can be pleasing to women. I think" he *wanted to interrupt but I had to get this out,* "let me finish, I think what happens when you meet these women is that they see you, a beautiful intelligent man who is sensitive, and they want the whole package. So they fall in love and quickly. I think you may play along at first because you are a decent guy but then you realize you are in for much more than you initially anticipated."

He sat there. Silent. Stunned.

"But let me tell you that I know Julie didn't leave you because of you. She left because of her own issues. You were an innocent bystander. I know that you need not prove your sexuality by jumping at any opportunity. Women, especially when they find out you are a doctor, will throw themselves at you. I know this. On behalf of women, you are a catch and we can get pretty aggressive when we see something we want. Take some time to find out what you want in a relationship, what you want in a woman before you make your move. I mean, did you really think Leanne was the woman for you?"

"No, but I was just having fun."

"Did she know that?"

"What? I'm supposed to tell her that from the start?"

"Yes. You start any relationship by stating what your needs are and you are much less likely to get hurt."

"So I should start a relationship telling a woman I just want to have a good time, nothing serious?" he asked.

"Exactly. But remember, that whoever you are with will be convinced on some level that she is the one who can change you."

"Shit," he said shaking his head, "I can't win."

"Now you understand." I laughed.

"Do you really think I'm fucking around to make up for Julie?" he asked me sincerely.

"It's not about what I think, it's about what you think. I don't know, David. I barely know you. It's just an idea. Its something to play around with in your own mind."

"Well," my pager went off to break the moment. It was the unit.

"Hold that thought," I said, rising from the chair and picking up the nearest receiver.

"Eve," it was Annie, one of the senior nurses in the unit, "get here now, Patricia Maxwell just had a seizure."

I put down the phone and ran to the unit. David was right behind me.

A Good Life

Tuesday, 12:12 A.M.

Patricia Maxwell had now had her fourth seizure of the night and I continued to give her enough Valium to level an elephant. I was at her bedside watching her as she remained seizure free for the last five minutes and was now on a continuous Valium infusion.

"Can someone page Steven for me, please?" I knew this woman was worsening but it was happening right before me and I was running out of options. The next step would be to put her in a Phenobarbital induced coma and I needed Steven's help on that one.

Moments later he was at the bedside, standing beside me. I told him of the events of the last half hour and what was left to do.

"The Phenobarb coma is risky and would likely add no benefit at this point. We'll continue with the Valium infusion for now. Let's call Infectious Disease and ask them if putting another dose of antibiotics into the shunt will help." Steven of course had options, a benefit of his experience.

I turned to grab the cordless phone behind me when it happened. Patricia's body went into violent convulsions and her ventilator alarm sounded. The monitor screamed and she had now coded.

Steven let me take control. I asked Michael to continue bagging the patient and called for the crash cart. Her rhythm was asystole, she was flat lined. The Nurse's aide started CPR and so it began again. I ordered the appropriate drugs and waited for any effect. Ten minutes later, the rhythm remained flat and I asked for temporary transvenous pacemaker. Twenty-five minutes in Steven tried floating a transvenous pacemaker in through the central line in Patricia's neck but the signal wouldn't catch. We continued the code for another ten minutes without success. Steven came up behind me and put his hand on my shoulder. I took one last look at the scene. This pale frame lay before me. The shunt in her head now spilled blood for the past twenty minutes, the monitor reading nothing.

"Let's call it," I said, my mouth dry, "time of death 1:04 A.M." I turned and walked away from the bed. I hated my job. I was angry and beaten and broken. My emotions were nothing in comparison to those of Jason Maxwell.

"Where's her family?" I asked Annie. Behind me the nurses were already cleaning up the scene in preparation for the family.

"Her husband is in the waiting room."

"I'll go talk to him," I said softly.

I turned and walked slowly down the hallway. In minutes I would give a well-rehearsed speech I had given many times before. In minutes, Jason Maxwell would be a widower.

73

Chapter 11

The rest of my night was surprisingly quiet. I had faced Jason Maxwell with the news smelling of his wife's death. He was alone in the waiting room and his eyes met mine when I walked in the door. I sat down beside him and made his children motherless. He sobbed uncontrollably into my arms for more than half an hour. Then as though on cue, he rose and walked into the unit. He stayed at Patricia's side until they took her to the morgue. From her bedside he made funeral arrangements, phone calls to families and held his dead wife's hand. It was an intense devotion that many might have found strange. I had long ago given up the idea that there was a "normal" response to such a magnitude of loss. I had seen so many reactions in the last few years that I failed to classify any of them as ordinary. If there were any words to classify these moments of last devotion, they were sacred, pious dedication. I wondered, no, I hoped Patricia was loved as much in life as she was in death.

And then the moment returned to me. Was my life blessed with this kind of precious allegiance? Did I marry a man who well after midnight would sit with my dead body and hold my dead hand, making phone calls to family, friends and funeral parlor? It was too late in the day and too early in my life to struggle with these self-indulgent exercises in personal deprivation. My married life was fulfilled. How could I predict what one man may do in a situation that was so far beyond his comprehension? Did Jason Maxwell ever expect his marriage would require such a grave commitment? Likewise I myself had never anticipated a life with Jack would require any semblance of the scene before me. I offered my condolences again to the new widower and returned to my call room. It was now early in the morning. I put my head to pillow and all I could wish for was a dreamless sleep.

After rounds were done, I finished up the last of my notes and signed out to Alex Connor. Smelling like a mixture of feet and a bad locker room, I walked out of the hospital and into the sunshine. This was followed by the usual climb to the parkade and the ten minute search for my car. Once safe inside the Valiant, Liza Minelli on the stereo system, I was on my way to redemption.

3:45 P.M.

I was at the computer finishing the last of my slides for the morning rounds presentation when the phone rang. Leaving the computer running in the den, I went to the kitchen to answer the call.

"Hello?" I said clearing my throat.

"Darling." It was Katarina's voice on the other end.

"Hey, my sweet. Are we still having dinner tonight?"

"That was just what I was calling to confirm. How was the rest of your night?"

"Oh, Kay, it was good and bad. That young woman coded and died. After that it was pretty quiet and I got some sleep. I hated it."

"Who were you on with?" she asked.

"David Auerbach."

"Don't know him."

"Oh, yes you do. Tall, Australian, Orthopedics?" I was stating the obvious buzzwords to stir her memory.

"My god, he's gorgeous. I know him. I even went out with him once."

"Really, when?" I had no idea Katarina had dated David. My world was getting smaller and smaller.

"About two years ago. He had just broken up with a girlfriend and I was free. He took me to dinner that was all."

"Did you sleep with him?" I needed to know.

"No. He was too needy at that point and I don't like the needy type." It was true; Katarina always went for men who were self-sufficient in the emotions department. Initially this made them seem cold and aloof but really, she had told me, it helped to not have them hanging on to her for dear life after she broke their hearts. I sometimes envied Katarina's freedom. She had sexual and emotional adventures far beyond my own. She was independent in the true sense of the word. Financially, her debt was long ago paid off. Career-wise she had her own practice. Socially she was betrothed to no one but herself. It was a classic case of surveying one's own assets and wanting another's. I'm sure there were days when Katarina herself surveyed her own self-sufficiency and craved an alternative.

"Well he seems to have recovered nicely," I said laughing and she laughed along with me.

"Anyway," she segued, "I've made reservations at Brava's for seven o'clock. Can we meet there?" Brava was one of my and Kay's favorite restaurants. It was a testament to our relationship that she would pick a place she knew I would love. Part of my deepest affection for her stemmed from the idea that although Kay was her own woman, I was her own woman too. She was the type of person who was able to guard her own interests while still maintaining an element of concern for others. Katarina never put herself above those she cared about; rather we were all on the same pedestal.

"We'll meet you there. I am going to have a nap and promise to be refreshed by the time I see you."

"All right, my darling. See you later. Ciao." She hung up the phone.

I returned to the den and checked my slides one last time. I saved everything to disk and transferred the presentation to my laptop. Then, still smelling of rotten jockey shorts, I headed to the shower. The hot water was welcomed as I erased the night's events with soap and shampoo. Its odors were replaced with the scent of promise and purity. All I needed now was a decent sleep and I would be a new woman.

The post call haze is a difficult time in which to sleep. Firstly you can never fully erase the smell of the night before. The stench of stale bodily fluids and your own sour stink mingle together long after the much needed shower. Accompany this with a tremendous feeling of over tiredness and you are doomed to remain awake for some time. Most people took over the counter sleep aids or cold pills to get over this. My drug of choice was a television set. It was without fail that if I could not fall asleep, all I need do was turn on the T.V. for ten minutes or so and I'd be unconscious. It often did not matter what show was playing, although golf tournaments and the Home Shopping Network worked best. A quarter of an hour of grown men's whispers over a tiny white ball or Ivana Trump's new face cream and I was easily rendered unconscious.

I called Jack's voice mail at work and reminded him of our dinner plans. Then, with the set in our bedroom turned to the Golf Channel, I set my alarm for six o'clock, put my head to the pillow and closed my eyes.

7:00 P.M.

We arrived just in time at the restaurant to greet Katarina at the door. She was wearing a sleeveless black sheath dress that served to accentuate every curve. Coupled with my favorite black stiletto boots and *I* would have slept with her that night.

"Hello, beautiful," Jack greeted her warmly with a hug and a kiss to both cheeks. I stood back admiring the exchange between the two great loves of my life. Where I might have felt a pang of jealousy watching my husband be so demonstrative to another woman, with Katarina, I felt only pride that she was my dearest friend and Jack, my husband. I hugged her tightly and the maitre dé led us to our table.

"You look amazing," she whispered in my ear, "new dress?"

"Hmmm," I nodded. The dress was new as were the shoes. Both were black, of course and bought two weeks ago in a moment of need. I had paid too much but it was well worth it. Nothing cures depression better than a fabulous expensive outfit. I had hid the dress and shoes in the back of the closet and brought them out tonight with the false caveat that Jack had seen them many times before and I just hadn't worn them in a while. Katarina was whispering because she knew my technique all too well. I did look good and I knew it. The clothes fit me perfectly. My hair was slicked back in a black knot and I had painted my lips red. My body was nothing like Katarina's goddess figure. I often called myself voluptuous when the word chubby was not welcome. I was a "bigger" girl, but I knew I was a babe and could easily get away with it.

On the way to our seats we passed one of Jack's co-workers. His name was Tony something and I remembered him for his teeth. We had met last year at the Christmas party where he and his wife had spent half an hour telling me about their teeth. They had come late to the party as they had just finished having dinner at the home of their dentist. I had remarked how close they must have been. Tony answered with a twenty minute detail of the $150,000 he had spent on his teeth and the $75,000 details of his wife's pearly whites. When the shock of spending nearly a quarter of a million dollars on mouth work wore off, I spent the rest of the conversation staring at their mouths. I was mesmerized with the fact that their caps combined could have paid off my debt and bought us a Porsche in the process.

"Honey, you remember Tony and his wife Linda?" The dental legends, who could forget?

"Of course," I said graciously, shaking both their hands, "nice to see you both again. And then I looked up at Tony and it hit me like a slap in the face. He had grown a moustache. $150,000 in dental work and he had the audacity to cover it all up with facial hair. This man needed therapy.

Katarina and I continued on to our seats and left Jack behind to wrap up the conversation.

"Who's that?" Kay asked.

"He works with Jack," I said smiling. "Remember the story about the teeth people? The ones who spent a quarter of a million on their dental work?"

"No" she said shocked to have met the famous couple, "them?"

I nodded and we both burst into laughter.

"There's more," I said pausing from my moment of amusement, "the moustache is new."

She keeled over. "You mean he spends that kind of money on his teeth and then has the nerve to grow a moustache over it?" Her remark was met with my laughter. By now tears were forming in the corner of her eyes.

"That's exactly my point."

Our giggling was truncated by the waiter's arrival. Katarina ordered a glass of Chardonnay and I elected for a Martini. Jack, who rarely drank, arrived in time to order a Caesar.

"Do you know who that was?" he asked me, laughing lightly.

"The teeth people!" I pronounced rather proud of myself.

"What's with the moustache?" Katarina asked.

"He thinks it makes him look smarter," Jack reported.

"No?" I laughed.

"I kid you not, my love. Personally I think it's stupid to pay that much for your teeth and then cover them up with a face rug."

Katarina looked at me and me at her.

"*That* is why I married you," I said, kissing his puzzled face.

The waiter arrived with our drinks shortly thereafter and a wonderful evening had begun.

9:00 P.M.

Katarina was a friend first and a colleague second. She was my soul mate. It was coincidence and an added benefit that we shared the same profession. As such, we got together and spoke of almost everything but our patients. Sure we discussed the profession itself, but the conversation usually centered on how we had gotten ourselves into the predicament in the first place. A dialogue of the dysfunctional individuals we had the privilege to work with usually followed. These were sessions of support and comradery and I only shared them with Kay. When Jack joined the conversation, we rarely spoke of Medicine. Partly because, not being in the profession, he could easily be made to feel alienated. More importantly, with Jack around there was always more to talk about than our habitual lives.

I had the seared tuna for dinner and more than enough wine. I had told myself to keep the drinking to a minimum given my rounds presentation in the morning and ignored my own warnings the minute the bottle of Chardonnay arrived. We drank and ate and talked and laughed and the evening flowed freely. I was surrounded by the *beautiful people*. They were the ones who ate out on a Tuesday night for no apparent reason. Here were the men and women, the executives of the world with their beautiful shoes and fabulous suits and perfect handbags. These were the men and women born with designer labels on their asses. Their hair was always perfect, their make-up pristine. They were in bed by dawn and up well past noon. These were the masters of the universe with money to spare. They were heir apparent to the ultimate world's fortunes. Regardless of my brain or my new outfit, I could never compete in their presence. I was stained with too many sleepless nights. I was condemned to a closet full of comfortable shoes and appropriate attire. I had lived several lifetimes in hospital greens where they only wore silk pajamas. I could never erase the smells of blood and shit and fear. No amount of perfume or aromatherapy wraps would cover the stench of my inadequacy. I was somehow tainted, fraudulent, less of what I wanted to be when surrounded by their Fendi purses and Manolo Blahniks. I could spend a lifetime in Saks Fifth Avenue and never be one of those beautiful people. I was an outsider and they held the keys to paradise. Try as I might, I would never fully gain access.

But tonight for a few brief moments in my fabulous dress and my shiny new shoes, with enough wine in my blood and a belly of tuna, I was one of them. With my fabulous friend and her stiletto heels, with my husband's stunning black eyes and his thick platinum wedding ring, I was a beautiful person. I sat back in my chair with the keys to paradise in my own hands and smiled at the open gates.

11:00 P.M.

We finished dinner and kissed Katarina goodbye. We continued casual conversation in the car on the way home.

"Nice dinner, wasn't it?" Jack asked.

"Hmmm." My mind was elsewhere. It was only Tuesday but I desperately wanted to call in sick tomorrow and avoid reality. That terrible feeling fell over me as I knew I had to give rounds in the morning and there was no way I could feign illness.

"You okay?" Jack asked, concern in his voice.

"Fine," I said feeling unconnected. There was so much of my life, so much of my days, which Jack knew nothing about. Much of it I assumed he would never understand and so I avoided telling him. More of it I could never bring myself to articulate without sounding pitiful and weak or egotistical and self-righteous. He could never understand the elements in my life that were a daily challenge. The stories of the Maxwells or Joe or Mr. Burnow could be easier told to strangers than to the non-medical man who shared my bed. As such I would always underestimate him. My silence would be a failure to appreciate Jack's insight or capacity to understand my world. This would serve to isolate me further in a time when I should have reached out.

I had always said that one doctor in the family was enough. I often looked at couples where both individuals were physicians and dismissed their interactions as being heavily laden with occupational jargon. The alternative was something I had never fully appreciated. This was a choice I had made. We would never consume our lives with only talk of work. As such, Jack would never fully understand my world and I would never be fully understood. There was a part of me that would forever be alone.

"Where are you?" his question broke the chatter in my head.

"Oh, just... It's been a difficult time at work lately. I've lost a few patients and well.... You know." He didn't, but I had lost the ability to articulate at this moment.

"How's the group you are working with?"

"Okay. There is the usual mix. One of my staff men is great."

"Anything else exciting?"

"There's a resident at work who I think is hitting on me."

Jack laughed. "He has good taste."

I joined him in a chuckle. "Oh, he's harmless. I think it's just he's looking for something and I'm the only woman in the unit right now."

"No, sweetie, you're a babe. That's what it is." Jack was not the jealous type. Firstly he had so much faith in me. I would always live up to his expectations and so there was never a need to doubt my fidelity. Would I ever give him cause to do so? I had never thought of being unfaithful. I had never met anyone worthy nor had I ever had the desire. David was of no exception. He did however make me feel ratified in a way I had long forgotten. Suddenly he had awakened a place in me I had thought was dormant long ago.

We continued the rest of the drive in silence. Jack had an early day tomorrow and went straight to bed. I went into the den to go over my slides once more. Almost an hour later, face washed, teeth brushed, I climbed in between the cool sheets next to my husband. My feet searched for his warm body and finding them I turned to face him and wrapped his warm sleeping body with mine.

Wednesday, 8:45 A.M.

"Interesting case, Dr. Solomon. How is the patient doing now?" Dr. Leonard's question rose from the audience in the hospital auditorium. I had finished my case report and review of the literature and was relatively unscathed. Now the questions, or "slings and arrows", would ensue.

"He's now in the burn unit. As I mentioned he suffered second and third degree burns to his face when he tried to have a cigarette while on oxygen."

A chuckle rolled through the crowd.

"But," I continued, "he's had skin grafts and is doing well. Furthermore," I made an attempt at humor, "he hasn't had a cigarette in over a week."

More light laughter.

I paused, surveyed the room and then spoke, "Well, if there aren't any more questions, I thank you for your time and attention."

Dr. Leonard nodded in my direction and I stepped down from the podium to safety.

Chapter 12

Thursday, 11:32 A.M.
I was on call again today and was trying my best to stay focused in rounds. Yesterday had been a slow day in the unit and we had too many empty beds. Someone was bound to fill them and I had a habit of doing just that. Health care professionals were fascinating on so many levels. They were highly intelligent but equally superstitious. The idea of karma was not just a belief but also a tangible fact in many circles. Within the hospital, people's fortune was common knowledge. It was called *"call karma"* and it was either good or bad. Good karma meant you got at least three hours sleep every night on call and rarely had a traumatic night. Bad karma meant you filled the unit with extremely sick patients and kept everyone on their toes. People may not know your spouse's name, but they always knew your *call karma*. It also meant that if you filled every bed on the unit you were somehow responsible on some supernatural level. Let it be known that I had a reputation, and justifiably so, for having terrible *call karma*.

My pager went off and I excused myself to answer the call from Emergency.

"Eve Solomon, ICU," I said into the receiver when the unit clerk answered.

"Hold for Dr. Wright." I waited to speak to the E.R. doctor while listening to *Rainbow Connection* on the muzak track.

"Ian Wright," his voice broke in moments later.

"Hi, Dr. Wright, it's Eve Solomon."

"Oh, Eve, do I have one for you. Twenty-nine-year-old man, no past medical history, presents with foreign body in the rectum. Shall I continue?" he was trying not to laugh.

"No, I'll be right there." Someone would have to tell me the story; I might as well get it first hand from the patient. I was on call with David Auerbach again and motioned to him that I had to see a patient in Emergency. He nodded to acknowledge that he would fill me in on the remaining three patients.

As I walked into ER, the smell hit me—shaving cream. I met Ian Wright at the bedside where a young man lay intubated, covered with shaving cream and feces. The smell was overpowering.

Evan White was a twenty-nine-year-old executive who apparently, while partying with some friends, slipped and fell on a can of shaving cream, which lodged itself in the man's rectum. His friends, in an effort to help him out of the difficult situation, tried to dislodge the can from his ass. They were successful but not before the can exploded and the man became septic. He was on his way to surgery to explore the area and remove what remained. He would come to the ICU thereafter.

Evan was unconscious and unable to tell me the story but his friend Jared was at the bedside. I walked over and introduced myself, knowing full well that Evan White had not fallen on anything. I had seen cases like this before in my Emergency rotation. Men came into the ER with cucumbers, shampoo bottles, and vibrators lodged in their rectums. The worse case I had seen was a man who perforated his bowels with a squash. This came to a close second.

I walked over to Mr. White's friend and introduced myself I turned to the patient and began a cursory physical exam. The man was in shock and Emergency had already begun the initial treatment. He had been started on antibiotics and Dopamine and his pressure was holding at 110/60. I was listening to his heart and lungs when the surgeons arrived to take the patient to the operating room.

"We'll take him to the ICU post op," I said to the staff surgeon.

"Thanks," Dr. Mackantyre acknowledged me.

I turned to Evan White's friend Jared and explained to him the situation.

"Can we talk somewhere?" he asked me nervously.

"Sure. Come with me." I led him to a conference room in the ER and offered him a seat.

"Evan didn't fall on the shaving cream can," he blurted out the moment he was seated.

"Tell me what happened," I said listening.

"There was a huge party. One of the guys from the firm was getting married and he had a floor rented at a hotel downtown." He paused and asked for a glass of water. I went to the sink in the room, filled a paper cup and returned to my chair. Once seated I looked to him to continue.

"There were half a dozen prostitutes there and a hell of a lot of coke." He continued, "We were high and things got out of hand. I mean, Evan's not gay, at least I don't think he is. But he wanted to try it, so we did and that's when the can got stuck. I panicked, I tried to use my pocket knife to get the damn thing out but it broke." He started to cry. "Fuck, now he's gonna die and I killed him. I was only trying to help; I mean we were really fucked up. Oh my god! If anyone at work finds out I could get fired. You won't tell any-one will you?" he looked up at me, tears streaming down his face, suit wrin-kled and still high from last night's events.

"No. The only people who will know are the doctors and nurses looking after him," I said. "Jared, why don't you go home and get some rest. Evan will be in surgery for a while. You can come back later tonight and see him. By then he'll be in the ICU and we'll know more about how he's doing."

Jared agreed and gave me his cell phone number should anything change. Evan hadn't any family in the city and would want this type of thing kept from them at this point. I agreed not to inform Evan's family unless his condition seemed grave. I shook Jared's hand and showed him the way out of the department. I then returned to the ER and wrote a quick consult note. I returned to the ICU and told the charge nurse, Ellen, of the new admission. Amidst her shock and shaking head, she wrote down Evan's name and bed assignment.

The group had finished its rounds and David Michaels was on call tonight for staff I found him at the back desk and told him about the pend-ing admission.

"He did what?" Michaels started to laugh.

"He put a can of shaving cream in his rectum and in trying to get it out, it ruptured. He's in the O.R. now and should come to us in the next few hours."

"Holy shit," he shook his head. "Okay, do we have a bed?"

I nodded and told him that I had already given report to Ellen.

"Eve, make sure you tell me before you start booking beds for patients." *Here we go.* The man was a power monger. *Choose your battles, Eve.* I told myself.

"Sure," I said, trying to get out of this situation as soon as possible.

I turned from the scene and walked to the desks at the back of the unit. I had progress notes to write and blood work to check. It would take me at least an hour to cool off from my recent interaction with the great Dr. Michaels. I was halfway though my last note when a cup of coffee was plant-ed beside me and I heard David's voice behind me.

"Skim milk latte, three packets of pink poison."

I looked up to his smiling face.

"David, you've got to stop buying me coffee."

"Why? I owe you for our talk the other night." He smiled.

"No you don't. I was just being a friend," I said, looking down at the cup and taking a sip.

"Hmm, thanks. Should we continue our little chat tonight if there's a chance?" He was really looking at me.

"Sure. Come get me when the dust clears later tonight." We were start-ing a trend. It was not a safe thing. I now had a secret and I wasn't sure what to do with it. "Listen," I said, interrupting his gaze, "I have to finish these notes. I'll catch up with you later."

"Great," he said smiling.

I focused again on my note, not watching him walk away. I picked up my pen and returned to safe and solid ground.

2:45 P.M.

I was at Harold Brown's bedside checking his afternoon lab results. My elderly bull rider had done extremely well over the past few days and would likely be extubated later in the day.

"Let's wean him off the Dopamine and then we'll check what his weanable parameters are," I said to the bedside nurse. I turned to Mrs. Brown, his young wife, and explained what the process would entail.

"Kathy, he's doing very well. We're going to see if he can breathe without the ventilator safely and then we can take the tube out." I smiled.

"Oh, good. I told you he was a tough old bastard." She laughed.

My code pager went off before I could finish our pleasant exchange. *"Code Blue, patient care unit 61. Code Blue, patient care unit 61."* Unit 61 was the Oncology ward. I could already visualize the scene in my head as I raced to the elevators. It would be a mother of three with metastatic breast cancer or a young father of two with a brain tumor. The scenes played in my mind as I put on my latex gloves and faced David in the elevator.

"May I, madame?" he smiled.

"Please do. I'm right behind you if you need me."

"I always need you, Eve." One of the code team nurses laughed and I was caught off guard.

"Stop flirting, David, you couldn't handle me," I snapped back. It was mean and meant to shut him up. It had done the job. He looked at his shoes and I felt like shit. The elevator doors opened and we were on our way.

We ran down the hall of Unit 61 to the room of Sal Gianni and the scene was like nothing I had anticipated. There lying on the bed was a ninety pound seventeen-year-old kid with a nurse on top of him pounding away at his chest performing CPR. David on cue announced he was running the code. He turned to me and asked me to intubate the patient. I went to the head of the bed and looked at this young boy's face. His head was bald from the chemotherapy. His eyes half open, were blue and glazed over. I called for a number seven endotracheal tube and a laryngoscope and tilted the boy's head back. To my right was Michael, the respiratory technician, with the suction and the oxygen. I placed the laryngoscope in Sal's mouth and moved his tongue aside. His throat was red and raw with patches of yeast lacing the insides of his mouth. The light on the scope would guide me to the back of his throat where I caught a glimpse of his vocal chords.

"Suction," I called and Michael handed me the tube. After clearing the mucous from the back of the throat, I could see the vocal chords perfectly, and I called for the tube. Moments later I slid the tube into the boy's throat, watching it pass between his vocal chords. I pulled the stiletto out from the tube. And I watched the humidity build in the base of the tube as Michael pumped oxygen into the tube using the bagging mechanism. One of the other respiratory techs at the scene took her stethoscope to listen to the boy's chest for air exchange. She gave me a nod indicating that the tube was in the lungs and not the stomach and then handed me the stethoscope so that I might listen for myself Hearing the breath sounds in the patient's chest, I announced that the tube was in place. I looked up at David. He had already surveyed the rhythm, which was asystole (flat line) and had started to give the appropriate drugs. We were now five minutes into the code and he looked at me. I could see the fear in his eyes.

"What's the history?" I asked, hoping to give him some guidance.

He smiled back at me and turned to one of the nurses at the foot of the bed, "What's the story?" he asked.

Sal Gianni was a seventeen-year-old man with leukemia. He had just finished the last cycle of chemotherapy yesterday. He had been feeling fine in the morning and when the nurse came in to do her usual assessment this afternoon she found him unresponsive. David looked at me after the story was finished.

"Labs?" I said softly.

"Labs?" he asked the nurse while winking at me.

"There aren't any from today," she said.

David ordered another ampule of Epinephrine and Atropine and turned to me. I asked Michael to run a blood gas right away and include potassium on it. I turned to David and said softly in his ear, "Hyperkalemia or another electrolyte abnormality from tumor lyses syndrome. Other possibilities are Pulmonary Embolus, Sepsis, and Aspiration. You can do this David. Give him Bicarb and lots of it and then Glucose and Insulin."

He nodded at me and ordered the appropriate drugs.

"Jackie," I said to the other respiratory technician, "can you keep giving him Ventolin through the tube?" She nodded and began to set up a nebulizer of Ventolin to attach to the oxygen.

David was now back in control. He had a list of diagnoses to work with and his confidence was rising. Michael returned with the blood work and confirmed what I had expected. The potassium was twice the upper limit of normal. Sal Gianni had tumor lyses syndrome. The chemotherapy was killing off his cancer by causing the cells to die. When the cells died, they ruptured, releasing all of their contents into the bloodstream. The body could usually handle most of this with the exception of some electrolytes, including potassium. Normal levels were between 3.0 and 5.0 mmol/litre.

Sal's potassium was 8.5 mmol/litre, a toxic number that had likely caused his heart to stop and was the reason we were gathered here today. The only chance we had at saving him was to get the potassium levels down. David was giving him every drug there was to cause potassium to shift back into cells and lower its concentration in the blood. CPR continued, as did the stream of drugs. We had been working for almost an hour when I heard it. It was as though the entire room was silent except for the beep. Sal's heart started beating. The beep was followed by many others and I looked at the rhythm. It was fast as hell but it was sinus. David looked at me, shocked and grinning. At that moment, he was the master of the universe.

"Call the unit, tell them we're on our way," he announced.

The rhythmic beeping of the monitor continued and within minutes we were wheeling Sal Gianni and his beating heart down the hall towards the elevator.

5:35 P.M.

I stood at Harold Brown's bedside waiting for Jackie to pull the endotracheal tube from his throat. She placed a blue pad of gauze across his chest to catch the mucous and cut the tape which fastened the tube in place. With Harold sitting up she instructed him to take a deep breath and pulled the tube in one swift motion. With a suction in the other hand she cleaned the saliva and mucous from his mouth. Harold Brown was now breathing on his own. With a mask on his face, his oxygen saturations were well above 90%.

"How are you feeling, Mr. Brown?" I yelled above the sound of the flow of oxygen. He nodded his answer and I grasped his hand in support. I left his bedside and walked down the hall to the waiting room to let Kathy know how her husband was doing. The family room was quiet with only a handful of faces. The fish tank's filter buzzed in the corner. It was one of the most beautiful freshwater tanks I had ever seen. I had heard it cost well over five thousand dollars. It was a one hundred gallon tank with two dozen cichlids of various colors. It was supposed to soothe families while they waited for whatever fate awaited them. No, really, psychologists would attest to this. Spend five grand on a bunch of fish and people will take bad news in a more civilized way.

I found Kathy Brown in one of the smaller rooms at the back. She was watching a talk show with a blank look on her face.

"Hi, Kathy."

"Oh, Dr. Solomon," she sat up from the television, "how's he doing?"

"Just fine," I smiled, "we took the breathing tube out and he's tolerating things very well. You can go in and see him now, if you like."

"Great," she said, standing up from the couch.

I waited for her to gather her things and we walked together back to the unit. Once at Harold's bedside, I glanced at the monitor above his bed. His saturation was 96% and he was breathing comfortably. I left Kathy with her husband and walked down the hall again to grab a coffee and snack before sign out rounds.

The doctors' café was closed so I elected to try the cafeteria downstairs. Why do all cafeterias look alike? This one was no exception. It was a large room with the decor of an auditorium with plastic chairs and sterile tables. The floor was of course linoleum and today's specials were etched on a black chalkboard on the wall by a stack of trays. I bypassed the serving line to the coffee station and grabbed two large Styrofoam cups. Pouring coffee in both, I put cream and sweeteners in one and left the other one black. I grabbed two blueberry muffins wrapped in cellophane and headed to the cashier. Five dollars and twenty cents later, I was on my way back to the unit. Once there I headed immediately to Sal Gianni's bedside where I knew I would find David. I was out of line in the elevator and had some apologizing to do. David was standing at the head of Sal's bed, inserting a central venous catheter into his neck.

"Hi," I said, holding up his coffee and muffin, "I brought you reinforcements."

He looked up from his sterile field and I could see he was finished with the procedure and was now suturing the line in place.

"Thanks," he said with a muffle through his mask, "I'll be done in a minute."

I watched him finish his stitches in the patient's neck. While he was dressing the line and cleaning up his mess I took the time to flip through Sal's chart. He was seventeen and had leukemia for the past three years. He had gone into remission a year after diagnosis and had relapsed four months ago. The cancer had returned with a vengeance. He was now undergoing a particularly aggressive form of chemotherapy and there had been minimal success thus far. Since his arrest we had normalized his potassium, and he was now stable. He had regained consciousness and was easy to ventilate. The breathing tube had since been fastened in place using white tape across his face and nose. He was able to communicate by motioning his head and hands, pointing to a board with letters on it.

"Hey," David interrupted my thoughts, "thanks for the coffee and muffin."

"David," I looked up at him to meet his gaze, "I was out of line in the elevator. I'm sorry."

"What about?" he looked so innocent. It always amazes me how you can read so much into something. Here I was in confession and David had let the whole episode slide off his shoulders. I was divulging my fault and David was oblivious. Still, I pressed on.

"I made a comment to you in the elevator before the code. I told you to stop flirting with me and I deliberately embarrassed you. I'm sorry, it was mean."

"Eve," he smiled at me, "apology accepted, but I was flirting with you."

He caught me totally off guard. My face turned red and I could no longer meet his gaze.

"Oh. David.... Listen... we need to talk. This isn't good."

"Have dinner with me." He was confident and perfect. I was a mess.

"What?"

"You heard me. Say yes."

"David, I'm married."

"I want one dinner, Eve, not adultery, just dinner." I couldn't believe what I was hearing. Suspecting someone's intentions is one thing, having those suspicions confirmed is quite another. My heart was racing but I couldn't deny how flattered I was. I loved Jack. I would never do anything to hurt him. Seven years together had been wonderful but there was a part of me that felt like an old maid. Here I was in front of the most sought after babe in the hospital and he was making me feel good. I was desirable, attractive, worthy. Here was an affirmation of my self-esteem. It was naughty, it was dangerous, but it was exhilarating.

"Pick me up at seven." I heard myself say.

He smiled at me with his fabulous face.

"Where do you live?" he said, looking straight at me.

I took a pen from my jacket pocket and wrote my address on a piece of hospital letterhead. I handed him the paper without saying a word.

"See you at seven," he said and turned and walked away from me.

I watched him strut down the hall towards the doors to the unit. I knew I was crazy for agreeing to this. It was dangerous on so many levels. The obvious was my husband. I had already decided I would absolutely tell Jack the truth. This was just dinner. We needed to talk anyway. I needed to clear the air. *It was only dinner*, I told myself. I figured if David understood where I was coming from he would agree to be friends and stop this charade. *It was only dinner*, I told myself again as I watched him walk down the hallway and my eyes glanced over his backside and rested on his perfect ass.

Chapter 13

Friday, 2:04 A.M.

I was at Evan White's bedside in green pajamas and with coffee in hand. He had returned several hours ago from a marathon surgery. The shaving cream can, in its attempt at removal, had once again ruptured and perforated several areas of his colon. He had arrested several times in the operating room and they were fortunate in bringing his heart back. Now the task was to maintain his blood pressure and continue keeping his heart pumping blood to his organs. He was on multiple antibiotics and several drugs to support the above tasks. The surgeons had removed nearly his entire colon and had spent hours washing out his abdominal cavity. The scent of wintergreen still hung about him. He now had a colostomy bag attached to his abdomen, to the right of his navel. Upon removing a good part of Evan's colon, the surgeons brought the remaining piece up through the skin in his abdomen and attached it to a bag. This would serve as his rectum for some months until it could be reattached to the stump, which remained inside his body cavity.

He was now in shock and his kidneys were shutting down. He was still making small amounts of urine and not yet requiring dialysis, but I could see that his struggle would be long and complicated. I looked through the computer for his last blood work and added serology for HIV and Hepatitis B and C. It was now a matter of supporting him through this insane ordeal and dealing with any surprises that should arise.

"His friend just called about ten minutes ago," Betty, the bedside nurse, announced.

"Is he here?" I asked.

"No, he phoned from home. He left a number." She handed me a scrap or paper. It was Evan's friend Jared, the man who had brought him to hospital. I told Betty to call me if Evan's urine output dropped below twenty milliliters per hour and walked to the front desk. I picked up the nearest phone's receiver and dialed Jared's home phone number.

"Hello?" a man's sleepy voice answered.

"Could I speak to Jared, please?" I said fully awake.

"Just a sec." I heard some rustling of what must have been bed covers and then mumbling.

"Who is it?" the voice came back on.

"It's Dr. Solomon from the hospital," I answered.

Again, rustling bed covers and hushed voices.

"Hello, Dr. Solomon, it's Jared. How is Evan doing?" It was now Jared's voice.

"He's stable right now, Jared. He had a long surgery and they had to remove part of his bowels. It is now a matter of time."

"When can I see him?" he asked, concern in his voice.

"At any time. We don't really have visiting hours. Does he have family in the city? Anyone I should call?" I asked.

"Yeah, I'll phone his sister and his mom." Pause. "Dr. Solomon, do they have to know how this happened?"

"No. In fact you can tell them he had a burst appendix and that's why he's here. I'll let the staff know. Okay?" I said.

"Thank you so much," he said with relief. "I'll be by to see him first thing in the morning."

"Sure. You can always call us at any time to see how he's doing," I said. I gave him the number to the direct line for the unit and said my goodbyes.

I put down the phone and put my head in my hands. I was tired and desperately needed a nap.

"Eve," it was Vicki, the night desk clerk, "they need you at bed four."

I nodded and walked over to Sal Gianni's bedside. David Auerbach was standing at the bedside. He looked up at me and I could see he was scared.

"He's bleeding out," he said.

"Can I help?" I asked.

"Please." There was fear in his voice.

I pressed the call button at the bedside and asked Vicki to page Dr. Michaels and to call the blood bank for six units of red cells. I then walked over to David and lifted the sheet covering Sal. There was blood everywhere. He was oozing from his rectum, nose, penis, and mouth.

"It's DIC," I told David. "We need to get some Cryo into him fast." I once again called Vicki and asked her for the clotting factor as well as twelve units of platelets. The scene was all too familiar. Sal was trying hard to die and we were scrambling to stop it. Lisa, the nurse, hung the first two bags of blood which David had ordered before I arrived. Sal's blood pressure was stable for the moment and I checked his last blood work in the computer. He was losing all ability to clot his blood and the only option we had at this point was to infuse clotting factors into his system and hope to temporize measures. I ordered broad-spectrum antibiotics as he easily could have been infected and this could be contributing. Likely the cancer and the chemo were the big players here but we had to cover all our bases. Moments later Dr. David Michaels arrived. He stood at the foot of the bed surveying us for a moment and then approached.

"What's the story?" he looked directly at David.

"I think he's in DIC. He's bleeding from everywhere. We've ordered blood and cryo and I started him on antibiotics. Eve was kind enough to—."

"Thank you, Dr. Solomon, I'll handle things from here." Dr. Michaels was dismissing me. I knew it would happen the moment he saw me at the bedside. David was sweet for trying to give me credit, but he had no idea what kind of history I had with this man. David smiled in my direction and I excused myself from the bedside.

"David, I've got the next admission," I said, waving in his direction.

I left the bedside and walked down the hall to my call room. Medically speaking my night had been pretty basic. Personally it had been tumultuous. I walked into the call room and brushed my teeth in the attached bathroom. The room itself looks very much like a hotel room. It's quite small but clean, with a bed, phone, and bathroom in the room. I sat on the bed and dialed my home phone number. It was late but I knew Jack wouldn't mind. The phone rang three times and his sleepy voice picked up.

"Hi sweetie," I said into the receiver. "Sorry I woke you. Just wanted to say goodnight."

"Love you," he said, half unconscious.

"Love you. Goodnight." I smiled and listened for him to hang up the phone. I took off my shoes and walked back to the sink to wash my face. I stared at my tired reflection in the mirror for some time. *What was I doing?* I repeated over in my mind. Without any answers and only more questions, I shut the light in the bathroom and crawled into bed.

8:06 AM

My pager woke me for the first time since I had laid down several hours before. I pressed the button to shut off the beeping and check the number on the screen. *Good Morning* flashed in green letters across the backlit screen. I could not believe I had slept through the night. Times like these are small gifts, few and far between. They must be cherished. I smiled to myself and sat up in bed. I checked the time and stood to stretch. There were two patients for me to see before rounds and I elected to use the shower in the call room to wake me up. I locked the door to the room and climbed into the hot spray. Ten minutes later I was dressed in a fresh pair of greens, my hair was still damp, and I was on my way for my morning coffee.

The doctor café was nearly empty. I stood waiting, with a blank mind, for my morning latte. I relished in the fact that I did not exude the usual smells of the night before. In fact, aside from the wet hair and pajamas, I could almost pass for normal.

"How was the rest of your night?" a voice broke my mental chatter. I turned around and it was David Auerbach. He was sporting wet hair and an air of exhaustion.

"Too good. And you?" I said, suspecting that he hadn't slept much.

"Awful. That young guy with leukemia died. You were right about the DIC. We couldn't stop the bleeding and he coded at least twice." He looked at his shoes and I could tell this was more difficult for him than he would let on.

"David, I'm sorry," I said looking directly at him, and I was. I had deliberately stayed away from this case because it harbored too much of a resemblance to times gone very badly. I had been where David was right now. I had felt the profound sense of failure as a person, the exhaustion, the irreparable injustice of it all. As much as I was watching David swim in a sea of sorrow, there was nothing I could say or do to ease the moment. I would search for the perfect phrase to make things "all better" and always come up empty. There was nothing to be said, there were no magic phrases to heal this moment. I was as powerless to help him as he was to Sal. By the very nature of his own self-loathing he would isolate himself. He felt weak and no one within these walls wanted to identify with fragility.

"I'm trying to think of something profound to say," I said, laughing at the absurdity of my words.

He smiled and looked up from his shoes.

"We still on for dinner?" he grinned.

"Sure, use the sympathy factor. If I cancel now I'm really a bitch," I responded, trying to bring humor to yet another awkward moment.

"Well..."

"Seven o'clock," I said.

"Wear something nice," he said.

"David, behave yourself. This is not a date," I scolded.

"I'll behave. You just wear something nice," he smiled.

The woman behind the counter called my attention. My coffee stood on the counter. I walked over and added the three sweeteners in my hand into the warm mix and took the ceremonial test sip. David watched me preparing my coffee and I could see him laughing out of the corner of my eye.

"What's so funny?" I said turning to him.

"You treat that stuff like it's a religious experience. It's just coffee, Eve."

I smiled and thought how much he had underestimated the power of a latte. If he only knew my true vulnerability when it came to coffee. The perfectly prepared cup could make a relationship. After all it had been his initial gift of milk and java that had won me over.

I picked up my cup and motioned that we should get back to the unit. Shaking a can of orange juice in his hand, David followed me out of the doctor café and into the fluorescent hallway.

1:42 A.M.

Rounds finished in almost record time. After all the unit was relatively quiet over night. We had one admission from the day and the only other admission had died in the night. My presentation of Evan White was met with a chuckle on Alex Connor's behalf. I stopped cold in the middle of my sentence and looked straight at him.

"What?" he had said, no longer laughing.

"Nothing. I thought you were going to say something," I said innocently.

Evan had done well throughout the night. His urine output remained stable and his kidney function was holding steady. He was still on a multitude of drugs, but he would likely do well. I had not had the chance to talk with his friend, Jared, as rounds had been going on. I completed a transfer note on Harold Brown and arranged for him to go to the Medical Teaching Unit. With the rest of my notes written, I left the unit and walked to the family room to see if I might be able to speak to Jared before I left the hospital.

The room was quiet except for the usual hum of the fish tank's filter. In one of the back rooms sat Kathy Brown who waved in my direction.

"Hi, Dr. Solomon,' she said.

"Hi, Kathy. He's doing just great. We're sending him to a regular medical unit today."

"I know," she smiled, "thanks for everything."

"Oh, my pleasure. You take care." I walked over to her and shook her hand.

I turned around and noticed two women sitting by the door. One of them stood and approached me.

"Are you the doctor looking after Evan White?"

"Yes, I am." I said, approaching the two women.

"Oh. Hi, I'm Evan's sister Angela, and this is my mother," she said motioning to the older woman seated in the chair.

"Hello. I'm Eve Solomon. I admitted Evan. In fact I was just coming to look for his friend Jared to let him know how Evan was doing." I sat down in the chair across from the pair.

"How is he?" Angela asked.

"He's very sick, but I think he's going to do well. He is on a lot of drugs to keep his blood pressure stable and to help fight the infection, but things look positive at this point. We'll have to wait and see."

"All this from an appendix?" Mrs. White asked. "Can I see him now?"

"Certainly, Mrs. White. Let me call the unit and let them know you are or your way." I stood up and walked to the phone on the wall. All family members had to phone from the waiting room before visiting their loved ones. It ensured that a mother did not arrive at her son's bedside in the middle of his cardiac arrest. I picked up the receiver and dialed the number to the unit.

"Hi, Becky, it's Eve, can I speak to Evan White's nurse?"

"Sure." She put me on hold and *Rainbow Connection* played in muzak. Halfway through the first verse, Betty, Evan' s bedside nurse, interrupted.

"Hi, Eve."

"Betty, Mrs. White, Evan's mother, would like to come see her son. I wondered if you had finished dressing his appendectomy site."

"What the hell?" she said and then after a moment's pause, "Ohhh, yeah sure. Appendix, good one, Eve. Send her back," she said.

I hung up the phone and told Mrs. White I'd walk her to the unit.

"Mom, I'd like to talk to the doctor for a minute. You go ahead. I'll meet you inside," Angela said. Her mother kissed her cheek and left to see her son and his appendectomy.

I sat down again and looked at Angela.

"Does he have AIDS?" she said to me frankly.

"Sorry?" I said, caught totally off guard. "He had his appendix out—"

"Dr. Solomon, I appreciate your respect for my brother's privacy. Evan is gay. Our mother doesn't know and our father has been dead for years. He thinks I don't know, but he's always been terrible at hiding it. Evan's thirty-three; he never had a girlfriend. Last summer I was cleaning out his apartment and found a box of gay porn. Evan told me he was doing research for a client. He's deathly afraid anyone will find out. Now, is this AIDS or not?"

"Angela, Evan is HIV negative. I have the test results to prove it. This is not AIDS. However, the rest of the story is confidential and without your brother's permission I really can't tell you much more. When he does wake up and this is all over, I suggest you have a long talk with your brother. I think he may find it a relief that you know about his sexuality and are accepting."

"Is he really going to be okay?" she said, tears in her eyes.

"Look, in my business there aren't any guarantees. But Evan is young and he's done well so far. We just have to wait and see," I said, putting my hand on her arm.

"Good," she said wiping the tears from her eyes, "and thanks for telling my mother it's his appendix. Evan would be shattered if she found out his way."

"No problem, Angela. How did you know Evan wasn't in the hospital for his appendix?" I asked, impressed by her astute evaluation of the situation.

"Evan had his appendix out three years ago while our mother was on vacation in Palm Springs. He made me promise not to tell her," she said laughing.

I couldn't help but smile, "I should have been more careful and checked for scars," I said.

We sat in the family room looking at one another, mourning with periodic spurts of laughter, the loss of Evan White's second appendix.

12:45 P.M.

I found my car on the first try. It's amazing what a few hours of sleep will do for you. The day was cloudy and cool, but I rode with the window open and let the fresh air blanket my face. Madonna played on the CD player and I was her backup singer.

Once home I ran a bath and poured myself a glass of wine. With the bubbles still building in the tub, I went into the bedroom and phoned Jack's office.

"Hi, sweetie," I said, bypassing his secretary and using his direct line.

"Hey. I remember you. You're my wife aren't you? Funny though, I can't quite recall what you look like," he said joking.

"I'm a leggy blonde," I said playing along.

"No, that's my girlfriend. My wife is a voluptuous brunette with eyes like the sea."

"Good one," I said, impressed by his flattery.

"How are you?" he asked.

"Good, listen, I'm having dinner with one of the guys from work tonight. Is that okay?" I almost hoped he'd say no.

"Eve, you don't have to ask my permission for these things. Of course you can go. Have fun. Do I know him?" he asked. Jack was too good for me.

"No, his name's David. You'll meet him tonight," I said.

"Great, I'll be home by five or so. Will you still be there?"

"We're not leaving until seven. See you later."

"Love you," he said sweetly.

"I love you too, Jack." I hung up the phone and stepped into the bathroom. Already bathed in a feeling of warmth and good fortune, I climbed into the tub.

Chapter 14

Jack answered the door and I could hear his voice echo through the loft. It was followed by David's Aussie twang telling him what a great place we had. I called from the bedroom to let them both know I'd be right out. As usual I was late. My bath was followed by a nap, which did not end when the alarm sounded. Jack woke me just after six and we sat in bed and talked before I realized how late I was.

"Can I offer you some wine?" I heard my husband say.

"Sure," David responded.

The acoustics in our home are such that you can hear everything echo from each room. With the exception of the den, which is an old elevator shaft turned into a room, sounds bounce off every wall. I put on lipstick and struggled with a pair of black boots. I had worn a black knee length skirt with knee high boots and a black short sleeve shirt. It was almost the end of summer so I knew I could get away with the outfit. Around my neck was the diamond Jack gave me for our first anniversary. My hair was back in a big black ponytail. I looked classy, unassuming and good. I walked into the living room to find Jack entertaining David with a story about a painting of ours. Both looked over at me.

"Hi, David. Welcome," I said smiling at him. Jack walked over and kissed my cheek.

"Eve, you painted this?" David said, referring to the monstrosity of a canvas hanging on our living room wall.

"Yeah. It's my therapy." I said laughing. I was a terrible artist but that never stopped me. I was never able to draw so I confined my paintings to large shapes smeared with thick acrylics. This painting was true to my usual form.

"Great. I was admiring it and Jack told me you painted it. I'm impressed."

"Don't be," I said walking to the kitchen and pouring myself a glass of wine. I took a sip of the Chardonnay Jack had opened and returned to the living room. This was insanity. My husband was having a perfectly decent conversation with a man who had openly admitted to flirting with me. The two were standing in my living room drinking wine, admiring my painting. One had seen me naked, the other hoped to. I felt my insides turning at the whole display.

"So, you work with Eve," Jack said, in an attempt at small talk. I began sipping my wine quickly as I knew he'd be out of polite chitchat in a few sentences.

"Yeah. She's awesome to work with." David smiled at me.

I was now gulping my wine.

"We should get going," I said, "it's a school night after all." I laughed and took the last sip of my wine.

"Where are you two headed?" Jack asked.

I looked at David.

"I'm taking your wife to dinner at Rococo's. Have you ever been?"

"No, but I hear it's excellent," Jack said smiling.

"Well, Eve's been really great helping at work so she deserves a real thank you," David said putting down his wine glass.

The three of us walked to the door.

"I won't be home late," I said to Jack, kissing him.

"Have fun, my love," he said smiling.

We walked through the door and I closed it behind us.

"You have a beautiful home," David said on our way to the elevator. "And Jack is just great," he added.

"Thanks, I feel very lucky," I said smiling.

There were those moments of uncomfortable silence in the elevator before we walked out of the building and towards David's car. As I expected he drove a sports car. It's amazing how people sometimes live up to your stereotypes.

David opened my door. As I was climbing into his testosterone mobile he caught my gaze. "You look beautiful, Eve," he said.

"Thank you, David," I smiled, "so do you." And he did. He was wearing a casual gray suit with a crisp white shirt. His blue eyes were shining amidst all of it. I sat in the passenger seat and waited for him to close the door, come around the front of the car and join me. Suddenly the moment was no longer frightening. In the comfort of a small but virile car, smelling of Calvin Klein cologne I was no longer afraid of what might happen between David and me. He was right, I was lucky, and there was nothing on this earth that would alter my conviction. I loved my husband and our life together. I couldn't believe I had even thought of betraying his trust.

Of course then David opened the driver's side door and slid in beside me. He smiled at me with his perfect face.

"Shall we?" he asked.

And my heart quickly fell into my stomach.

7:35 P.M.

The car stopped in front of Rococo's and David left the engine running. The sound of his techno music entered the air the moment I opened my door. He handed his keys to valet and waited for me to come around the car. I joined him at the door to the restaurant. Rococo's is a beautiful, very ornate Italian restaurant in the heart of downtown. It was a fairly new place and Jack and I hadn't a chance to try it. The entrance to the room was covered in Italian glass chandeliers and beautiful paintings with gilded frames. A man in a tuxedo showed us to our seat. The room itself was exceptional. The floors were a mix of white marble and plush navy and gold carpeting. The ceiling was studded in painted gold with more of the chandeliers like the ones in the entry. It was a bit much, but it was certainly breathtaking. We were seated at an intimate corner table with a velvet booth.

"This is extraordinary," I said to David.

"Isn't it?" he responded, sliding into the booth next to me.

"Can I offer you a drink?" the maitre de asked.

I ordered a martini and David ordered a scotch.

"That's quite the man's drink," David commented when we were alone.

"I hate sweet alcohol," I said laughing. "Jack and I will go for dinner and I'll order the typical boy drink and he'll have a daiquiri. It's quite humorous when the drinks arrive," I said, trying to maintain a steady flow of conversation. David was looking at me, I mean really looking at me.

"What is it?" I asked, feeling once again uncomfortable.

"You are a very attractive woman," he said smiling.

I looked back at him. That was it. Enough. The flirting was over and I had to draw a very definite line.

'Okay, David, out with it. What do you want from me?" I was almost afraid of the answer.

"Why do I have to want something from you?" he asked coyly.

"Please stop playing games. David, I like you. I find you very attractive, and I think you are a real catch. But I am very happily married and I'm not comfortable with the way things are between us. Now maybe I'm totally reading too much into your behavior, but I can't help but think that you have motives beyond friendship here." I took a deep breath and looked over at him. He was smiling. Had the man not heard one word I had said?

"You're right," he said softly.

"I am?" I was acting on a hunch and now it was confirmed.

"I like you, Eve…a lot. I've been with lots of women before but you're different. I can't deny that I could see us having a relationship," he said, looking straight at me.

Was this man crazy?

"David, this is madness. Firstly, I am not available. Secondly, we work together. I can't have you acting like this."

"Why not?"

"Because I am not comfortable with this. Please, I'm asking you as a friend to leave me out of this."

"What do you mean leave you out of this?" he said laughing.

I had to be cruel. There was no other way of getting through to this man.

"David, come on. Part of the reason you are interested in me is because I'm a challenge, a conquest. I am totally not your type."

He didn't say a word.

"Well, I'm telling you that there is no future here. I would love to be your friend but that's all," I continued.

He kept looking at me in silence. Our drinks arrived and I took a sip of my martini and stared back at him. I couldn't tell if he was hurt or pleased with himself. All I knew was he was in full control of this conversation and it was starting to really piss me off. Who the hell did this man think he was? He sat there, a smug bastard and I was doing all the work.

"You know, this is crazy. I don't care how gorgeous you are. I need to go home. Thank you for the thought, David, but this isn't going to work." I put my hands on the table to stand up and his hands were suddenly on mine. His fingers moved up my arm and every cell in my body was screaming to leave.

"Stay," he said softly. His hands were warm and soft. I pulled my arms back.

"David, please, we can't do this." I had now moved out of the booth and to the end of the table.

"Thank you anyway," I said. I was suffocating and I needed to get out or there. I was now a babbling mess. I had lost control. I turned and walked quickly to the door.

Once outside the restaurant the night air hit me quickly. I needed a cab and fast. I asked the man at the valet to call me a cab and stood in the darkness and waited.

"Eve." David was beside me. Why is it men never follow you when they are supposed to and then always go after you when you absolutely don't want them to? I turned to him. Now was my turn to pull the silent act. I had been wooed by his flattery. His smile was like a new toy I had to have and it had tricked me into forgetting myself. The conquest and not the consequence became the key. And now, with reality and the cold night air in my face I had come to my senses. Why must I always search for more? Why is it that whatever lies before me is never enough? I have suffered an insatiable appetite for too long and if allowed, it will lead to my downfall. I looked over at David.

"Stay and have dinner with me," he said, touching my arm. I took a step away from him and remained silent.

"Oh come on, Eve, don't pull that innocent act with me. You wanted something as much as I did," he said. I looked at him. He had lost his luster. All of the sudden he was no longer a sophisticated soul I might connect with. He was a horny college boy with another conquest on his mind. And to think I had even thought of sleeping with him. This would have been so easy for him. I would risk my entire happiness and he would get off easy. He would never understand, nor appreciate the sacrifices I had made to be with him. I now understood the true betrayal unraveling before me. I had forsaken my honor, my life's code for a cheap promise of passion.

He stood there beside me waiting for a reaction. My cab arrived and I opened my own door. "David," I said, climbing in to the back seat, "go home. I'll see you at work." I closed the door and after telling the driver my address, sunk into the back seat of the cab. I sat there watching the city pass by me, angry with myself. I hated David for tempting me; I hated myself for being so easily tempted. But mostly I marveled in a mournful kind of way the ease at which I had lost my sense of self. I took little comfort in the fact that I had-n't consummated anything. Rather, I sat in the back seat of a cab racing across town and thought of how effortless it would have been to betray myself. This time it was not about the loss of a patient or the loss of my inno-cence. I sunk into the cracking leather around me, having lost the core of what I held dear. I sat in the darkness, tears streaming down my face with a new emptiness inside of me and the knowledge that it would take more than a bubble bath to wash myself clean again.

8:45 P.M.

I wiped my face in the elevator in the hopes that Jack would be in the den when I arrived home and could not see my tear-stained face. Nonetheless I did my best with a Kleenex and some lipstick to wipe the guilt from my face. I arrived at our door, put the key in the lock and walked into the apartment. As I'd suspected, Jack was at the computer in the den and the music was on. He loves techno shit, which I'm not crazy about and plays it all the time when I'm not around.

"Hello," I called from the door.

"Hey, you're home early." He poked his head out from the den. "How was dinner?"

"It wasn't. David got called into the hospital for an emergency," I lied. It was an easily believable lie and it had slipped out before I could even think of telling the truth. I would confess the whole story to Jack at some point, but I decided that it should be years from now, when the benefit of time would turn the insanity of the situation into a humorous and harmless tale.

"You hungry?" he asked from the den. "I ordered Chinese food. It should be here any minute."

"Great. I'm going to put on my pajamas and I'll join you in a bit," I said holding back the remnants of tears. I walked into our bathroom and took off my tainted outfit. I hung everything neatly in the closet and returned to the sink to wash my face. Minutes later the tearstains were gone and I slipped into my flannels. I heard the doorbell ring as I buttoned my top, followed by a brief exchange between Jack and a deliveryman.

"Supper," he called as I walked into the living room.

"Hi," I said, kissing him.

"Well, it's too bad you missed out on dinner," he said sympathetically, "but I promise to make it up to you." He pulled plastic cartons from the large paper bag.

"We have ginger beef, sweet and sour chicken balls, fried rice, dumplings, and beef and broccoli," he said proudly. Jack had ordered all of his favorites.

"Were you expecting an army?" I said, laughing at the amount of food before us.

"No, I just got carried away," he said laughing.

He pulled two stools up to the counter and with chopsticks in hand, proceeded to eat straight from the boxes.

"Jack, get a plate," I said.

"Hey, this is my dinner. We're eating my way." He smiled, a mouth full of dumpling.

I conceded. This was a man who made everything in life an enjoyable experience. Jack's primary goal in life was to have fun. His needs were so simple and yet sheer entertainment was at the heart of everything he did. I smiled lovingly at my husband and buried the secrets of my evening deep within myself. I reached over him for my own pair of chopsticks and climbed in the stool next to him. We sat there beside each other with a feast before us, eating Chinese take-out straight from the boxes. He began to tell me about a new project at work with his usual enthusiasm.

Between dumplings and chicken balls the conversation flowed. I was an old maid in flannel pajamas. I had traded in black boots for bare feet and high class Italian for low budget beef and broccoli. Amidst all of this, I would look up at my husband from time to time and with a mixture of gratitude and guilt admire his perfection.

11:30 P.M.

A post Chinese food coma followed dinner. We lay together on the couch in the living room flipping lazily through the channels and settled on watching *Suddenly Last Summer* on cable. We had both seen the movie before but could easily use it as background noise for the evening. I tried like hell to stay awake but periodically closed my eyes in certain scenes. Finally I conceded and wound up falling asleep well before Elizabeth Taylor makes her climactic confession to Montgomery Cliff. I woke up in time for the credits and Jack led me to bed. Head to pillow, his feet entwined in mine, I fell asleep without even thinking how in the turn of a moment I might have lost it all.

Chapter 15

Saturday, 8:30 A.M.

The phone woke me with a start. I picked up the receiver and looked at the alarm clock on the bedside table.

"Hello?" I said exaggerating the sleep in my voice. I think people who call before 11:00 A.M. on a weekend should be made to feel their error.

"Hi, sweetie. Did I wake you?" It was my mother. She was notorious for this kind of behavior.

"Yes. What's wrong?" I asked, assuming that if she had the nerve to call at this hour there must be another family crisis.

"Why does something have to be wrong for me to phone?" she asked, inhaling. It was well before noon on a Saturday morning and my mother was smoking. Something was definitely wrong.

"It doesn't, Ma," I said, sitting up in bed. "How are you?"

"Oh, I'm okay. I got into another fight with your sister last night. She thinks I'm too controlling."

The fact is Penny couldn't find her way out of a paper bag without my mother and her complete dependence on my parents occasionally angered her beyond reproach. Penny was in her mid thirties and my mother still did her laundry and balanced her checkbook. For the most part, I think Penny saw this as a real bonus. It served to further her life philosophy of "no stress, no responsibility". However, there were times when she would have to take the benefit of my mother's secretarial duties with the disadvantage of her advice and instruction. It was in these times when Penny called my mother controlling and lashed out verbally in any way possible. My mother, who despite her faults was part saint, took Penny's shit with grace. In fact these outbursts were now such a common place that I really believe my mother completely sailed through them by just ignoring the beast.

"Yes dear, your sister is in one of her moods again." I almost resented the term "your sister". Penny and I really did not like one another. There wasn't any salvageable connection between us. My mother's attempt to help me identify with "my sister" was useless.

"Hmmm." My standard response. I was trying my best not to get sucked into yet another conversation about Penny's dysfunction. It was too early in the morning and talks such as these always ruined my day. It was amazing how one woman miles away from me in mind and body could still torture me as often as she did.

I used to envy women who had sisters to be close to. I would sit with friends and strangers listening to their family tales of how their sisters had brought them through many a trying time. And then they would turn to me and ask the obvious next question, "Do you have brothers or sisters, Eve?" And I would obligingly tell them that, yes, I had an older sister and no, we weren't close. This was usually met with "That's too bad". Now in those moments of sympathy I no longer feel a loss. In fact I no longer feel anything. Penny and I stopped being close long before I can remember. My memories of good times with her stop at around the age of ten. It's difficult to form a sense of loss for someone you haven't seen for over twenty years. It is as though you have a parent die when you're seven or eight and all you have to remember them by are the black and white movie memories that play once in a while in your brain. With Penny, these movies are tainted so badly with her bitter words and actions over the past twenty years that they will never come clean. And so when I sit in a group of people, all from big, fabulously functional families, I don't envy their good fortune. I don't even mourn the loss of my own good fortune. In fact I sit there listening to their tales as though they are speaking another language. I smile in all the right places, nod in others. But the details are completely foreign to me. I no longer remember what it is I am missing.

I suppose the source of our discord began when Penny was fourteen and I was eight. She found drugs and sex earlier than some and began a course of self-destruction. My parents were less than pleased by their eldest daughter's rebellion. From what I can remember she was a pain in the ass. She would hide men in her closet on a regular basis. She was high on cocaine or out of it on heroine more times than not. She went beyond the teen rebellion and in the process never really grew up. I stood by watching her take us all down with her and somewhere it became my responsibility to save my parents from Penny. As much as she failed, I strove to succeed. I grew up doing what I was told. Above all I behaved myself. I did well in school, didn't sleep around and stayed sober. This of course was not well received with my doped up sibling who felt my good behavior was a deliberate personal offence. I was motivated to be anything but Penny. She saw my every action as a way of making our parents love me and hate her.

Penny used to beat the shit out of me. She found any excuse to get violent. This went on until I was sixteen and Penny tried to kill me with a pair of scissors. I don't even remember what I had done to strike her fuse. What I do remember was that she jumped on top of me, high as a kite, and held a pair of scissors above my chest, threatening to drive them into my heart if I made a sound. My father came into the room just in time and pulled Penny off me.

Penny was kicked out of the house that day. The truth is, Mom and Dad found her an apartment downtown and began to pay her rent until she found a job. I suppose this is where it all began. Penny blamed me for her 'bad fortune', and I began hating her with a vengeance. The bitch tried to kill me and she got her own apartment. It's pretty much been that way ever since.

And now years later, she's still doing it. Penny lives in a house my parents paid for and when she can, she pays the monthly mortgage. She now has a daughter she uses as leverage to get what she wants. She still blames me for her 'bad fortune', only now she calls me a self-centered snob. Now it has become a class war. I am the white collar capitalist that will always keep her, the single working mother, down.

You know she is right on some levels. All of this between us isn't only her fault. I don't like Penny. On some levels I'm ashamed she's my sister. I do feel superior to her. I will never forgive her for fucking with our family, even to this day. So we will never heal the pain and animosity between us. So every time I find myself in a group of friends or strangers, the talk of their amazing connection with their siblings will always be something I will never understand.

The issue at hand was that Penny was not speaking to my mother. Mom was a master at dealing with her older daughter's anger. Mom would just dismiss it and let her "cool off". Two days later she would get a phone call from Penny as though nothing had happened and that would be the end of it. The fact was, Penny needed my parents and they knew it. She could rant all she liked about my mother's controlling ways, but Mom felt it was only Penny's way of expressing her frustration over her situation.

"Just ignore her, Mom, she'll cool off." I said exactly what she wanted to hear. I felt sorry for my mother in moments like these. She did things for my sister because she truly believed in helping her. Sure they treated Penny like a child. But hey, she deserved it. Was my Mom controlling? Sure. She balanced Penny's checkbook, paid all of her bills, and had an opinion about everything Penny did. My sister would allow it up to a point and then lash out. It was madness.

My mother quickly changed the subject and began to tell me about a new suit she bought at a warehouse sale.

"Is Isaac Mizrahi expensive?" she asked.

"Yes, Ma, why?"

"Well I got this gorgeous black suit that's by him. I paid two hundred dollars for it. Did I get a deal?" she asked and took a puff of her cigarette.

"Big time," I said.

"Ohhhh." She was thrilled.

I looked at the clock. It was now almost nine in the morning. I was not ready to get out of bed just yet. I was on call tomorrow and this would be my only day to sleep in. If I got out of this conversation now, I still had a chance at getting back to sleep.

"Mom, I'm going back to sleep. I'll call you this afternoon. Okay."

"Sure, sweetie, speak to you later," she said exhaling.

I hung up the phone and unplugged the cord from the base. I fluffed up my pillows and looked over at Jack's sleeping face. He hadn't stirred once in the entire conversation. This had come from years of sleeping through calls from the hospital in the middle of the night. I moved over to his warm body, putting my arm around his belly. He rolled over and wrapped an arm around me, pulling me into a sleepy embrace. I closed my eyes and tried not to think of the conversation moments before, now replaying in my mind. I listened to my husband's rhythmic breathing and tried to time it with my own. It was not long before I fell into a deep and dreamless sleep.

11:45 P.M.

I woke up with the smell of coffee filling the loft. Jack's side of the bed was empty and had already gone cold. I sat up in bed and stretched and then got up to brush my teeth.

"Good morning," I called from the bathroom.

"Hi, sweetie." He poked his head into the room, "Coffee?"

"Please," I said, rinsing out my mouth. I washed my face and after drying it with a towel, saw that Jack had left a cup of hot coffee on the shelf in the bathroom. I took the coffee cup into the den where Jack was working on the computer. I kissed him on the mouth and sat down on the couch facing him.

"How'd you sleep?" He smiled at me.

"Great. My mother woke me up early this morning, but I managed to get back to sleep," I said, sipping my coffee.

"What do you want to do today?" he asked.

"Absolutely nothing," I said, looking around the room.

"Okay." He smiled.

"I just have to pick up the ticket for New York and then I'm going to rent some movies. Want to be a sloth with me?" I smiled. I loved days where I did not have to justify staying in my pajamas.

"Sure. I just have to finish this one part of the program. I can do that while you're at the travel agent. Okay?"

"Perfect. The travel agency closes at four o'clock, so I have plenty of time," I said stretching. "I'm going to lay here for a while."

"More coffee?" Jack asked getting up.

"No, I'm fine," I said. The phone rang and I called to Jack that I was not home and he should take a message.

"Sorry, David, she's not in. I'll have her call you when she gets in." I heard him say from the kitchen. I was less than pleased with the phone call. Jack put down the phone and called to me that it had been David.

"Thanks," I said, picking up my ICU book and turning to the chapter on ventilators. I would have a quiet day at home reading with my husband followed by an evening of videos. I would not call David Auerbach. I would avoid the whole subject entirely. I continued to read and sip my coffee, trying my best not let David and last night's incident into my thoughts. The chapter on ventilators was less than stimulating. I had spent so much of my life studying that now even on a small scale any such task required huge motivation on my part. In short I had lost momentum long ago and no longer had it in me. Amidst the ticking of Jack's fingers on a computer keyboard, I recited in my head the requirements for Pressure Support Ventilation versus Assist Control Ventilation. I went over the necessary weaning parameters for extubation. I knew, however, that I would likely forget most of this information in another two weeks. The expanse of medical knowledge became greater with each day while my brain continually strove to keep up. I had long ago resigned myself to the fact that I would always know less than half of what there was to know. I had entered into a field as an extraordinary achiever and emerged the other end as average. It was an amazing process. Medicine recruits these high achievers with amazing minds. As individuals they are special. In a group, they lose their uniqueness rather quickly. Instead, one's accomplishments melt into another's. What emerges from this fabulous primordial soup is an average person in an exceptional field. When outside the doors to the compound, you have greatness. However, once inside you will always just be ordinary.

I had long ago learned to live with this. In fact I rather liked being ordinary. With it came certain freedoms. Being outstanding is a truly exhausting experience. When you are on top, there will always be the ones below you trying to grab a piece of the pie. As such you spend countless hours being that which people measure themselves up to. The middle ground, once accepted as such, is quite a comfortable place to be. No one looks over your shoulder trying to throw you off. There isn't the need to compete to stay alive. You float along in an average way and try and take pride in your own little unique abilities. It was a system that was really working for me.

The ring of the phone surprised us both, and without thinking I reached to answer it.

"Hello?" I said into the receiver.

"When are you coming to visit? I'm lonely." It was my father.

"Hi, Daddy." How are you?"

"Your mother is driving me crazy. You know if I wasn't dying, I'd leave her," he said laughing.

My father's approach to death was a combination of comedy and obsession. When he wasn't making jokes about the way he "wanted to go", he would drift off into existential talk with a far away look on his face and tears in his eyes. He had been living with a diagnosis of end stage cancer for almost two years now. This did not go over well with his oncologist who had the bedside manner of a cockroach. My father would walk into the illustrious Dr. Frank Wohl's office every two months and was met with the surprise statement, "You know, Isaac, I can't believe you're still alive! I thought you would be dead by now. I can't explain it. Are you sure you have cancer?" This was usually met with my father reminding his oncologist that it was he who gave him the diagnosis in the first place. These little visits did nothing to bolster my father's faith in the medical profession. They did, however, ruin him for about a week at a time.

"How's everything else, Daddy?" I asked, interrupting my father's explanation of how my mother is now chain-smoking.

"Well my CEA count is nine, which Frank says is good. Jerry's CEA is forty, which is not good and Eddie is having prostate surgery next month." Jerry and Eddie were my father's closest friends. Jerry had been diagnosed with metastatic colon cancer five years ago and had since had six surgeries to remove the spreading tumors from various organs. Doctors had told him they couldn't do any more surgery and he was now awaiting a salvage chemotherapy program. He and my father now had the same oncologist and would exchange "Frank" stories as well as CEA counts. Carcinogenic Embryonic Antigen (CEA) is a blood test which helps physicians monitor patients with metastatic disease. For my father and Jerry, it was like taking a final exam. Every two months my father would sit in Dr. Wohl's office and await the news. If his CEA rose even one point it would destroy him. If it dropped two points from a previous visit, he went out and celebrated. I know I have no right to form an opinion about my father and his diagnosis. It was his cancer and he was the one dealing with it. It was not up to me as his daughter to pass judgment on his tolerance level or lack there of. I had afforded my patients, perfect strangers, a better understanding of their actions and reactions. He was somehow exempt from this understanding because he was the hero of my youth. Despite the fact that I had long ago accepted my parents weren't gods, there were certain things I wasn't willing to give up.

"How's Jerry feeling?" I asked, knowing full well as Jerry called me every few weeks with a report.

"He's coughing up blood. It's bad, isn't it?" he asked.

"Yeah, Daddy, it's not good."

"How long does he have, Eve?" I hated these questions.

"I don't know, Daddy, maybe months, I said.

"Ohhh."

Long silence.

"How's Eddie feeling?" I asked to break the silence.

"Oh, he's okay. Millie is driving him crazy." Millie was Eddie's wife and my mother's best friend. They had been close for as long as I can remember. She chain-smoked in a manner consistent with my mother and learned everything she needed to know about medicine from the *Ladies Home Journal*. As such she would entertain us all with a slew of diagnoses every time a new issue emerged. Considering Aunty Millie had been a subscriber for the past thirty years, she had amassed quite a knowledge base. My father and Uncle Eddie often referred to her as Dr. Millie over brunch with the boys every Wednesday.

"What's wrong with his prostate?" I couldn't believe I was asking this question, but it was an attempt to get my father to focus on something other than his own death.

"Oh, it's benign. But apparently it's as big as a grapefruit and he can't pee properly. He keeps getting stones in his bladder. So they're gonna take out the prostate and while they're in there, remove the stones as well. He goes in three weeks from Thursday."

"Hmm," I said, between my father's breaths.

"Millie thinks it's cancer even though he's had six biopsies which show it's benign. They even went to the Mayo clinic, you know?"

"Yeh, Ma told me."

"Well the Mayo thinks it's benign, but Millie's convinced it's cancer. Go figure. So she's driving him crazy."

I chuckled. My father was born to be an entertainer. He could tell a story like no one else.

"How are you, Daddy?" I asked sincerely.

"Eh, fine... (Pause) I'm dying, what else is new? (Pause) Listen, I need Jack to show me sometime how to install that new software I got. Ask him when he's free," my father said.

I turned to Jack and relayed the message.

"Tell him I'm free all day tomorrow," Jack said.

I relayed the message back to my father.

"Well darling, I'm going to go have a nap. I just took a Valium and it's kicking in. I'll call you tomorrow," he said, yawning.

"Bye, Daddy. Love you."

"Love you too, dear." He hung up the phone.

I returned to my chapter on ventilators and Jack continued on the computer. An hour and two cups of coffee later, I was finished with the chapter and ready for a shower. I walked into the bathroom and began to run the water. I let my pajamas drop to the floor and stepped into the hot spray.

3:40 P.M.

I had picked up our tickets for New York from the travel agency and was on my way to the video store. I reached for the cell phone and dialed our home number. Jack picked up.

"Pack your bags, baby, I've got the tickets." We were both very excited about this trip. This would be our first time together in New York and I couldn't wait to show Jack my favorite places.

"Great! Are you on your way home?"

"No, I'm going to stop at the video store. Should I pick up sushi for dinner?" I asked, looking forward to a quiet night at home before my day on call.

"Sure," he said.

"I'll see you soon," I said, hanging up the phone.

The Indigo Girls were playing on the CD player and I sang along on the way to the video store. I parked the Valiant in front and walked into Blockbuster. This place is like a bad addiction for me. It is an endless pit into which I throw my money on overdue rentals with the promise that I will never do it again. However, despite the negative consequences, I continue to return in search of my latest escape. I walked into the fluorescent video superstore to be hit with a wall of yellow and blue and the sound of the latest action movie playing over the loudspeaker.

Surveying the "New Releases" wall, I chose three movies, two bottles of Diet Coke and a packet of popcorn in accordance with the latest movie deal. All were due back tomorrow and there was no way I would watch three movies tonight. This meant that I was setting myself up for late fees once again. It was a vicious circle.

The sixteen-year-old at the counter informed me that I owed sixteen dollars in late fees. He smiled and offered me a free promotional Blockbuster cup and rang in the movies. I hated the people who worked at Blockbuster. They were condescending teenage assholes who never paid late fees and never gave me a break from mine. Standing in front of me was just the prepubescent "cool dude" with a mouth full of metal and jeans three sizes too big.

"Can you give me a break on the late fees?" I asked, knowing this would not happen but it was worth a try.

"Sorry, but I'll give you an extra cup." He smiled, the ass of his jeans practically down to the floor, "That will be thirty-eight fifty." He smiled again.

I looked up at him. His hair was badly bleached and his face was oily. He was wearing a Blockbuster tee shirt with a nametag reading CHIP in big letters on a chain around his neck. I handed CHIP my bank card and waited for him to process the Interac transaction. I was the only person in the world who found going to a movie cheaper than renting one.

"Would you like a bag?" he asked.

"Sure," I said. If I was paying thirty-eight fifty, he should carry the shit home for me.

CHIP placed the bag containing my movies, popcorn, drinks, and two Blockbuster Video cups on the counter behind him and handed me my card and my bill. I walked though the gates of hell theft detectors, picked up my forty dollars worth of entertainment and exited the store. I hated that place, but I knew I'd be back. Much to my dismay, CHIP was my dealer and I was helpless to the beauty of his wares.

I sat in the Valiant and called Kyoto's to order the sushi. Having a few minutes before the food would be ready, I left the car in the lot and walked across the street to the Starbucks to grab a coffee. After spending forty dollars on videos, I like to wash things down with a five-dollar coffee.

Half an hour later, latte in hand, I was back in the Valiant and on my way home from the Sushi house with sixty dollars worth of raw fish. I had been gone less than two hours and had managed to spend a total of $1,105.42 including the tickets to New York and my fix at Blockbuster. I was on my way to New York City with my husband and I no longer had any late fees at Blockbuster! The latte had officially kicked in.

Chapter 16

Sunday, 6:45 A.M.

The buzz of the alarm was offensive. I had always kept it at the maximum volume to ensure that it would wake me. As such it often woke me with such a start that I would automatically slap the SNOOZE button and, once recovered from the palpitations, fall back asleep. Jack was almost programmed to sleep through these episodes. There was no mental debate this morning about getting out of bed. I was on call. If you were dying, you didn't call in sick when on call. We all had horror stories of doing call while on our own deathbeds.

I had pneumonia last year and had refused to go to the hospital. Instead I had ordered home oxygen for myself in order to keep my oxygen saturations above 90%. Ill as can be, I couldn't get anyone to cover my call day and wound up doing an in house, overnight call for Internal Medicine while carrying my home oxygen on my back. There was no calling in sick.

On the second alarm I sat up in bed and shut the clock off. I turned to look at Jack who was sleeping soundly spread eagle over the bed. The man slept like a turtle with attitude. Firstly he always slept on his stomach with his head under a pillow and hands tucked under his body. As such if you woke him, he looked like a turtle poking his head out of a shell. Furthermore he slept diagonally. With Jack there wasn't any point to having a "side of the bed". He took it all. When we were first dating I used to wake up at night with him sleeping on top of me. In retrospect it was quite comical. I had terrible sleeps in the first year of our marriage, but vowed to myself to persevere. Now several years of practice had allowed me to be used to the idea.

I suppose we could have bought a larger bed or even slept in separate beds. My parents slept in separate beds. They have been doing so since I was nine years old. My father snores and wakes my mother who then spends the remainder of the night poking him in order to keep him quiet. This would culminate in my father waking periodically and finally neither of them got any rest. So around the time that I was nine, my mother moved into the guest room down the hall and has been there ever since. As a child, kids at school would look at me funny when they found that my parents didn't sleep together. To this day, I still get the occasional look when people discover my deep dark secret. I've grown up with it. I'm so accustomed to it. In fact I think the idea is rather practical. They go so far as to rent two hotel rooms when they travel. In fact my parents haven't slept together in over twenty years and are still happily married. How many people can say that?

As practical as it was, I would never choose this potion. Jack would have to try and kill me in my sleep before I'd move to the guest room. That was all there was to it.

The hot shower was a nice way to wake up, considering the apartment was cold in the morning. With its high ceilings it was hard to keep warm in the morning and in the winter months. I washed my hair and stood under the spray for a moment to warm up. I closed my eyes and in the silence of the morning my mind turned to David. It is amazing how good we are at pretending. I had pretended that honesty was the key to any good relationship. I had pretended to myself that I was a woman of honor. Yet here I was standing in a shower with the memory of an emotional infidelity. Is it worse to have committed the act or have contemplated it? By thinking about sleeping with David had I already taken that step? Was the actual act of fucking him just a geographical consideration or could I still be redeemed? It was in these times I needed advice the most and yet could never ask for it. I was alone in this journey and I knew it. The tears mixed with the shower water as I stood in the spray. I had always sat in judgment of the men and women who would stoop this low. I took pride in standing above them in my moral tower and passing my latest opinion. And now I was sliding down the stairs to the castle to join the commoners below.

And on top of it all, I was late for work.

I shook off the haze of my existential crisis and grabbed a towel. I no longer had time to dry my hair. I grabbed a brush and put my wet hair back in a tight bun. My body still wet, I put on a sundress and a pair of close-toed shoes. I grabbed my makeup bag, running shoes, and a change of underwear. I put them into my call bag along with my deodorant and an extra pair of hospital greens. I kissed Jack on the cheek without waking him and headed for the door. Without any traffic and a bit of luck and I might just make it.

7:50 A.M.

I drove into the staff parking lot which unlike the resident lot, is directly across from the hospital. This of course meant incurring a $30 parking fine in the morning, but I accepted it as a necessary cost to allow me the time to grab a coffee before getting sign over. Grabbing my bags from the car, I ran into the hospital and got in line in the café in the lobby. I ordered my latte and looked at the clock. With four minutes to spare I could breathe easily. It was not that I was anxious about being late; it was more that I was always late and hated to continue to draw attention to myself in this manner.

I grabbed my coffee and headed for the unit. Once inside the doors, I knocked on the first call room door and hearing no answer opened it and put my bags inside. I proceeded down the hall to look at the unit board where all the patients' names are written. I noticed that none of the names looked familiar. This meant that all of the people I had been looking after had left the unit.

I found Ethan Baker, one of the surgery residents, at the front desk. He looked tired from a night on call and was holding a coffee with both hands.

"How was your night?" I asked.

"Hell," he said.

"Do you have anyone you'd like to hand over to me? All my patients have left the unit," I offered.

"Sure, Eve, let me get a list," he said, proceeding to the other side of the desk and grabbing two copies of the patient census.

"Ethan, did Evan White go to surgery? I don't see his name on the board," I said.

"Who?"

"Evan White, the young businessman who had punctured his large bowel with a can of shaving cream," I said reminding him.

"Oh yeah, him. He died yesterday night."

"What?" I said with shock. He'd been doing so well on Friday afternoon.

"Yeah, poor guy. He coded early Saturday morning. They think it was septic emboli, but they're not sure. We got a post mortem on him, though. Great case, eh?"

"Hmm," I said. My mind was racing. *Had I put him on the appropriate antibiotics? Did I have him on Heparin? No, not this close after surgery.* Were there any signs I had missed. I repeated the vain dance in my head that many of us do when a patient dies in our care. How could he die on *ME?* How could *I* lose a patient? What had *I* done? A woman had lost her gay son and his gay secret and I was obsessing about my own ass. It was amazing.

"Eve?" Ethan's voice brought me back.

"Yes?"

"Let me give you some patients," he said.

And just like that, the world went on.

11:15 A.M.
We were making our way around the unit in the usual manner. Ethan had given me two patients in his handover whom I'd seen before rounds. The first was Mrs. Nessie Silverman, a seventy-eight-year-old woman who was admitted from home with a gangrenous foot and was septic. An echo (ultrasound of her heart) yesterday showed she had endocarditis (heart valve infection) of her aortic and mitral valve. To make matters even more interesting she had a myocardial infarction (heart attack) last night and was now in heart failure. I ordered repeat blood cultures and gave her an extra dose of Lasix to help her diurese. I checked all of her current medications and made sure we had her on the appropriate mix for heart failure. I ordered a repeat echo for today to check her heart function given the recent events and called the lab to see if she had a bug from her last blood cultures. I paged orthopedics and asked them to come by and assess her leg for possible amputation. Steven Woo was the staff man on call and he also suggested we get Cardiovascular Surgery to see her to get an opinion about possible valve replacement.

The second patient was Ava Gardiner (that was her real name), a twenty-five-year-old transsexual prostitute with HIV who was admitted yesterday with Pneumocystis Carnii Pneumonia (PCP). Ethan was more than happy to give me this patient as I had recently developed a reputation for being very good at taking care of society's interesting members. Ava was intubated and sedated when I arrived at her bedside. A man, who I was later told was Gus, her pimp and boyfriend, was seated at her right, holding her hand. I did my cursory assessment and asked Gus if he had any questions. He shook his head and I proceeded to check Ava' s blood work as well as her medication list. She was on the right dose of Septra in addition to steroids and I ordered a repeat chest x-ray this morning to check her nasogastric tube placement.

Finally in rounds I listened to Alex Connor present the case of a twenty-year-old Asian boy named Soon Lee, who was had been shot twice in the chest in a gang related incident. Since Alex was going home, I offered to take care of Mr. Lee for the day.

With three new patients under my care and a coffee in my system, I proceeded to finish my progress notes, so as to be on top of things should I get a new admission. I was on call today with Brian Ellis, a family doctor who was moonlighting picking up shifts in the Intensive Care. Brian was a good man and I had enjoyed working with him in the past. Of course I couldn't help but have a pang of envy at the $1800 Brian would make for his extra shift today while I was still being paid an average of $5.00 an hour as a fellow. I had done these extra shifts over the year when I wasn't scheduled in the unit. They served to pay down my loans from medical school. Jack affectionately called them "thousand dollar nights".

Just as I was finishing my last note, my pager sounded and I walked to a phone to answer the call. It was unit 61, one of the medical teaching units.

"Hi, it's Eve Solomon, ICU, you paged?" I said into the receiver.

"Just a minute, DID SOMEONE PAGE A DR. SOLOMON, ICU?" she yelled into the crowd at the other side of the phone.

Some shuffling of the receiver ensued and a moment later I was talking to a third year medical student.

"Uh, hello uh, Dr. Solomon?" said the scared voice on the other line.

"Yes."

"Yah, it's Michael Dennis, I'm a clinical clerk. My senior resident wanted me to call you. She says to come quick."

"What seems to be the problem, Michael?" I asked, not running upstairs without knowing what I was getting into.

"Well, we have this lady here and her...well, she was admitted yesterday and she...well, she was admitted with liver failure from alcohol and now she's seizing and well, she won't stop," he said, and I could tell he was on the verge of tears.

"Okay, Michael, tell your senior I'm on my way. In the mean time, has she had any Valium or Ativan?"

"Uh, no, my senior says her liver won't tolerate it."

"Well tell your senior I said it is okay and to give five milligram every five minutes until she stops seizing. And get the crash cart at the bedside. I'm on my way, Michael."

"Um, yeah, thanks, Dr. Solomon."

I walked towards the doors of the unit, stopping at the desk to tell the head nurse that we may have an admission in the next few minutes but that I'd call from upstairs. I asked Ian, one of the respiratory technicians, to come with me and we proceeded to the elevators. On the way up to unit 611 I went through the list in my head of what could be waiting for me. *Delirium tremens, alcohol withdrawal, liver failure with hepatic encephalopathy, spontaneous bacterial peritonitis, a gastrointestinal bleed. And of course, poor Michael.* The memory of his fear was all too real for me. He was now officially a doctor in training and totally unaware of what the hell he was doing. On top of it he was at the bottom of the barrel and his existence was barely noticed, let alone valued. If he had a nice senior resident he'd learn a great deal. If he was working with an idiot, he'd be fetching coffee and x-rays and doing what we called *scut work* for an entire year. I had been privileged to have both in my medical training which had indeed served me well. I had promised myself never to become the latter. Whether or not I had been true to this vow remained to be seen. You always set your sights on being wonderful and live life day to day, hoping you don't wind up another person entirely.

We arrived on the unit and were ushered into the room where Amber Baird lay seizing on the bed. There was no crash cart to be seen and no Valium in sight. Instead the senior resident was standing over her yelling,

"Amber, can you hear me?"

I walked to the bedside and introduced myself.

"Where's Michael?" I asked.

"Here," said a short man in hospital greens with a short white coat on.

"Michael, go get me the crash cart from down the hall. Can I get ten milligrams of Valium now, please? And Ian, can you get a mouth guard into her and start high flow oxygen?" I asked.

"I'm Dr. Joe Flanders, the Senior Medical Resident. This patient has no liver. I don't think Valium is wise," he said, looking down at me.

"Well, Joe, I think despite her liver failure, it's the safest thing to stop her seizing. Do you mind if I take it from here?" I asked. Clearly Joe was an idiot and an arrogant one. A very dangerous combination stood before me.

"Well she's our patient, you know," he said getting defensive.

"Right. I'm just here to help. You called us and here we are. What would you like me to do?" I said, meeting his less than favorable gaze.

A syringe filled with Valium arrived, as did Michael pushing the crash cart. I took the syringe in my hand and asked Michael to get out the intubation bag. I then looked at Dr. Joe, whatever his name was, and said, "Well, have we decided?" I was now officially being a bitch, but I had lost my patience and Amber Baird was losing brain cells while we had this cockfight in front of her. Dr. Joe moved aside and I reached for Amber's intravenous line and pushed five milligrams of Valium into the line. She continued to seize. I watched the clock and asked the nurse to get me some more Valium. Five minutes later she was still seizing and I pushed another five milligrams into the line. Within moments of the second dose, Amber settled. Her breathing was slow and I told Michael to bring me her chart, while Ian proceeded to intubate her to protect her airway.

Michael whispered in my ear, "Sorry, Dr. Solomon. I told Dr. Flanders what you said and he wouldn't listen."

"That's okay, Michael, and please, my name is Eve," I said smiling. "You did well, Michael. Is she your patient?"

"Yah, I admitted her last night."

"Great, why don't you tell me about her?" I said, holding the chart and reaching for the nearest phone to tell the unit we were on our way.

"Well," Michael started and was interrupted.

"Kelly," I said to the head nurse on the other end of the line, "I have a lady up here who needs to come to us. Her name is Amber Baird; she's got liver failure and was in status epilepticus. She's no longer seizing but she's intubated."

Kelly told me she could go into bed five in five minutes. I turned to Michael and asked him again to tell me about the patient while we walked to the bedside. Amid Michael's struggle to give me the details, he was sweating profusely. I listened to Michael and told Ian to get ready to take the patient to the unit.

Within ten minutes we were in the elevator with Amber Baird on our way down to the unit with Michael continuing his story of Amber's admission. Although Dr. Joe Flanders was nowhere to be found, I knew I hadn't heard the last of him.

Amber was a fifty-six-year-old woman who had been an alcoholic for thirty years. She had been admitted two days ago after her skin turned yellow and she felt unwell. It turns out she had fulminant liver failure. In short, her liver had finally given up. Michael informed me that her last drink was five days ago, which meant this was perfect timing for alcohol withdrawal. She had been started on antibiotic yesterday as a precaution against bacterial peritonitis. This morning when Michael went in to assess her, she started seizing and wouldn't stop. The senior resident had thought she was drug seeking and wouldn't give her anything. It was only when she was on her third seizure in half an hour that he elected to call the ICU.

Amber continued to remain seizure free and once settled, I started her on a Valium drip to ensure that she wouldn't seize again. I then took the time to assess her. She looked well beyond her fifty something years. Her skin was bright yellow in color and her belly swelled, filled with fluid. She was emaciated except for her massive mid-section and when she breathed I could see her spleen moving on the right side of her abdomen. Her breath smelled of ammonia and her hands were tremulous despite her sleepy state.

I examined her closely, checking her heart and lung sounds and feeling her abdomen. I could feel both a large liver and a large spleen through her thin skin. I asked the bedside nurse to prepare a peritoneal drainage tray, as we needed to send a sample of the fluid in her belly to the lab to confirm infection. I pulled a chair up to her bedside and prepared for the procedure. After cleaning the area, I stuck a small needle in the lower right quadrant of her abdomen, well away from her liver edge and injected some Lidocaine. I waited a few moments for the freezing to take effect and then put a larger needle through the already small hole I had made. Yellow fluid flowed out easily and I collected some of it in a three sterile containers to send to the lab for analysis. I then pulled out the needle and held a piece of gauze to her skin. Fluid was leaking slowly out of the hole, staining the gauze yellow. I placed another layer of gauze and waterproof tape over the wound and told the nurse to keep an eye on it for further leaking. I cleaned up the area and disposed of my sharps and then went to the computer to enter my admission orders.

I knew Amber Baird had liver failure and the reason for her seizures was likely a combination of alcohol withdrawal and hepatic encephalopathy. When the liver fails, its ability to filter toxins, such as ammonia, from the blood fail with it. These toxins build up in the blood and affect the brain causing hepatic encephalopathy. Amber Baird was a prime candidate for this. I also checked her coagulation parameters given her liver had likely lost the ability to form clotting factors. I called for a CAT scan on Amber's head to ensure she hadn't had a bleed in her brain and ensured she was on the appropriate antibiotics as well as a laxative to keep the toxins from accumulating further. With my orders complete, I took the chart to the back of the unit to finish my note.

As I was completing my admission history, I lifted the phone to call Steven and let him know about the new admission. He agreed to go over the case with me at the bedside in half an hour. I signed my name to the note and put the chart back at the bedside. With a few minutes to spare, I left the unit to grab a sandwich and a coffee in the cafeteria. Lunch had long ago passed and I needed to eat while I had the chance.

On my way to the cafeteria, I heard my name called in the hallway. I turned around to see Dr. Joe Flanders standing behind me.

"Can I speak to you for a moment?" he said sternly.

"Sure, I'm just on my way to the cafeteria, why don't we talk while we walk?" I said, trying to make light of the situation.

"How is that patient doing?" he asked me.

"She's stable. I think she has a combination of hepatic encephalopathy and ethanol withdrawal. I'm meeting my staff man shortly to discuss it," I said.

"Are you doing a moonlighting shift?" he asked.

"No," I said.

"Well what year of residency are you in?" I couldn't believe he was trying to pull rank with me.

"I'm an ICU fellow," I said.

"Oh." He backed off knowing now that I had two years on him.

"Why does it matter?" I said, not letting him off easy.

"Well, I wouldn't have given that patient any Valium given her liver and I wondered where you got the idea," he said condescendingly.

"I'm not sure why you're hesitant to use it, especially in her case. She basically had status epilepticus and that is the first line treatment. As for it hanging around in her system too long, given her liver, that may be of benefit. We don't have to use too much of the drug and we can still keep her seizure free while she gets over this," I said, entering the cafeteria and grabbing a sandwich from the glass case.

"Well I don't like the way you handled the situation," he said once we were at the coffee station.

"I'm sorry you feel that way, Joe, but I think I was acting in the best interest of the patient. Besides you asked me to come and assess the patient and when I did you basically dismissed me," I said, pouring my coffee.

"Well, that's because you were wrong," he said.

"Listen, Joe," I said, looking straight at him, "before you make accusations, you'd better have the information to back yourself up. I appreciate your feedback on the situation, but I think this conversation is over." I grabbed my coffee and walked over to the cashier. I was trying hard not to tell him where to go.

"Well, I want you to know I'll be reporting you to my staff man," he said, trying to scare me.

"Great." I smiled, "I look forward to discussing the case with him." I took my change and walked out of the cafeteria, leaving Joe and his ego behind.

Perhaps I was wrong. Perhaps I had taken over the situation too prematurely. But when I got to the bedside it was clear that someone needed to be in control or the patient would die. So rather than take into account the emotions and ego of one Joe Flanders I acted as quickly as possible and now it looked as though I was going to have to explain my actions. Joe Flanders, motivated by one hell of a bruise to his rather large sense of self, was going to make me pay for his lack of knowledge. I could hardly wait for the shit to hit the proverbial fan.

I returned to the unit and walked to Amber's bedside. Steven was already there going over my note.

"Hi," I said, sipping my coffee.

"Interesting case," he said, looking up from the chart. "Did you do a pericentesis?"

I told him that Yes, I had taken fluid off the abdomen and sent it for analysis. Steven told me we needed to watch the patient's renal function very closely to make sure her kidneys didn't fail as well.

"Good work, Eve. Any questions?" he said.

"Can we talk for a minute? I need to run something by you," I said.

He nodded his head and walked towards the back of the unit where it was quieter. We sat down and I told him the story of my initial assessment of Amber Baird, followed by the interaction I had with Dr. Joe Flanders afterward.

"What do I do?" I asked Steve once the story had been told.

"Nothing, Eve. I don't have to tell you that people will expect you to be a wallflower. Because you are anything but a wallflower, they take it personally. The point is, Eve, if you retreat every time someone's ego gets in the way of the right thing to do, you'll never get any work done."

"He's telling his staff man," I said, looking down.

"Good. That will give his staff man the opportunity to see what a jerk he really is. Hold your ground. You did the right thing, Eve. That's what's pissing him off." Steven smiled.

"Thanks," I said. My pager went off and I stood up to answer it.

"I'll finish my note here on this patient. Nothing fancy, I agree with your plan," he said.

I walked over to the front desk with my ego in tact. My faith restored, I answered my page.

Chapter 17

I was changing into my greens when the unit paged me. "Eve, Amber Baird's family is here, can you come talk to them?" Kelly, the unit clerk, asked on the other line.

"Sure, I'll be there in a moment," I said, tying the drawstring on my pajama pants.

"They're at the bedside," Kelly said and hung up the phone.

I took my hair out of the bun it had been in since early yesterday morning and ran my fingers over my scalp. I closed my eyes and enjoyed the release from the pain of a tight head. It had been a long afternoon and evening to match. We had two codes and two consults all before midnight.

Earlier in the day I had met with Gus (last name unknown), Ava Gardiner's pimp and boyfriend. He was listed as her next of kin. According to Gus, Ava had a sister she still spoke to and she was on her way into town from Connecticut. Ava's parents had disowned her after the sex change operation. She still had a few friends in the business who might be by in the days to come. Despite my preconceived notions of the pimping world, Gus was really supportive. He had been taking care of Ava since her diagnosis and supporting her financially, as she was no longer working as a prostitute. It was odd to see such sensitivity flowing from a huge leather-clad body. Gus was over six feet and weighed at least three hundred pounds. He had tattoos over much of his body and several piercings in rather randomly placed locations. I explained to Gus about Ava's current condition and what the plan of action was.

"Oh, yeah, Doc. We've been through this before. She's had PCP twice in the past three years," he said.

"Well, is she on any prophylaxis at home?" I asked wondering if we could prevent a fourth occurrence.

"No, she's just on the usual AIDS cocktail. She stopped taking the Septra a year or so ago because it made her nauseous," he said.

"Well we can put her on a different medication once this is over. When is her sister coming into town?" I asked.

"Tomorrow. But Doc, she doesn't know Ava's got AIDS. So, I wondered if you would tell her. Ava's sister won't talk to me," he said, looking at the floor.

"Sure, Gus. Anything else?" I asked.

"No. Thanks for everything," he said.

Amidst his social deviant appearance, Gus emerged as a caring, pragmatic next of kin. They may have been a circus act on the surface, but beneath the facade and preconceived presentations there was compassion and concern.

I finished massaging my scalp and put my hair back in the bun. I washed my face quickly, trying to erase some of the exhaustion from it and left the call room to meet Amber Baird's family. As I rounded the front desk and made my way to her bedside, the smell of alcohol became ever so apparent. At Mrs. Baird's bedside stood what I assumed was an elderly man and woman and a younger man. I walked up to the group and introduced myself.

"Hello, I'm Eve Solomon, one of the doctors working in the Intensive Care Unit. I transferred Amber down from the unit upstairs," I said, holding out my hand.

"Hi, Burt Baird, I'm Amber's husband," he said with the stench of alcohol on his breath. "This is my sister Joanne and her friend Fred," he said. I looked into their eyes as I shook each of their hands. All sets of eyes were glassed over. The Bairds were severely intoxicated. The whole family was drunk.

"Did you have any questions?" I asked.

"No," said Burt, swaying from side to side, holding onto the bed for balance.

"Amber's very sick," I began, "she has liver failure from longstanding alcohol abuse. Because her liver doesn't work anymore, she has poisons building up in her blood. What we're doing now is supporting her through this with the hope that her liver will recover," I said, looking up at them for a response.

"Yeah," Burt said.

"Unfortunately she doesn't qualify for a liver transplant given her history of alcohol abuse," I said, trying to be sympathetic; but wondering how much was getting through to this family amidst their drunken haze. I looked at Burt closely. He had all the physical signs of chronic liver abuse. Amidst the smell of whisky and stale cigarettes, Burt looked up at me.

"So when can she come home?" he asked.

"Burt, she's very sick. If she survives this she will be in the hospital for some time. And she can't ever drink again," I said. My suspicions were confirmed, they had little insight into the situation.

"Oh," he said.

"Do you have any questions?" I asked again.

"Nope," he said.

"Well, why don't we meet again tomorrow during the day and I can update you on your wife's progress," I said. I was hoping a second meeting might help me get my point across.

"Okay," Burt said.

"Well, it was nice meeting you. If you have any questions, I'm here all night," I said. I walked away from the bedside and Peggy, the bedside nurse, followed me. She grabbed my arm and led me around to the other side of the unit.

"Eve, they're hammered," she said.

"I know," I said, putting my head into my hands.

"No, Eve, they're drinking at her bedside. The husband's got a flask and he's passing it around," she said.

"Well as long as they're not waking anyone else, let them stay. As for the booze, if you see him pull it out again, just ask him to wait until he's out of the unit," I said, one of my hands still on my forehead. If I were waiting for a dull moment, it wouldn't happen anytime soon.

I yawned, stretched, and smiled as Peggy burst into laughter.

"Jesus, what a scene," I said.

We composed ourselves quickly and walked back to Amber Baird's bedside. Her family was in the process of leaving.

"We'll call you if anything changes," I said to them.

"Actually, Doc, we talked about it. We don't need a meeting tomorrow," he said, handing me a piece of paper.

"What's this?" I asked.

"It's the funeral home where to send the body," he said and turned and staggered out of the unit.

I stood behind watching him go in total disbelief. Three beds over was a transsexual with a loving and supportive pimp. Here lay Amber Baird, an elderly alcoholic from an alcoholic family who had arranged her funeral before she had even died. Yes, she was deathly ill, and yes she would probably not live the week. But I never expected that alcohol would kill her body and her soul to this degree. It was in these times, in the early morning hours, with the smell of whisky still lingering in the air and the glow of the bedside light, that the world no longer made any sense.

"Call me if anything changes," I said to Patty and turned and left the bedside.

I checked on my other patients and found Brian at one of the bedsides. We split up the unit, assigning ourselves equal amounts of patients. I ordered all my lab work for the morning and returned to the call room. I took my white coat off and hung it on a hook on the wall. I slipped off my running shoes and climbing into bed, pulled the elastic out of my hair. I removed my pager from the waist of my pants and placed it on the bedside table, checked that the phone in my room was working and shut out the light.

5:02 P.M.

My pager went off. This time it was a code blue beeping. I checked the little green screen and it read *Code Blue, ICU Bed 5*. I grabbed my pager and my jacket and ran to the bedside in my socks. Amber Baird lay there with a Unit Aide on top of her, performing CPR. The baseline rhythm was asystole (flat line). I ordered Epinephrine and Atropine and two ampules of Bicarb. Terry, the respiratory technician, was at the head of the bed pushing air into her endotracheal tube with the bagging contraption. My mind was racing for what would have caused the sudden deterioration. And as if on cue, my answer came to me when bright red blood spilled out from Amber's nasogastric tube. She was bleeding out into her stomach.

"Page G.I. (gastroenterology) for me stat and call Steven as well, please," I said. "And can we get two units of blood set up on the rapid infuser right now? She needs a Blakemore tube to stop the bleeding."

Within moments things were happening around me. The rapid infuser was set up with blood being pushed into Amber. The unit aide continued CPR while I ordered more Epinephrine and Atropine. Steven arrived at the bedside and I updated him on what had happened.

"How long has it been since she coded?" he asked.

"Twenty-two minutes," Peggy said checking the clock on the crash cart.

Steven looked over at me and said nothing. I placed a Blakemore tube down Amber's throat and into her esophagus. It has a balloon on the end that can be inflated and pressed up against any blood vessels in the esophagus to stop them from bleeding. We continued in vain. After eight units of blood and more than enough Epinephrine and Atropine I looked again at Steven.

"G.I. called back, they said she has gastric varices and has failed gluing five times before," Steven said. "They're on their way in but it will be at least a half hour."

We continued. Thirty-three minutes into the code, blood poured up over the Blakemore tube. I looked at Steven.

"Call it, Eve," he whispered in my ear, "the only definitive treatment here is transplant and she doesn't qualify."

I ordered one more ampule of Epinephrine and Atropine almost as though I was going through the motions. Thirty-nine minutes after the code, I heard myself say, "Let's call it. Time of death 5:45 A.M."

I looked over at Steven.

"Any family?" he asked.

"Yes. They were here a few hours ago. I think they were too drunk to understand what was going on. I'll call them," I said looking down at the socks on my feet. "I need to put on my shoes," I said.

"You okay?" Steven asked.

"Yeah, I'm fine, Steven," I said sighing. "It's just the usual, you know?"

He nodded. "I'll sign the death certificate, you go get your shoes," he said softly and smiled.

I walked back to the call room. My head hurt. My socks were covered in blood. I sat down on the bed in a daze. I took of my socks and checked that I had not cut my feet on any sharps. My feet were clean. I put the socks in the garbage can and put my running shoes on my bare feet. I felt this tremendous feeling of sorrow fall on me. It made me feel heavy. It made my head throb and my stomach turn. I closed my eyes and took a few deep breaths. I rose from the bed and walked towards the sink to splash cold water on my face. I patted my face with a towel and opened the door to the hallway.

With my bare feet squeaking in my running shoes, I walked down the hallway to the front desk. I found the Baird's home number in the patient list at the front desk and dialed the number. After at least five rings, a sleepy voice picked up.

"Mr. Baird?" I asked.

"Yeah." I recognized his sleepy voice.

"I'm sorry to have to tell you this, sir." I paused, "Amber died a few moments ago sir, I'm so sorry," I said.

"Yeah, well you know where to send the body," he said and hung up the phone.

I stood at the front desk staring at the receiver and its now empty dial tone. I searched my pockets for the piece of paper Mr. Baird had given to me hours before. 'Chapel Funeral Home on fourth' was scrawled on it in black pen. I turned to Kelly at the front desk and relayed the message.

"We can send Mrs. Baird's body to Chapel Funeral Home on fourth," I said. My head continued to throb, my heart ached in my chest. It was now past six in the morning and I might as well start seeing my patients and writing my notes. I walked down the hall in my squeaking feet towards the cafeteria for my morning coffee.

Sorrow or no sorrow, there was work to be done.

8:25 A.M.

I saw the remainder of my patients and managed to write my notes early. With it being the start of a new week, I knew we would be late starting rounds and late finishing. The earlier I had things in order, the earlier I could expect to be home. I asked Karen, the day unit clerk, to page me when rounds were starting and walked towards my call room. I put my hand on the door handle and heard my name being called behind me.

"Eve." It was David.

"Hi," I said, still holding the door handle.

"How was your night?" he asked.

"Fine, David. Thanks," I said, turning the door handle and opening the door. "Do you have a minute?" he asked. My heart started racing.

"Maybe later, David. I have to get changed before rounds," I said, the door now fully opened. I wanted to run inside and slam the door.

"Sure," he said smiling.

Asshole, I thought. *He's smiling and I'm having chest pains.* I walked into the call room and closed the door behind me. I sat on the bed and put my head on the pillow. I was so tired. My head hurt, and I felt sick to my stomach. I sat up and went to the shower. Perhaps, if I scrubbed really hard, the soap and the water would wipe my mind clean.

1:45 P.M.

I had walked halfway to the residents' parking lot before realizing I had parked my car in the staff lot the night before. Wandering like a zombie around the hospital grounds, I made my way to the Valiant to find the expected parking ticket displayed on my front window. Retrieving the consequences of my never-ending tardiness from the driver side windshield wiper, I opened the door and fell in to the driver's seat. Drunk from exhaustion, like many mornings previously, I was essentially driving under the influence. As well, despite my shower, I still smelled of a men's locker room and my headache was now a brain tumor. I started up the car and the rush of music began. Searching for the right music to drive home to, I realized I had successfully avoided David entirely. My notes were all written before rounds and having known most of the patients from the night before, I handed them over to Ethan Baker and slipped out. I don't even remember trying to avoid him. I do know that when I don't get enough sleep, I tend to burst into tears for no apparent reason and this would be very bad form in front of David. It's best I make my get away now and make excuses later.

The day was really quite nice. The sky was this perfect blue and the wind blew in from the car window to keep me conscious. I sang along with Jan Arden on the CD player and my mood lightened as the distance between me and the hospital increased.

My work has forced me to consider basic needs a luxury. Where most people with an afternoon off would find themselves on a patio with a beer, I hadn't slept in thirty hours. My treat for the day would be a head on a pillow. I would sit at a table and eat lunch without watching the clock, rather than standing in an elevator or walking to Emergency. Sleeping, sitting and eating, taking a moment, coffee breaks, and two consecutive week days where one was guaranteed self assurance; these were the staples of life that were my luxuries.

I know I chose this life, but at the start of it all there were much different promises, much greater hopes. I had been seduced by the glamour of being able to make a difference. I had been captivated by the glory of a life changed and my own vanity restored. I was charmed and it forbade me to see the headaches and heartache of a life less ordinary. As such it was now ten years later that I sat behind the wheel of a beat up car, driven by a beat up lady, trying her best to stay awake long enough to make it home. The stars had long faded from my eyes. I thought of Michael, the medical student, who had called me, terrified to see Amber Baird. He was still new, still fresh, not yet tainted by the perpetual process which expects you to be more than human and which does not relent. Sure there was fear in his eyes and yes, the process had begun. But amidst the panic and self-doubt there was still that flash of wonder. The world was full of possibilities and he was not "stuck". He was someone. He was going to be a doctor, god damn it, and so soon, he could taste it. I envied his magic. I wanted so badly to taste my own hope again. I was weary of having become someone who had lost her way. And I wondered if we all started out like Michael, embracing his miracles while surrounded by fear? And if we do all begin that way, are we then destined to end up like me?

Chapter 18

Monday, 2:08 P.M.

I called Katarina's office from the cell phone in the car. "She's with a patient. Can I ask who's calling?" the secretary said.

"It's Dr. Solomon." Once you say 'doctor' they always put you through.

"One moment, doctor, I'll ring you through." Bingo. The muzak mixed poorly with my CD.

"Dr. Vlahov speaking."

"Kate, it's Eve."

"Hi, Boobie." I loved her pet name for me.

"Can we meet for coffee? I need you," I said.

"Tonight. Seven o'clock. I'll come get you," she said.

"Perfect," I sighed.

"You okay, Boo?" I could hear the concern in her voice.

"Just small. That's all," I said.

"Well, *I* love you. And I have fabulous taste," she said.

She made me laugh. "I know. I love you too." I smiled and ended the call.

I rounded the corner of our apartment block and opened the door to our garage. I drove in and parked the car in our underground parking spot. I rode the service elevator up to our loft, stopping on the way to get the mail. Once in the apartment, I put the mail on the kitchen counter and my bag on the floor. I went into our bedroom and fell into the unmade bed. Within moments I was fast asleep.

6.30 P.M.

I woke to the sound of Jack entering the apartment.

"Hello, I'm home," his voice followed.

"In the bedroom," I called from the bed.

I sat up and stretched as Jack appeared in the doorway. "How was your night?" he asked.

"Long, tiring," I said.

"Want to go study tonight?" he asked.

"I'm having coffee with Katarina," I said.

"When?" he asked, walking into the room and sitting beside me on the bed.

"At seven. She's picking me up here," I said and he kissed me warmly on the cheek. I stood up and went into the bathroom where I turned on the shower.

"How was your day?" I called from the bathroom.

"Pretty good," he said joining me. I looked at Jack in the bathroom mirror. He was such a handsome man. His body was tall and lean, his skin chocolate brown and smooth with almost no hair. His face was kind and chiseled. I turned and fell into his embrace. I put my head on his chest and breathed in his scent. He stroked my hair as the steam from my running shower built up in the small bathroom.

"I have to get ready," I said, pulling away reluctantly from him. I took off my pajamas under his admiring gaze and climbed into the shower.

I let the warm water wash over me for some time and welcomed the calming sensation of the spray on my body. I so wanted to go out and talk to Kay but part of me was just too tired to make the effort. All I really wanted to do was sleep for a day or so. I thought of Jack and the peace he brought to my life. I thought of our coming trip to New York City. In less than a week we would be there, enjoying one another's company and visiting with friends. We so needed some time away. I so needed the time to regain my perspective, to clear the haze from my life. I shut off the shower and stepped out to wrap myself in a bath towel. I dried off quickly and grabbed a simple black dress and a pair of clogs from the closet. I got dressed and tied my hair back. I dried my face and put on mascara and lipstick. The doorbell rang as I was looking for my jean jacket and I heard Jack answer. Katarina' s warm voice filled the apartment and I heard her embrace Jack.

"Boobie!" she called from the living room.

"In here," I yelled from inside the closet. My jean jacket was still missing.

"Hello, my sweet." She walked into the bedroom.

"Hi, Boo. I'm just looking for my jean jacket and then we can go, "I said.

"This one?" she called from the bed.

I poked my head out of the closet to see Katarina holding up the very jacket.

"Of course," I said. It could happen to anyone. I took the jacket from her and put it on, giving Kay a kiss on both cheeks. She looked dazzling as usual. Her dark brown hair was down in loose curls at her shoulders. She was wearing a tight black top which accentuated her bust and a pair of black hot pants with healed sandals.

"Let's go," I said standing over her. She rose from the bed and linked her arm in mine.

"You still small?" she asked.

"We'll talk," I said, escorting her to the door. We called our good-byes to Jack and left the apartment.

7:15 P.M.

We drove to La Cantina for lattes and chocolate cake. In the car I confessed to the evening with David.

"You did nothing. What's the problem?" Kay asked.

"The problem is I almost did something. That is as bad as doing something."

"Oh, Eve, you're being too hard on yourself. What's really the problem here?" she said.

She was right. Why was I so angry with myself?

"Did you want to do something?" she asked.

"I don't know. I feel terrible. I feel so cheap."

"Why? Because it was easy for him and wasn't for you. You thought you were special and you found out you were just a conquest?" Kay said.

I thought about what she said. I had thought I was special. I felt this connection with David. In my mind I was this sophisticated unattainable woman whom he fantasized about. Instead I fell into a class of silly women whom David had been with.

"You're right. I feel cheap," I confessed.

"Anything else?" she asked.

This woman knew me well. "Yah. The sick thing is I think I still want him." I said.

"Yah, you still do," she said pulling into the public parking lot.

She shut off the engine and turned to look at me.

"Everything okay with you and Jack?" she asked.

"Kay, don't pull that shit with me. Are you saying I went looking for David because I'm not satisfied with my marriage?"

"It happens, Eve."

"Not to me it doesn't. I love Jack. We're very happy. He treats me better than anyone I've ever known," I said.

"Yes. But are you satisfied? We both know that Jack is wonderful. Is he enough for you is the question?" she said, unlocking my door and signaling us out of the car.

That was the question. I was happy at home. I loved my husband and he worshipped me. But the reality was I had stopped falling in love with him long ago. I had felt that rush and moved on to being in love with him. Despite the deepening of our feeling and my emotions, there lacked that initial excitement. Perhaps it was that which I was longing for. Theo, my New York friend with his bad history with women once told me he much preferred falling in love to being in it. He always blamed this flaw for the downfalls of his relationships. I always thought this reflected his free spirit. At the same time I thought it was his greatest weakness. It never allowed him a mature loving experience. Would I be destined to suffer the same fate? Was I bored with Jack because he loved me for so long? Would this be my downfall?

"I'm mad because I'm weak," I said

"How do you figure?" she said, linking her arm in mine as we walked to the café.

"Well, for one thing, I gave in to David's game and that's not like me," I said.

"Bullshit that's not like you," was her answer.

"Why bullshit?" I was getting defensive.

"Because, Eve, you're a woman, he's a man. Contrary to the Joan of Arc image you have of yourself, not even you are immune to hormones. So cut the drama. You wanted him and he called you on it and now you're pissed off because your world isn't as perfect as you'd like to believe."

As I listened to her words I realized how right she was. Medicine could be a disaster and my world would be fine as long as Jack was perfect. When my home life was unsatisfying my world would crumble. Furthermore the fact that I wanted David was a sign that something was wrong. The question was who was at fault? Me? Jack? Both of us? And why did someone always have to be faulted?

"So are you going to tell Jack?" she asked as we were shown to our seats.

"What is the point? All that would do is to make him feel badly over something which is really not important," I said.

"Can you handle keeping this a secret from him?"

"I'll have to." I sighed, "Oh, Kay, I don't know why I'm making such a big deal about this. It's really quite pathetic. I can guarantee you David Auerbach is not having this kind of conversation with his buddies right now."

"Of course he's not. First of all he's a man. They aren't built this way. Secondly, you're a woman. You are designed to persevere over an issue with other female friends and chocolate." She smiled.

She had made me laugh.

"Okay. Here's what I do. I only have this week left of the rotation and then we're going to New York. In the meantime, I will not tell Jack. If David approaches me to talk I will tell him that the issue is closed and I want to be his friend and that's all. And as for my feminine desires, I will channel all of that sexual energy into my gorgeous husband. And that," I said, taking a sip of my coffee, "is my plan."

The waiter arrived with our cake and Kay asked for a wine list.

"I think we need a drink," she said smiling at me.

"Now, enough about me. How are you?" I asked.

"Eh, fine. Looking for love in all the wrong places. How about a Merlot?' she asked, looking up from the wine list.

"What about Nico?" I asked.

"He's Roman Catholic, I'm Russian Orthodox. His mother is having a fit and he already promised her he wouldn't marry me unless I convert. I told him if he's going to choose his mother over me, our marriage has already failed," she said looking for the waiter to order the Merlot.

"Oh, Kay, I'm sorry," I said. Nico and Katarina had been dating on and off for almost a year. I knew she really cared about him and this couldn't be easy.

"Oh, Eve, I'm not like you. I don't think there's one perfect person for me. Even if there is, Nico wasn't him. The man believes in God, for Christ sake. I believe in Capitalism. I can just see it. He'd be in church on Sundays praying for my soul, I'd be worshipping at the temple of Prada," she said laughing.

"I know but it can't be easy to end things this way," I said.

"Oh, we didn't end things. I'm still sleeping with him. I'm just not marrying him," she said. "Yes, we'll have the 96 Merlot please," she said to the waiter.

"Kay, are you sure that's the best?" I said concerned.

"Of course not, Eve, and besides, darling, don't pull that mother shit with me, it doesn't become you. Look, I don't love Nico, but I do love sleeping with him. So I figure, why should that end while I'm looking for the man of my so called dreams?" she had a point.

"I envy you," I said sipping my coffee.

"Why?"

"Well, because if you really do believe this bullshit it makes you very self-sufficient," I said challenging her.

She smiled knowing I had caught her. "Don't flatter me sweetie, it's all an act," she said.

"I know," I said softly.

"But it's a very good act, isn't it?" she laughed.

"Excellent," I agreed. She was quite a woman.

"And if I continue it long enough, someday I may actually believe it," she said taking a sip of the drops of wine the waiter had poured in her glass and then motioning to him to pour for both of us.

"Well then here's my toast," I said raising my glass, "To someday."

She raised her glass in the air and clinked it with mine. "To someday, darling," she said, accentuating a thick Russian accent.

9:30 P.M.

We drank our Merlot in honor of that day. The conversation flowed between us mixed with wine and laughter. Here was a person with whom I was totally myself. Gone were the pretense and the pursuit for excellence.

"So how's work?" Kay asked.

"Eh," I said sipping my wine. "The usual. They'll never offer me a job next year."

"Why don't you stop this ICU fellowship thing and just be an Internist?" she asked.

"Because I'd be bored," I said.

"So what's so wrong with being bored with your job? I'm bored at work. But overall, it's okay. It provides me with the kind of life I want." She had a point.

"You know, Kay, after a while of doing something for so long, it is sometimes best not to question why you are doing it but rather just finish. When I have all my credentials and I can write my own ticket, then I'll ask myself what I really want out of Medicine," I said.

"Are you going to apply for jobs when you're in New York?" she asked.

"Maybe, why not?" I said.

"What does Jack think about all this?" she asked.

"You know Jack. He's up for any adventure," I said. It was true. Jack was so easy going. He'd move anywhere. "Anyway, enough about my job, you're starting to sound parental."

"So how is your family?" she asked laughing.

"Oh in summary, my Dad is dying, Mom's now embraced chain smoking and Penny is... as Penny does," I said, laughing with her.

"And Ahava?" she asked referring to my niece.

"She is three, she's adorable. But my sister refuses to toilet train her. So I told my mother, when I'm home for Yom Kippur next month, I'll train the kid," I said.

"Excellent," she said. Kay knew my family history as well as anyone. She also knew that going home for the Jewish holidays would always take the most out of me. I was not a practicing Jew. In fact if not for my parent's insistence, I would ignore the holiday all together.

Jack was agnostic by choice. By birth, his mother was Jewish, his father was Baptist. We were married in a synagogue because by Jewish Law he was one of the tribe; a fact my mother clung to throughout our courtship. I had gone to Hebrew School until the age of eighteen and had enjoyed it at the time. I was sheltered beyond belief and in retrospect it was a nice feeling. I remember at the time, however, wanting to break out of the small world I was in. But I was living under the yolk of Penny and I understood that I was expected to behave myself. University followed where I intentionally rebelled without telling my parents. By that time I had firmly established my reputation as 'good girl' and so it was easy to misbehave. I slept with men I would never bring home to meet the parents and to this day, they still think I was at all night study sessions. I knew I would have to marry a Jew. I'm not sure if that is what I wanted or if it was more to keep the peace. That's about the time I met Jack.

Jack was raised in an interfaith, interracial home. His parents divorced when he was thirteen and Eileen, Jack's white Jewish mother, was left to raise her three half black, half Baptist children on her own. He tells me they were raised more Jewish than anything except for Christmas, which they had once a year at their father's. We now spent the Jewish holidays with my parents and Jack's mother and on Christmas Eve we got a phone call from my father-in-law who now lived in Florida. We had been to visit him several times, but he was more of a stranger to Jack than a father. Jack could never forgive the man for leaving his mother for the babysitter. I stayed out of it just as Jack stayed out of my family politics.

"What about New York?" she asked.

"Well, we leave on Saturday and we're staying a week. Theo comes back from Paris this Thursday so I'll be able to spend time with him when we're there, and I have to call Nina to see what her schedule is," I said.

Nina was my other 'sister'. She and I had been friends for more than ten years. We met in Paris on my year abroad. She was a student in the same program as I was. I met her at a bus stop after our first orientation. I knew no one and she was with some geek she knew from high school who wanted her all to himself. I could understand men wanting Nina to themselves. She was strong and beautiful with a sharp wit and a no bullshit attitude. Three weeks after our meeting we found an apartment together off campus and became roommates. It's been love ever since.

Now she lives in New York and is a chef at a new upscale restaurant. We can go weeks without speaking on the telephone and then it is as if no time has passed. I couldn't wait to spend time with her.

Kay and I continued our evening. She heralded me with tales of her mother and her new boyfriend and of gossip from our medical school class. At the end of it all, my headache had been replaced with a warm feeling of wine and content. It had been a truly cathartic evening for both of us and the laughter still remained in the air as we fought over who would pay the check and made our way to the door.

"Thanks," I said when we were outside in the cool night air.

"Hmmm," she said smiling at me. "We sure are good together, aren't we?"

"We certainly are," I said.

"Now," she began with the question that always made me laugh, "do we get married in a synagogue or a church?" she asked grinning.

I smiled, linked my arm in hers and walked with her to the car. I had found my sister on my own and she was all I could have ever hoped for.

Chapter 19

"It's official, I'm calling in sick. I have no desire to ever leave this bed. I will stay in my pajamas and drink coffee all day. I will read the newspaper over breakfast and go for a walk at lunch. I will be a lady of leisure/housewife/ glamour girl/woman with no care in life whatsoever. But first I will go back to sleep."

"Sweetie, time to wake up." Jack was poking me.

"I'm calling in sick," I said.

"Can you do that?" he asked.

"Don't give me a conscience. I need a day off," I said, sitting up and reaching for the phone. I forcibly coughed a few times to roughen my voice and dialed the direct number to the ICU.

"Hello, ICU, Becky speaking," a voice on the other line said.

"Becky," I whispered in my best 'fake sick' voice, "it's Eve."

"Oh, Eve, you sound terrible." It was working.

"Yeh, I was up all night vomiting. I'm not coming in today. Will you tell the staff men for me?" I asked.

"Sure, Eve. You're not prego are you?" she asked.

"No. I've just got the flu," I said.

"Well, get well okay? Stay in bed," she said sympathetically.

"Thanks," I said, hanging up the phone.

I lay back down in bed and stared at the ceiling. I was wide awake. I could hear Jack contemplating life in the shower.

"Everything okay?" he yelled from inside the spray.

135

"Yah," I answered.

"What?" he yelled.

I got up and walked into the bathroom.

"I said yes," I answered again.

"Good. What are you going to do today?' he asked.

'You know they thought I was pregnant," I said.

"Who?" he asked.

"The unit clerk at work. I told her I was vomiting all night and she asked me if I was pregnant," I said, sitting on the toilet looking at the shower curtain.

"You're not are you?" he said poking his head out from the curtain.

"Of course not," I said. "Relax. It just pisses me off that if I'm puking all night they have pregnancy at the top of their list of diagnoses like I should be by now."

"No you should not," he said. He so didn't get it. These were the times where having a man as your best friend had its downsides. How could you explain this to someone who by nature of his sex at birth was automatically a master in his own right? How could a man understand that despite a woman's achievements she is not fully successful until she has pushed a piano through a hole the size of a walnut and raised the damn thing into a well functioning member of society? These were days, especially when pregnancy was the issue, when I wished I were a boy.

You know most women think it's amazing that they have the ability to nurture a life inside them and to give birth to it. Although I think the concept is fabulous, I'd be just as happy if Jack were to wear the maternity hat in the family. In fact I think we as woman should relinquish the skill of childbirth to our male brethren for a while and let them carry the task of repopulating. Frankly the thought of letting my body change to that degree and then suffer the worst pain imaginable was less than fascinating to me. And as for people who think pregnant woman are sexy, they're just trying to make them feel better. How is it that fat people are never sexy but pregnant women are? It's society's way of saying, 'Don't worry sweetheart, nine months from now and several fitness classes later and you'll be back to your old self...' Then once you push the thing out you spend the rest of your life, forever changed, making one sacrifice after another with the hope the little shit will take care of you when you're older and not, God forbid, put you in a nursing home and forget you.

Call me insensitive but I'd rather have the flu. You vomit for twenty-four hours, lose a few pounds, drink lots of fluids and before you know it, the whole thing's over and your life returns to normal. You can then spend the next three days eating ice cream for breakfast as compensation for your previous illness. I hate to admit it and don't punish me for having an opinion, but I'd take influenza over pregnancy any day of the week.

Jack emerged from the shower dripping wet. I handed him his towel and watched him dry off. Jack was one of those people who was born with a good body. It was maddening. He ate whatever he wanted and never gained weight. He exercised when he felt like it and always seemed in shape. I watched him dry off and begin to brush his teeth in the sink and thought how I could do this every morning. I could sit on the toilet with nowhere to go and usher my man off to work. A feeling of true content washed over me.

"You want coffee?" I asked.

He nodded with a mouth full of toothpaste foam. I rose from the toilet seat and made my way to the kitchen. The timer on the automatic coffee maker had been set the night before and had brewed in cue. I pulled two cups from the cupboard and added cream to both and sweeteners to one. I lifted both cups and, taking a sip from mine, carried them back into the bedroom. Jack was standing in front of the closet in his underwear. I handed him the coffee and sat on the bed.

"Where's my gray suit?" he asked.

"At the cleaners. Wear your blue one," I said, sipping the coffee.

"Where's the blue one?"

I put the coffee cup on the bedside table and walked over to the closet, reached out and pulled his blue suit from the front of the rack.

"Thanks, babe," he said.

I sat back down on the bed.

"Where's Lapine?" Jack asked.

"I forgot to let him in," I said.

Lapine is our excuse for a pet. Lapine is a velveteen rabbit that runs free in the apartment. He's perfect for us. He is not a cat as Jack is allergic to cats. He is not a dog and therefore never needs to be walked. He is litter trained and despite the fact that he eats the walls in our house, he's perfect. He usually spends the nights out on our rooftop deck eating his way through the flowerbeds. I rose from the bed once more and walked to the patio door to let him in. Jack hated Lapine at first but has since grown to love him. His fur is like silk and he's very low maintenance. Moreover he's the size of a small cat and eats everything, which only adds to his charm.

I opened the patio door and walked onto our deck. Our loft is on the top floor of an old remodeled warehouse. Lapine has a small rabbit hutch by the patio door which has a small hole in it should he want to come inside at night. The deck overlooks the city and is the reason we bought this place. It's a large area enclosed by a fence where we have a garden and a patio. In the summers we sit out here for hours drinking wine and watching the river below. The sun was already casting shadows on my flower and vegetable gardens. The garden itself is pathetic. It consists of wooden boxes filled with various plants, which the cleaning lady, Lisa, waters twice a week. The flowers are for appearances only and the vegetables are for the rabbit that I found lying in the middle of the tomato plants having breakfast. He is white with one huge black spot on his face and another one on his belly.

"Lapine," I called, and the little rodent looked up and ran over to me. I picked him up and brought him inside hugging him to me and kissing his fur. He smelled of tomato plants and morning as he snuggled into my chest.

"Here he is," I said to Jack who was now fully dressed in his blue suit and white button-down shirt.

"Can I get away without a tie?" he asked, walking over to me and petting Lapine.

"Sure. They don't expect you to wear a tie do they?"

"No," he answered.

"Then no tie is fine," I said, putting the rabbit down on the floor. He immediately ran into the living room in search of his litter box and his water dish.

"What are you going to do today?" Jack asked putting on his shoes.

"Nothing. Pet the bunny, drink coffee, phone my mother. Maybe I'll finish that canvas I was working on," I said. Jack had bought me an easel for our wedding anniversary last year and I had put it on the patio. Every few months I'd buy a new canvas in an attempt to awaken the artist within. I was a terrible painter but still I endured. I would sit outside on the weekends and my days off and slap acrylic paint onto the canvas while looking out over the city. The pictures were extremely juvenile but I felt like an artist and that is all that mattered.

"I gotta go," Jack said and left the bedroom.

I followed him to the front door and watched him put down his coffee cup and gather his keys and briefcase. I kissed him goodbye and closed the door behind him. I looked around the empty house and put down my coffee cup next to Jack's. I had the entire day before me and I knew exactly what I would do first. I found Lapine's water bowl and refilled it. Then I walked to the bedroom, turned off the lights, pulled back the covers, and crawled back into bed for at least the next few hours.

11:30 A.M.

I had now officially slept the morning away. My opportunity to lie around and drink coffee all morning while watching CNN had long since past. Instead I now contemplated whether there was any point getting out of bed at all. Lapine jumped up on the bed and began licking my face. It is truly an adorable gesture once you get past the idea that this animal also eats his own shit. Nonetheless it's a need for the salt in my skin, but I pass it off as unconditional love and take it anywhere I can get it. I pushed the rabbit off me before he started on my nostrils and grabbed the remote from the bedside table. I turned on the television and flipped to CNN. It is now near noon but I can still enjoy the day. With the drone of world events in the background I began to run the bath and went into the kitchen for a fresh cup of coffee. Coffee poured and appropriately sweetened, I returned to the bathroom to check on the bath. The water had not even reached halfway so I decided to set up my easel on the patio. I went into the den and collected the half-finished canvas from the closet as well as the box of acrylics and brushes I had collected over the past year. I walked out onto the deck with my arms full and Lapine followed. I placed the canvas on the easel and put down my box of paints on the small table next to the set up. Lapine returned to his place in the tomato plants and I left him out there as I returned inside for my bath. With the bath now at the ideal height, I shut off the water and grabbed the cordless phone from its cradle before taking off my pajamas and climbing into the warm water. I closed my eyes and began to soak. Moments later the phone rang. I sat up in the bath and reached for the cordless.

"Hello," I answered remembering to try and sound somewhat unwell, should it be someone from work calling.

"Thank God you're home," said a friendly voice.

"Theo, you're back! I didn't think you were home until tomorrow." I was so glad to hear his voice.

"I missed you so I came back early," he said.

"Yah, right. Everything okay?" I asked.

"Perfect. The meeting I had for today was cancelled so I took an earlier flight. How are you? When are you coming? I can't wait to see you," he said.

"I'm fine and we leave on Saturday," I said, splashing around in the water.

"Where are you? You sound funny," he asked.

"I'm in the bath," I said laughing.

"Oh, so you're naked then? Excellent. I have this naughty picture in my mind already." He laughed.

"Behave, you shit. How was your trip?" I asked smiling.

"Wonderful. Paris is not as fun without you but it was wonderful," he said.

"That's because when you're with me you can drink shamelessly. How's work?" I said.

"Excellent. I am climbing up the corporate ladder so to speak. How's the medical profession treating you?" he asked.

"The usual," I said. "Just trying to keep my head above water."

"Any news for me?" he asked.

"Lots, but I will tell you most of it when I see you next week," I said.

"Intriguing. Anything good?" he asked.

"Well there is this guy at work who hit on me," I said. Why I was getting into the whole David thing now was beyond me.

"Ooh. Dirty. What does Jack say about all this?" he asked.

"Jack doesn't know the whole story," I said.

"Interesting. Secrets and lies are great in any relationship, Eve. Just look at me," Theo said.

"My dear, those women left you because you are too good for them. Speaking of women, how's Jennifer?" I asked.

"Don't want to talk about it," he said.

"That good?" I asked sarcastically.

"I'll tell you when I see you. Where are you staying when you get here?"

"We're at the Plaza, thank you very much. The conference is at the Hilton Towers and *I* will call you as soon as we get to the hotel," I said.

"When are you arriving?" he asked.

"We land at four in the afternoon. So are you free for dinner on Saturday night?" I asked.

"Perfect. I will make reservations. How's Jack?" he asked.

"Perfect, wonderful, happy as hell," I said smiling.

"Man, it's gotta be hard being married to someone that wonderful," he said making fun.

"Yah. He's great," I said. "So talk to me, what is doing? I miss you," I said.

"Nothing. I went to Paris and now I'm back in New York. I'm working like a dog and my girlfriend is not a subject of conversation right now. I miss you terribly and I can't wait to see you, but I have to go because my boss is now standing in my office," he said smiling.

"All right, I'll speak to you later. Love you."

"Hmm," he said smiling, "love you too. Don't forget to wash behind your ears." And he hung up.

I continued to smile, putting down the phone and laying back in the bath. He could always put a smile on my face. I was blessed. I had married the man of my dreams and had the perfect friends. If not for my never-ending existential crisis, life would be great.

3:00 P.M.

I finished the last few touches on the canvas and left it on the easel to dry in the sun. I packed up my paints and brushes and took them inside to wash. I soaked the brushes in the kitchen sink and went back on the patio to check on Lapine. He was lying on his back in the tomato plants, licking himself I scooped him up and brought him inside to keep me company. I put Lapine down in the living room and went to rinse out my brushes and wash my hands. Once cleaned and dried, I put my supplies back in the den and checked my e-mail which was cluttered with the usual junk mail and the latest table of contents from the *New England Journal of Medicine*. All of it went into the trash bin without even being read.

I looked around the den and thought about doing some filing but decided instead to eat lunch. I went into the kitchen and found the book of take out menus. I called China Rose from down the street and ordered Wor Won Ton soup and rice. I then went back into the den to pick out a video. I had seen *Breakfast at Tiffany's* almost thirty times now. It was my favorite movie of all time, followed by a close second with *Auntie Mame*. I owned both movies and watched them repeatedly. I put *Auntie Mame* into the video machine and sat on the couch in the den watching my movie while I waited for my lunch to arrive. Rosalind Russell is a goddess. Theo and I always argued over who was better in the role. While he liked Lucille Ball, I was ever so faithful to Ms. Russell. She was perfect. I got comfortable in my seat and put a blanket over my legs.

Half an hour into the movie and the doorbell rang. I stopped the video and went to the door to collect my soup. I paid the deliveryman, took the brown paper bag from him and closed the door. I grabbed a spoon from the kitchen drawer and took the bag into the den. Seated back on the couch, I put the video back on and proceeded to eat my soup straight from the carton.

Overall, from my view on the couch, I was having a lovely day.

Chapter 20

Wednesday, 12:45 P.M.

My mental health day was over before I knew it and I found myself back in rounds trying to stay awake. I had already been to the washroom twice and a third trip would not go unnoticed. I had missed the remainder of Monday and all of yesterday. As such, I knew only four patients. Changeover in the unit was variable. We always said that if a patient wasn't getting better by the fourth or fifth day in the unit it was going to be a very long haul. We stood at the bedside of Ms. Ava Gardiner, my young transsexual lady with AIDS. She had done very well in my absence and was ready to be extubated. I had seen her earlier in the morning and had put together my plan.

"Dr. Solomon," said a voice of authority, "what's your plan here?" It was Dr. Jacob Dean. Dr. Dean was the emperor of the Intensive Care Unit. He had been here forever and this place was his baby. To his credit he took a dinky little unit and made it into a trauma center and one hell of an efficient place to get sick in. He had a reputation, as did everyone who was here long enough to get one. He took wonderful care of his patients, took no bullshit and had absolutely no tolerance for incompetence. If you were honest and hard working, he was wonderful to work with. If you slacked off and tried to talk your way out of things, he'd be sure to make you cry. He had always been very good to me. I think he saw that I really did give a shit and was trying my best. He never once made me cry.

"I've reviewed all of her issues. The respiratory techs did weanable parameters this morning," I said, handing him the sheet with her parameters. "She improved dramatically over the past few days and her infection has responded to the Septra. All of her other lab work is in order and the cultures from her BAL came back showing only PCP. I think she can be extubated, I said.

"Anything else, Eve?" he asked.

"She's followed at the AIDS clinic downtown and I've been in touch with them to update things and get all her records. Ava wasn't on Septra before because there was some confusion as to whether she didn't tolerate it before. I think this admission shows that she should be on prophylaxis in the future and I've conveyed that to her and the people at the clinic," I said.

"Good," he said softly and you could hear a pin drop within the group. When Dr. Dean spoke, no one else did. He commanded a combination of fear and respect. I always wondered if he went home at the end of the day and secretly laughed his ass off at the way people acted around him.

"Anything else, Eve?" he asked.

'No, sir, not unless I'm missing something," I said.

"No," he said and smiled at me.

We moved on to the next bed. I motioned to Mike, the respiratory technician, to pull the tube. I stood on the periphery of the group so as to be in earshot should something happen.

Alex Connor was presenting an interesting case of a patient who had Myasthenia Gravis and was now post op. This was a case of a fifty-six-year-old man with a progressive disease of the receptors on his muscles. As such he suffered from progressive fatigue to the point where he couldn't lift his head or chew his food. In a crisis it would affect the muscles he used to breathe. Alex Connor was presenting the case.

"Who's his Neurologist?" asked Dr. Dean.

"He doesn't have one," Alex Connor answered.

"Yes he does," said Dr. Dean.

"Oh. I didn't know that," Alex said. Wrong answer. He'd been caught in his lie. Alex knew the patient had a Neurologist but since he rarely talked to patients and their families he found out only the information that was in the old charts. Dean had caught him and he knew it.

What followed was not pretty. Alex was pretty much told to keep quiet from then on as Dr. Dean continued presenting the case. Alex looked as if he'd been hit in the face. Despite my feelings for him, I felt sorry for him. Public humiliation wasn't something you wished on just anyone. A plan was put in place for this patient and rounds were over. We dispersed and I went to the back of the unit to complete my notes. I only had Ava as my one patient and offered to pick up any new admissions during the day. Alex was summoned into the small staff doctors' office for what would be a reprimand. I wasn't smiling this time as the door closed behind him. He would be crushed like the others before him. The process had begun. He was an asshole and he would now be beaten into submission. This would serve to make

Ali Zentner

him not only more of an asshole, but it would give him the excuse someday to do the same to someone else. And so the cycle continued.

I was in the middle of my note when I felt a tap on my shoulder. I turned around to see Annie, the fourth year medical student, standing before me.

"Hi, Dr. Solomon. I'm Annie Taylor. I'm the new clinical clerk," she said, holding out her hand.

"Hi, Annie, I'm Eve," I said looking at her. She was average height and looked very clean. I mean she literally shone. Her hair was perfect and her makeup pristine. She was wearing a navy blue tunic dress and her short white coat. Her stethoscope was draped around her neck and she was looking to me to teach her something.

"It's my first day. Is there anything to do?" she asked.

"Sure," I said smiling. I had two days to go before my vacation and here I was stuck with Miss Congeniality in search of a purpose. "Why don't you pick a patient on the unit and familiarize yourself with his/her chart? Look at how we write our admissions and daily notes, and then when the next admission comes you'll be ready to do it. Okay?" I suggested.

"Sure," she said, walking over to the chart rack.

"Annie, I'll be here if you have any questions," I called after her.

She turned and smiled at me and I knew I was now in hell.

As if on cue, David passed her on her way to the charts and walked straight up to me.

"Hey," he said, sliding himself up on the counter next to where I was writing my note. "Who's the new recruit?" he asked referring to Annie.

"Her name's Annie Taylor," I said.

"Cute," he said.

"I'll put in a good word for you. She's my responsibility for the next few days," I said putting my head into my hands.

"Oh really?" she said.

"Dr. Dean himself has asked me to take her under my wing," I said.

"You free for lunch now?" he asked changing the subject.

I looked at him. There was no way to get beyond this situation other than to go through it.

"Sure. I can't ignore you forever," I said, trying to make light of things.

"But you were getting so good at it," he said putting his arm around me.

"Hey. Don't touch me, I'm still angry," I said laughing.

We walked past Annie who was standing at the chart rack and I told her I was going to get some lunch.

"Oh, Annie, this is David Auerbach. He's one of the residents here," I said introducing them.

"Hi," Annie said enthusiastically, shaking David's hand.

"Pleasure," was David's response, smiling.

We walked down the hall, leaving Annie to her work.

"What's this 'pleasure' shit? Where do they teach you that stuff?" I said making light of his recent interaction with our new recruit.

"Just being polite," he said grinning. "Don't tell me your jealous."

"What?" I said laughing.

"That's it, Eve. You can't have me and no one else should," he said.

"David, don't flatter yourself. Furthermore don't provoke me. I am not jealous. You want Annie, she's yours. I have nothing to do with it," I said. I was starting to get angry again.

"That's it, Eve. You're pissed off because I'm the one in control here, not you," he said as we approached the door to the unit. I stopped just before the door and turned back to the door to the call rooms. I opened the door and walked inside. He followed me.

"Sit down. We're not going for lunch. We're settling this now," I said, taking a deep breath. David sat down on the bed and I pulled up a chair from the corner of the room.

"David, I've thought about this a great deal, more than I care to admit." I was composed, poised, this would be good, "Please let me finish all I have to say and then you can talk." He nodded. "I've come to the conclusion that what really bothers me is that for you this is so easy. This would be another fling for you and that's it. For me it would be a breakdown of my moral code and it would really hurt my marriage and me. And now I feel as though I've gotten myself into something I can't get out of. So I'm asking you as a friend to let me out of this. David, we need to end this and let it go." I looked up at him for a reply.

"What do you suggest? We just pretend this never happened?"

"No, we don't pretend anything. There is nothing, David. I can go on ignoring you forever if I have to. I'd rather be a friend," I said.

"Can I think about it?" he asked.

"What's there to think about? I'm asking for a break here, this isn't some deep proposal." I stood up. I could see the game he was playing. God forbid I should have the control, but this was one situation I wasn't losing.

"Okay. Fine. I'll be your friend," he said, standing up to hug me. He put his arms around me and pulled me to him and I willingly went. His hand was on my hair holding my head to his chest. He ran his fingers through my hair and then over my face. I forgot where and who I was. I could feel my heart pounding in my chest and all I could see was his perfect mouth. He lifted my face to his and put his lips on mine. I closed my eyes. His mouth was warm and wet. I could taste his lips with my own and I felt my whole body come alive beneath his kiss. And then after what seemed like forever, he pulled away from me and looked at me smiling.

"Just checking," he said. I looked at him; he was smiling and very proud of himself.

"What were you checking?" I asked.

"Just checking to see if you really believe your own bullshit." He was smiling.

I was shocked. I felt sick. I looked at him grinning at me, taking comfort in my pain and as if in an instant he lost his luster.

"You sick bastard," I said softly. I turned to the door, opened it and walked quickly back onto the unit knowing he would not follow me this time.

I found Annie still at the chart rack surveying the charts intensely. She hadn't moved in the past ten minutes.

"Annie, come on, I'll buy you lunch," I said, welcoming my new distraction.

We walked back down the hall to the unit and passed David on his way out of the call rooms.

"Where are you going?" he asked as I passed him quickly.

"Lunch," I called halfway through the door to the unit.

"Can I come?" he called.

"No," I answered.

And that was all.

7:15 P.M.

I drove home to Barry Manilow singing *Looks Like We've Made It* on the CD player. Barry is considered by most to be an all time low in music history. I'm ashamed to admit it, but I like him. He's easy to sing to. I smiled at the thought that I had literally kissed David goodbye. In one swift move he had proved his point. He had played the game to his perfection and he had won. In the end I was weak. I wanted to be kissed and I had gotten what I wanted. And as I looked at him in the light of his true colors he was nothing but a fraternity boy out to prove his manhood. He was no longer a mystery. He was no longer desirable and he was no longer my friend. The situation was now very simple. I would go home, tell Jack a somewhat tame version of what had happened and we would have a very good laugh about the whole thing. In two days I would be finished in the unit and my path with David would rarely cross again. He would fade in my memory along with his kiss, and I would heal in time.

I think in those moments that I understood the "Davids" of the world. On some level, they really did want to be loved. They wanted the whole romance thing with flowers and moonlight as much as we did. But when it all came down to it, at the end of the day, they really just needed to fall in love. It was the fall that was the victory for them. They were addicted to the first twenty minutes of every relationship. When the sun rose the next morning and there was a bed to be made and a bill to be paid, they were on to the next conquest. Men like David would fall forever if life would allow it. And women like me would always be there at the bottom of some great cliff trying to catch them. We would stand there regardless of age or hour with our arms in the air waiting for that fabulous landing, only to be disappointed when he never touched ground. Here I was living and loving a man who was nothing like that. Jack never played the game. Hell, Jack never even knew the rules. Sure he had his moments. He was more of a child than a man on certain days but he wanted the whole package and not just the first few chapters. It all became very clear to me in those moments at the end of my day, with the sun setting behind me and Barry singing his heart out. I had left that cliff permanently behind and was on my way home to my husband—the man who had taught me to fly.

10:00 P.M.

We were sitting in the den. Dinner had been macaroni and cheese eaten standing up over the counter. It was my husband's turn to make dinner and his culinary forte was somewhat limited. Although Kraft Dinner would not have been my choice, I didn't complain when it wasn't my night to cook. Other hit items in Jack's repertoire were tuna melts, grilled cheese sandwiches, omelets, and pancakes. I was sitting on the couch flipping through the television channels and Jack was on the computer.

"David hit on me," I blurted out.

"Who's David?" he asked. Typical. I had been replaying this scenario over in my mind a thousand times and he didn't even remember the name of the man who took me to dinner.

"He's the guy from work who took me for dinner," I said. Suddenly my confession was no big deal. I had debated telling him the whole story and had finally elected for an edited version. I figured I could fill in any necessary blanks in a few years and we could then have a good laugh about the situation.

"Hmm," he said, focused on the computer.

"He kissed me," I said, looking at the back of Jack's head.

"Really? Any good?" He turned around to face me. He was smiling.

"Jack, don't make light of the situation," I said. Why did this man have to be so perfect?

"Was it a big deal that he kissed you?" he asked, trying to prove a point.

"No. I just wanted you to know. I don't want us to keep secrets," I said, being mostly honest.

"So, was he any good?" he asked. "Come on, no secrets."

"Yes," I said smiling.

"As good as me?" he asked.

"Never."

"Good answer," he said and turned back around to face his computer.

"Jack, don't you want to talk about this?" I asked.

"Eve," he turned around again, "some David guy kissed you. He was good but not as good as I. Hey, I saw the guy. He's a beauty. The fact is that

I knew what he wanted the night he came here for dinner. And my darling if you think I believed your little story about him getting called into the hospital you are more naïve than I thought. So, the point is, I love you, Eve. You love me and what is more, I trust you. David's not going to be the last beau hunk to hit on you so anytime you want me to pull that 'you're my wife' bullshit and let the guy have it, you let me know."

I walked over to my husband and embraced him. He held me very tightly and kissed my neck.

"Where did you get the word 'beau hunk' from?" I asked laughing.

"You like it?" he said grinning.

We began to laugh very hard and I continued to hold on to Jack.

"So you love me, Jack?" I asked batting my eyes.

"Sweetie, I adore you," he said smiling.

I stood up and took Jack's hand and led him into the bedroom. I turned down the bed and turned to face him. He was beautiful in so many ways and in this moment my life made perfect sense.

I kissed his neck as I unbuttoned his shirt and began to savor his body. It was as though in some way, I was making love to him for the first time. I kissed his face and his chest. I took my time, taking pleasure in the nuances that were so familiar to me. We made love slowly and passionately and when it was over I lay in his arms with the taste of him still lingering.

"You're one hell of a beau hunk," I said.

And we laughed ourselves to sleep.

Chapter 21

Saturday, 11:30 A.M.
Jack hates to fly. He is deathly afraid of heights and is convinced the plane will one day fall from the sky. On solid ground the man is a prince of peace. Put him in the air and he turns into a sweating, anxious idiot who fears his own mortality and makes regular trips to the bathroom to deal with the devil in exchange for his safety. My father once told him that it was the five minutes after takeoff and before landing that were the most dangerous. Consequently, he spends the first and last twenty minutes of each flight clutching my hand for dear life with the fear of God in him. I've tried medicating him through these episodes but all he does is sleep through the entire flight. This prevents his in flight terror, yet leaves him unconscious until at least three hours after we reach our destination. On a trip to Europe, Jack took an Ativan my father had given him. He fell asleep somewhere over the East Coast and woke up in our hotel room in Italy. It was his most enjoyable flight. However, he left me to literally carry him through customs and across the threshold.

So here we sit on flight 767 to New York City. My husband is sweating bullets and squeezing my hand tighter with every small movement of the plane. Thanks to Jack's business, we've been upgraded to first class. So here I sit among the beautiful people, holding my husband's sweaty palm and working on my third champagne and orange juice.

First class is wonderful. Don't let anyone tell you otherwise, there is a difference. Firstly the seating arrangements are extraordinary. As a pauper back in coach you find yourself sandwiched between two individuals, one of

whom inevitably has a crying baby or body odor. Furthermore the seats force
you to eat your knees and no yoga in the world will help your cause. Up here,
among the masters of the universe, the seats are reclining lazy boy chairs and
the only one on the verge of tears is my husband. The service in first class is
exemplary. Gone are the flight attendants with attitude who feel that getting
me a blanket is like giving me a kidney. While sitting in my couch riding the
friendly skies, I have 'Carrie' and 'Jeff', two lovely people who can't do
enough for me. My meal is a solid attempt at restaurant quality food and I
have more blankets, pillows, newspapers, and white little hand towels than I
know what to do with. The champagne has taken full effect and I sit at ease,
the world below, holding Jack's hand and whispering soothing words in his
ear. I'm a saint. I am sitting in first class. I am queen of the world. I'm drinking champagne well before noon at 30,000 feet and I'm surrounded by opu-
lence. If this plane goes down right now let it be said that I died truly happy.

'Jeff' hands out our earphones and announces that the in flight movie
will begin shortly. I unclench Jack's hand from mine and retrieve my bag
from the overhead bin. In the side pocket is the treasured Valium. I take out
one pill and hand it to Jack.

"What's this?" he says looking scared.

"It's Valium, sweetie," I say, handing him the pill.

"You don't mind getting me to the hotel?" he asks.

"I'll get a porter. Please, you look like you're going to have a coronary."

He nodded his head briskly in agreement and put the pill under his
tongue. I put a pillow behind his head and covered him with the blanket.
Within ten minutes his eyes were heavy. I put my earphones on and waited
for the movie to begin. By the time the previews were over, Jack was fully
unconscious and no longer clutching my hand. He had a look of pure con-
tentment on his face as the drug took its full effect. I pulled the blanket onto
his lap and reached up to touch his face. A smile crossed my lips as I sat back
to appreciate the humor of the situation. 'Jeff' offered me another champagne and orange juice which I declined, knowing one of us would have to
be sober for our arrival. He returned a few minutes later with plain orange
juice and another pillow for Jack. I smiled and thanked him and returned to
my movie. There we sat in our respective couches, Jack in dreamland and me
in heaven.

5:45 P.M.

We landed safely at La Guardia and 'Jeff' got me a porter to help with the
baggage and my husband. Jack was now awake, as he'd been given a coffee
before landing, but he was still groggy from the earlier Valium. Once we
retrieved our suitcases the porter found us a cab and we were on our way to
the Plaza. Jack slept in the cab and I woke him once we reached downtown
Manhattan. I sat him in the lobby while we checked into the hotel and then

had the bellhop take up our bags while I took up my husband. Once safe in our room, I put my husband in bed and surveyed the room.

I love hotel rooms. Everything from the tiny soaps to the room service speaks decadence to me. The room at the Plaza was the ultimate in decadence. I ran a bubble bath in a tub twice the size of our one at home and went to the phone to call Nina. I dialed the number at her restaurant and left a message on her voicemail as to where we could be reached. I then called Theo at the office.

"Hello from the Plaza," I said when he picked up the phone.

"Are you in heaven?" he said, referring to my love of hotels.

"Absolutely. I'm just about to get into the bath. We still on for dinner?"

"I've made reservations at Nobu just for you. How was your flight?" he asked.

"Great. We were moved to first class courtesy of Jack's business," I said.

"How's he doing?" Theo said, laughing in reference to Jack's flying habits.

"I had to drug him halfway through. He's sleeping it off," I said smiling.

"Does that mean I have you to myself for dinner? he asked playfully.

"Probably. When's dinner?" I asked.

"Eight o'clock. I'll come to the hotel and we can ride together from there," he said.

"Well, we'll see how Jack is in a few hours. I've put him to bed so he may very well be out for the night," I said laughing.

"Eve, what the hell did you give him?" he asked.

"Just Valium. But he's very sensitive," I said, defending myself and laughing.

"Well, I'll see you around 7:30. Okay?

"Great," I answered. We said our good-byes and I hung up the phone and returned to the bathroom to check on the tub. I shut off the water and went into the other room to change into a robe. Jack was now snoring loudly and I smiled, watching him sleep. I went back into the bathroom and took off my robe, hanging it on the back of the door. I lowered myself into the bath and let the bubbles and the warm water surround me.

The phone in the bathroom rang.

"Hello?" I said, answering the phone from the bath.

"Eee vee!" It was Nina.

"Hey, babe. How are you?"

"I'm so glad you're here. When can I see you?" she asked.

"I'm having dinner with Theo in a few hours, why don't you join us?" I asked. Theo and Nina had met several times on my behalf and got along well.

"Can't for dinner, how about drinks later?" she asked.

"Perfect," I said. We agreed to meet at her restaurant at eleven o'clock and we'd decide on drinks from there.

"How's my boy?" she asked, referring to Jack. Nina and Jack had a love affair. They were like brother and sister every time they were together. I loved watching them interact.

"He's unconscious. I gave him a Valium on the plane. He's still sleeping it off," I said laughing.

"I've got to go. I'll see you tonight," she said laughing.

I put the phone back on the receiver on the wall and finished washing my hair and my face. I stepped out of the bath, wrapped myself in the robe, and used a small towel to wrap around my head. As I was opening my suitcase to unpack, there was a knock on the door.

"Who is it?" I called.

"Room service," a voice called back.

I went to the door knowing full well I hadn't ordered room service. I opened the door and there stood a waiter with a tray filled with Champagne and truffles. The man handed me a card and put the tray on the table in the corner of our room. I handed him a few dollars and thanked him for his services, closing the door behind him. I opened the card, which came with the wonderful gift and read:

Dr. Solomon, So glad you could attend the conference. Looking forward to your participation in the days to come. Welcome to New York, Sincerely, Denise Johnson, Pfizer Pharmaceuticals.

It was in these moments that I could honestly say I loved being a physician.

7:20 P.M.

Jack was still sleeping soundly when the phone rang. It was Theo calling from the lobby and he was on his way up to the room. I had tried to wake my drug-induced husband earlier but it was useless. There was a knock on the door and I opened it to find Theo smiling. He embraced me and kissed my face.

"Hell beautiful," he said. "I missed you."

"Oh, it's so good to see you. Let me look at you." I stepped back from his hug and surveyed the man before me. Theo was an attractive man. He had gotten better with age and the graying of his hair only furthered his charm. He was very tall and lean and had lovely hazel eyes and an interesting face. He was not a typical beauty but rather had an appeal many women would call 'interesting'. His personality shone from him and only furthered his appearance. He stood there before me with steel-framed glasses and a casual black suit with a white button down shirt. I invited him into the room where Jack still lay motionless in the bed.

"I just have to get my purse and we can go," I said.

He took one look at Jack and began to laugh.

"Eve, what did you give him?" he said within the laughter.

"Theo, it was one Valium and trust me, he needed it. He was a mess," I defended myself.

"I take it he won't be joining us?" Theo asked.

"No. I tried to wake him earlier but it was useless. He'll likely sleep through the night," I said grabbing my purse. I took a pen from the bedside table and quickly wrote Jack a note, letting him know where I was should he wake up before I returned.

"Shall we?" he asked.

"Oh, I asked Nina to join us later. We just have to swing by the restaurant and get her. It's not far from Nobu," I said.

"Great." Theo opened the door and we left the hotel room.

We walked down the hall to the elevator and he told me about his trip to Paris. He had been working very hard and had the company in the palm of his hand. His time off was spent with friends at the various cafes in the city. He looked directly at me when he spoke, just as I had remembered. The conversation flowed between us as though we had seen each other yesterday. I listened to him tell me about the business and his job as we waited for the doorman to hail a cab.

"How's Jennifer?" I asked when we were inside the taxi.

"Good," He said, looking out the window.

"Theo, cut the bullshit. What's going on?" I asked.

"She wants to get married," he said, looking at me for a reaction. I had long ago learned to keep my mouth shut when it came to Theo's love life.

"Oh," I said looking at him.

"What, oh?" he asked.

"Nothing, just oh," I said laughing.

"Well what do you think about all this?" he wanted my opinion regardless of whether or not I would give it.

"I really don't know Jennifer, but you seem very happy," I said trying to be very diplomatic.

"Eve, come on, tell me what you really think."

"Can't it wait until after dinner?" I asked.

"Why?"

"Because, that way, regardless of what I say, we don't ruin a lovely evening," I said laughing.

I looked at him and he was staring intently back at me.

"Okay, we'll talk about Jennifer over dessert. How are you?" he asked.

"Good, Theo. Really good. You know, the usual."

"How's work?" he asked.

"The usual. I still don't know what I want to be when I grow up," I said.

"So, you've decided to be a doctor in the meantime?"

"Yes, something like that," I said.

"You're too smart for your own good, you know?" he said.

"Why? Because I question my vocation on a regular basis?" I defended myself. "Just because I refuse to be blindly happy at every moment doesn't make me brilliant," I said.

"No, it's just that with you, nothing is ever simple, Eve," he said.

"Oh and your life is so free of complications?" I asked.

"No," he said.

"Then back off with the judgment calls!" I said.

This always happened when Theo and I were together. We misunderstood one another on certain issues and it always lead to our conversation taking a defensive tone at some point. The truth was I hated Jennifer. I had met her the last time I was in New York. Theo was receiving an award from his company and I decided to surprise him by coming to the awards dinner. Jennifer was a self-centered bitch who took ownership of Theo. She even went so far as to call him 'my Theo'. I looked at her and saw Theo's life stretching out before him, an endless stream of obligations and misery. She would take his sense of duty and his need to look after others and twist it into some sad sense of obligatory shame. Jennifer was the type of woman who took far more than she ever gave and Theo was perfect for her. He would dote on her with all of his being until there was nothing left in him. Then he would find some way to sleep around and express his distaste for the relationship through a series of infidelities. It would only end in the same way all of his former lovers had fallen.

He leaned over in the back of the cab and took my hand.

"So, you don't want me to marry Jennifer?" he asked smiling.

"I thought we were going to wait until dessert." I smiled back.

"Oh come on. You're my best friend. You are the only one I can discuss this kind of shit with, and I know you'll be honest with me."

"You know what it is Theo. I don't dislike her, I just question her motives in all this," I said.

"Well, it's only marriage, Eve. I can get out of it," he said half joking.

"Lovely. That's the attitude," I said.

"Oh, and your married life is blissful?" he asked. "Why is it when people don't want to discuss their own shortcomings they feel the need to highlight yours?"

"We're not talking about my marriage right now. We're talking about you and Jennifer," I said.

"Fine. Sorry."

"Theo, it's just that I think you're rushing into this. You've only been with this woman for a few months and you've never even said you love her. Now she's proposing marriage and you're agreeing, with the caveat that you can get out of it."

The cab stopped in front of the restaurant and we both got out. Theo paid the driver and met me on the curb. He held the door open for me and we entered the restaurant. Nobu was one of the top restaurants in New York and one of my favorites. The food was extraordinary. It was an amazing mix of flavors. We were seated at the bar while we waited for our table to be ready. Theo ordered two ginger martinis and we continued our conversation.

"So, I'm not good at relationships," he said.

"That's not the point. It's not like a skill you acquire. Just because you aren't good at relationships doesn't mean you resign yourself to having shitty ones for the rest of your life. Don't you think you deserve better?" I asked.

"I never thought of it in those terms," he admitted.

"Well think about it. Just because your history with women had been less than ideal doesn't prevent you from having a healthy relationship. Instead Theo, you walk around with this albatross around your neck, fulfilling your own prophecy," I said as our drinks arrived.

He lifted his glass and looked at me sweetly, "Here's to you," he said.

"You are such a bullshitter." I laughed and clinked my glass to his.

The martini was perfect. It was the right mix of ginger and sweetness and I sipped it happily. I had a habit of always drinking too much with Theo. On some level I felt that I had to be the hedonist in the relationship and with that came the culture of excess.

"So are you going to marry her?" I asked, trying to bring him back to the issue at hand.

"Well, I guess so. After all, the woman of my dreams is already taken," he said grinning.

"Go to hell. We'd kill each other and you know it," I said.

"Tell that to my mother. She still wants to know why I haven't married you," he said.

"Are you mad? Forget it Theo, I'd exhaust you and you would make me crazy," I said. It was true. I loved Theo very much but he was too logical and too fatalist to capture my heart. Everything with Theo had to have a reason. He would never be the dreamer I so needed in my life, and I would always need the worship he could not provide. On some unspoken plane we would always be anything but lovers.

"Not to worry, I let my mother know you had married a prince and she rescinded," he said.

"I did marry a prince, didn't I?" I said, relishing in the thought of Jack. The events of the past few days had only deepened my conviction.

"Yes, Eve. He's perfect for you," he said, sipping his martini. "Maybe that's why you expect the rest of us to have such wonderful relationships," he said.

"Of course it is. If I have had such a great experience wouldn't logic have it that I would want the same for my friends?" I asked.

"Fine. So what's wrong with Jennifer?" he asked.

"Well, do you love her?" I asked.

"That depends. What's your definition of love?"

I had to think for a moment.

"What is my definition or the definition?" I had to clarify as it gave me time to gather my thoughts.

"No, not dictionary shit, what is your definition of love?" he repeated.

"Okay," I said sipping my drink. "It's when you lose yourself so complete-ly in someone that you can't imagine your life before them. And," I continued, taking another sip, "the thought of a life after them is not only unthinkable but unbearable." I sat back rather proud of my little analogy and looked at Theo. I could tell he was processing my words and I gave him a minute.

"So," I said, "do you love her?"

"Well, by your definition I don't," he admitted.

"Fine. Then what is your definition of love?" I asked.

"Well it's not a definition really. It's more of a feeling," he said.

"So describe the feeling to me."

"Fine," he said, sipping his drink and shifting in his barstool. "You know that place between sleep and wake?" he asked.

I wasn't sure where this was going.

"You know when you're lying in bed and the pull of the world is a mil-lion miles away? When you've climbed out of your obligations and your head is on the pillow waiting for dreams to come?" His voice became softer. You close your eyes and just before you fully fall asleep there this magical feeling that passes over you and you submit. You let go. You could be sleeping on your arm or need to shut the light out, but none of it matters. You just let go and let yourself fall into that safe warmth."

"Hmm," I said smiling, watching the magical look on his face.

"Well, that's love. It's that 'never shall I care about another thing in the world-feeling,' safe-perfection, embodied in another person," he smiled. "And of course there's great sex."

"Oh, of course," I said laughing.

So we took a moment and drank to love in all of its definitions. Then moments later a waiter came and took our drinks and showed us to our table.

We'd only been seated for a few moments when I turned to him and con-tinued the previous conversation.

"So, do you love her?" I asked.

"Who?"

"Jennifer. Theo, have you been asleep for the past hour?"

"I'm just teasing, Eve, relax. Do I love Jennifer?"

"Yes," I affirmed.

"No," he admitted with a perfectly straight face. "I mean, she's a great lady. She's bright and we do have a good time together, and hell, the sex is pretty good when I can get it. But in no way shape or form do I love her."

"Hmm," I said.

"What's this 'hmm' shit? I've known you for more than ten years and all of the sudden you're muttering 'hmm' all the time."

"Stop changing the subject," I said chuckling.

"What subject?" Now he was just trying to be annoying.

"You don't love Jennifer."

"Not at all. I can totally picture my life without her and I'm completely awake when I'm with her," he stated.

"Then why marry her?" I asked.

"Because I'm lonely."

I looked straight into his lovely green eyes and admitted the only truth I knew at that moment. "Marriage won't make you less lonely, Theo, regardless of how hard you try," I said softly.

"Hmm," was his only response.

Chapter 22

We talked and ate and laughed throughout the evening. Theo told me about his job and I confessed my tales of the hospital. I know he did his best to understand and empathize but he would never really understand my position. Theo was his own master of the universe. He was a businessman and a successful one. He never felt powerless or self-loathing. He was a king.

"How's your family?" he asked as we worked our way through the main course.

"What can I tell you?" I began. "My father's doing well physically but the cancer continues to chip away at his spirit. My mother is the same but has now taken up smoking as a means of coping with any life issues." I laughed at the whole situation.

"And Penny?" he asked, lifting a piece of sushi to his mouth.

"Penny is Penny. I don't want to talk about it."

"Oh, come on, this is me."

"Theo, we devote far too much time talking about Penny. I'm tired of it. She can monopolize an evening without even being in the room," I said, putting a piece of sushi in my mouth.

"Okay. Moving on. How's Jack?" he asked.

"Wonderful," I smiled.

"So what's it like living with that?" he asked. I could tell from his question that he was hurt about my earlier comments about Jennifer.

"Theo, I was just saying that marriage isn't just the next step in a relationship. You don't just get married because you're lonely," I said.

"Eve, I'm not like you. I don't have these fabulous dreams and big time illusions. It doesn't have to be magic every minute of every day," he said earnestly.

"Why can't you want magic every minute? I mean what's wrong with that?" I asked. This was getting too personal. We had gone from discussing his love life to critiquing my life's mission all in the same meal.

"Because it's exhausting," he said.

"So what's wrong with making that extra effort? Don't you think you deserve true happiness?

"Oh, don't give me that bullshit. It has nothing to do with what I do and don't deserve. It's a matter of what's realistic. I'm thirty-eight and I've been married twice already. It's not about what I want. It's about what I can get," he said, sipping his sake.

"That's crap and you know it. Stop with this 'I've been burned and now I'm playing it safe' crap. It doesn't suit you, Theo."

"I'm not playing. I'm just saying that I'm perfectly happy to settle," he said.

"Really?" I wasn't completely surprised. Theo approached life with logic. He was very practical in his dealings with what life had to offer. I remember the last time I was in New York and we went for a walk in Central Park for our usual intense conversation. I turned to Theo in the middle of the park and asked him, "Theo, what's your biggest dream? I mean what's your ultimate life wish for yourself?" He stopped in his tracks and told me blankly that he didn't have any big dream or life wish.

Now sitting before him, talking about his capacity to settle, I realized that Theo wasn't a dreamer. He would settle for Jennifer or someone just like her for the pure reason that, in love, Theo accepted life's offerings rather than creating his own terms. It's amazing how you can know someone for such a big part of your life and only stop to realize a part of their life's work has been hidden from you for so long. I suppose it is part of a real relationship; one that grows with you.

I had known Theo since high school. We had both grown up in the same small Jewish community and gone to a small private high school. Theo was five years older than me and was near graduation by the time I had started at the school. I was in awe of him. He was in the "popular" crowd and I was an awkward teenager. I became friends with him after I joined an activist group that Theo was working for. I admired him for his passion and his mission in life and I loved him for his stature and his position. Over the years we both grew up. Theo moved to New York and became successful in business and unlucky in love. We kept tabs on one another through his parents, whom I had adopted as my own second family Theo's mother had always said she wanted me for her daughter-in-law, but I knew it would never be. We never once dated nor had anything but a platonic friendship. Theo was now the brother I had always wanted and there wasn't an alternative arrangement.

Now he sat before me after years of conversations and arguments; after years of discussions and confessions and another realization was before me. Theo took what life had to offer and I always expected more. It was the great divide between us and it had always been there. I had not allowed myself to see it, for it would contradict all of my own notions of the man.

I smiled at Theo and he returned my gesture.

"Your mind is working, Eve. I can see it. What's up?" he asked.

"Nothing. Just thinking." I smiled.

"Hmm," he said smiling.

"I'm just glad you're my friend, that's all. I mean sometimes I realize how different we are. We're not different in a bad way, but we are very different people. And I'm glad for what you bring to my life," I said.

"You're drunk," he said.

"I am not, just content."

"Come on, Eve, every time you drink you get this wonderful, 'self reflective love the world' thing. Don't get me wrong, it's great, but you are drunk."

"Fine, I may be tipsy but that doesn't mean I can't appreciate you. I just hope you realize how special you are, Theo. I hope some day you don't settle for what comes your way and that you do fight for what you deserve."

"Nice thought, beautiful, and I do thank you for it, but I'm too old to fight," he said, raising his glass to mine.

"You're never too old, Theo. You're just too tired," I said correcting him as I raised my glass to his.

10:45 P.M.

We had paid the check and were now in a cab on our way to Nina's restaurant. Nina was the head pastry chef at a French bistro in SOHO called "Les Villages." Her talent was finally becoming appreciated by the culinary world and her career was beginning to blossom. I had always said that Nina and I would have made the perfect lesbian couple. Moreover, Nina was the perfect man. She had been raised by her father from a very young age and had been sent to the finest boarding schools on the east coast. All of her private school training was quickly put to shame by a trip through the culinary world. When I met Nina in Paris, she had barely acquainted herself with the four-letter word. Now ten years later her vocabulary not only was filled with them, but she had invented a few of her own. In short, she was now learning her trade from the daily vocational challenges she faced and learning to talk from the teamsters who delivered her pastries.

Nina was one of the most honest people I had ever known, She had an uncanny ability to show you yourself as though she were holding a mirror to your face. Nina cut through the pomp and pretense she had grown up with and emerge a true soul. It was amazing. She had been raised surrounded by money and opportunity. Her father had come from the slums in London and emerged a self made man. It had been his life's mission to be very rich and he spent his days in excess, somehow hoping it would cover the memory of his impoverished childhood. Her parents had divorced when she was very young and Nina hadn't seen her mother in years. She had been her father's best friend and confidante until a younger woman took over. Now years later, Nina was left to be her own woman. Nina's father was infuriated with his golden daughter's choice of profession. Here he had spent a lifetime running from a blue-collar life and Nina, by nature of her profession, found herself immersed in it. She had gone to the best schools in the best cities and had now found true happiness working side by side with a dishwasher from Peurto Rico. It was her father's greatest shame.

Nina had now dismissed the man and his empty expectations and chosen a life of passion. Her entire existence reminded her father that there was nothing wrong with an honest day's work.

The cab stopped in front of Les Villages and we both got out on the curbside. I paid the driver and we went into the restaurant together. Les Villages was a quaint midsize space that was decorated in a style that combined old French Country with Art Deco. It was a strange mix of motifs but it somehow worked. We walked up to the bar and I asked the bartender to tell Nina we were here. Moments later Nina emerged from the back in her usual strut. Nina had a presence about her. She had the most amazing hair, which was a long light brown Afro. It was well past her shoulders and there were mountains of hair. Nina had the kind of look that intimidated men. She would walk down the street and people would literally turn their heads to look at her. Now she stood before me, hair flowing, dressed in black cargo pants and a black sweater with bright pink running shoes. Typical Nina. She had her own style that was a mix of "club kid wear" meets stylish chic. She bounced her way towards me and wrapped her arms around me in an embrace.

"Hello, my sweet," she said in my ear.

"It's so good to see you," I answered.

She pulled away and looked over at Theo.

"Hi," Nina said enthusiastically.

"Hi, Nina," Theo answered, shaking her hand.

"Come, let me show you my kitchen," she said to us proudly.

Nina took me by the hand and led me to the back of the restaurant. The place was still quite full of late diners and I was struck by the charm of the restaurant.

"This place is great, Neen," I said.

"It's a bad French acid trip, but it's home," she said smiling.

Nina led us into the small kitchen at the back and took pride in showing me her workspace and the various goodies she had made that day. She led us into the large walk-in freezer and took out two spoons. She then proceeded to offer us various samples of the ice cream she had prepared. I could tell Theo was in heaven. Here we were with just enough alcohol to make life interesting, standing in a deep freeze surrounded by homemade ice cream. Life was good.

Nina led us out of the "tasting area" and on through the kitchen, introducing us to the various staff members with whom she worked. After our short tour through the very small space, we left the kitchen and moved back to the front of the restaurant.

"Where should we go for drinks?" Nina asked.

I looked at Theo and he shrugged.

"Anywhere you like. You pick," I suggested.

Nina went behind the bar and grabbed her black workbag and a pink purse as well as her cigarettes. She opened the package and put a smoke between her lips, lit it and inhaled.

"All right," she said exhaling. "I know just the place. Wait, where's Jack?" she asked.

"He had a Valium on the plane. Now he's unconscious in the hotel room," I said laughing.

Nina started to giggle. She took her bags in one hand and her cigarette in the other and led us outside the restaurant.

"So, how was work?" I asked as she stood in the street smoking and trying to hail a cab.

"Nina, you stand with Eve, I'll get a cab," he said being the gentleman.

Nina returned to curbside while Theo went into the street.

"Work was great, busy night. How was dinner?" she asked.

"Wonderful. We went to Nobu. Have you been?" I asked.

"Mmm," she nodded, inhaling again. "It's amazing. What did you have?"

It was so clear that Nina loved food. You could tell her you'd been to McDonald's and she would still want to know what you had eaten and how it had tasted.

"We started with this amazing sashimi dish with cilantro and ginger. Then I had a noodle dish with seared tuna as my main course and Theo had a teriyaki thing. It was fabulous."

"Mmm. Sounds wonderful," she said smoking away.

"So, how's everything? Talk to me. What's new?" I asked.

"Not much. I've been working like crazy," she said.

"How's Mark?" I asked referring to the man in her life.

"Eh," she said exhaling. "I got bored," she admitted.

When it came to love, Nina was very in touch with her masculine side. Nina was the type of woman who would make love to a man and then lay there afterward smoking a cigarette and wondering how long she would have to cuddle with the poor bastard before she could find her underwear and go home. I remember trying to fix her up with a man whom Theo knew from work. They went on three dates at which point the poor guy admitted to her that he would like a relationship. Nina chastised him afterwards, saying, "What the hell was he thinking? It takes years to get to know someone and already he wants a relationship? My God, what a candy ass." As for Mark, they'd been together for about six months. Mark was a sous chef at another restaurant in Manhattan. He was a very nice person and he worshipped Nina. According to Nina, he became too possessive and wanted to move in with her. Nina, of course, would have none of this and promptly cut him loose.

"You got bored?" I confirmed.

"Eve, he wanted to move in. Here we are sleeping together for six months and he has the nerve to try and take over my life. Besides," she said still smoking, "he was a cheap bastard and we had nothing in common."

"Anyone new since?" I asked as we walked towards the cab Theo had gotten for us.

"Well there is a new waiter at work who I wouldn't mind taking home," she said laughing.

"Oh?" I asked getting into the back of the cab.

"Hmm," she confirmed throwing her cigarette onto the curb and climbing in behind me. She told the cabdriver where to take us and continued, "He's all of twenty-five but he has lips that could suck the chrome off a bumper," she said.

Theo looked a bit shocked as I began to laugh, knowing this was typical Nina.

The ride in the cab continued in much the same vain. Nina heralded us with tales of her work and love life as we made our way through the village and into Chelsea to her favorite Vodka bar. It should be said that as far as drinking went, Nina was true to her profession. The woman could drink anyone under the table. She not only had the tolerance for large amounts of alcohol, but she knew her booze. Nina was raised on Cognac and Champagne and had spent much of her college life at wine tasting events. As such she could single-handedly finish a bottle of Hennessey while letting you know exactly what food would go best with it.

We stopped in front of Glasnost, a Russian vodka bar, and Nina paid the driver before getting out of the cab and walking to the door. Once inside she hugged the maitre dé and introduced me to "Yuri" as her best friend. Yuri asked if I was visiting New York and I nodded. With that we were led to a plush red velvet booth at the back of the bar.

"I've done wedding cakes for most of Yuri's family, including his own wedding cake," she said to me as we slid into the booth.

"She did an amazing job," Yuri said. "This woman is a master."

"She's wonderful," I said beaming.

"What can I get you lovely people?" he asked.

I ordered a vodka martini as did Theo, and Nina asked to see a wine list. Yuri left, promising to return with our order.

"Isn't this place great?" Nina asked.

I looked around the room. Glasnost looked like an old Russian hangout where Communists may have mingled with royalty. The walls were stained cement and the floor was dark hard wood. The tables were black lacquer and there were red velvet booths lining the walls. Old Russian newspapers decorated the walls along with Warhol type prints of Lenin and Marx. It was a great space.

"How did you find this place?" I asked.

"I did the pastry for the opening and it just grew from there," she said.

"Do you do a lot of openings?" Theo asked.

"Not a lot," Nina answered lighting a cigarette. "I do a big event about one every two weeks."

Theo began to ask Nina questions about her work and she entertained us with tales from the culinary underbelly. Yuri returned with our drinks and I excused myself to go find a phone, thinking Jack may be awake at this point. I slid out from the booth and straightened my dress.

"You look so good," Nina commented.

"Yes, you do," Theo agreed.

I did a little dance under the influence and the circumstances and made my way to the bar to ask for a phone. Yuri insisted I use the house phone and placed it on the bar. I dialed the hotel number and asked the operator for our room number. The phone rang six times before a generic automated answering machine clicked in. I left Jack a message letting him know where I was and that I would be home in a few hours. If he wanted to join us we'd likely be here well past midnight. I put the phone back on the receiver, thanked Yuri for his kindness and made my way back to the table. Nina and Theo were in the middle of a discussion about the food in Paris. I could tell Nina was dazzling him. Her knowledge of good food was matched only by her passion for it. Nina could talk about crème Brule as though she were describing an erotic dream.

The evening continued into the early morning. The vodka continued to flow to our table as the laughter flowed from it. I had forgotten how nice it felt to spend an evening with old friends. There is a bare honesty that comes with sitting around a table with those that "knew you when". Here were the ones who loved me not in spite of my flaws, but because of them. I paused amidst the moments and the laughter and looked at them both. Nina, with her vodka and her smokes, was in her element. She occasionally pulled her mane of hair back from her face and continued in her usual self-confidant way. Theo's cheeks were colored slightly from the evening and the alcohol and was now joining Nina in his third cigarette.

They both caught me staring at them in admiration and Theo broke into my thoughts, "What's up, Eve?" he asked.

"Nothing." I smiled, "I was just admiring you two, that's all."

"Eee vee, you are the most lovable drunk, man," Nina said laughing. "You know," she turned to Theo, "she can be a royal bitch, but get a few hard drinks in her and she's anybody's date," she said putting her arm around me.

"Stop it, you bitch," I reprimanded her. "I'm happy, that's all."

"You certainly are, sweetheart," Nina said, taking a drag of her cigarette.

3:30 A.M.

Theo and I shared a cab back uptown once we had dropped Nina off at her place in the village. I was still enjoying the effects of the vodka when the cab pulled up in front of the Plaza.

"I had a great time, Eve. Thanks," he said, kissing me on both cheeks.

"Thank you, Theo. That was perfect," I said, getting out of the cab.

"I'll call you tomorrow," he said, waving from the open window.

I turned and made my way up the steps to the hotel. It was well into the morning and for the first time in a long time I was awake because I had spent the night laughing. It was three A.M. and I had not yet slept, not because someone was dying, but because I was living. It was a great feeling.

Chapter 23

I washed my face and changed into my pajamas in silence, trying my best not to wake Jack. After drinking my obligatory four glasses of water as hangover prevention, I crawled into bed with Jack. He was snoring soundly and I moved my body to fit into the curves of his. I closed my eyes and smiled my way into sleep.

6:45 A.M.
The alarm woke me with a start and I reached over to hit the snooze button. I was alone in the bed and looked up to find Jack sitting on the couch reading the paper and sipping his coffee.

"How did you get up so early?" I asked shocked.

"I've been up since six. You drugged me, remember?" he smiled.

"Hmm," I said, dropping my head back into the pillow.

"How was last night?" Jack asked, looking up from the paper.

"Oh, we had a great time," I said crawling to the edge of the bed.

"Coffee?" Jack offered.

I grunted my approval and made my way to the bathroom. I still felt the effects of the alcohol as I ran the shower and turned to my reflection in the mirror. I looked a little worn at best as I splashed cold water on my face. Jack brought a cup of coffee into the bathroom and I kissed him good morning before stepping into the shower. The stream of water did little to help me wake up as I tried in vain to get ready for the morning. The conference began at seven-thirty with registration and breakfast. I had planned to go to the morning sessions and to meet Jack for lunch. I was giving a talk on septic shock to a group of physicians and drug reps at two-thirty and Jack wanted to be there. After today I knew I could relax and enjoy the city with him. I let the warm water wash the soap from my hair and body as Jack came into the bathroom wide-awake.

"So," he chirped, "what did you do last night?"

"Theo and I went for dinner at this place called Nobu and then we met Nina for drinks," I said, shutting off the water and opening the curtain.

"How's Nina?" he said smiling. I knew he wouldn't ask me how Theo was. Jack adored Nina. The same could not be said for Theo. They had never really spent any time together. Theo represented a part of my past and Jack had always thought he was strange man; one he did not want to get to know. He once told me that I was all the two of them had in common and I knew he was right. Where Jack stood by his rules of integrity, Theo was a hedonist. Jack had a code of honor and Theo had a code of pleasure.

"Nina is wonderful," I said, smiling back at him and wrapping a towel around my head. "She wants to see you," I said.

"Can we have dinner with her tonight?" he asked.

"I'll leave you her number and you can make plans," I said, sipping my coffee and making my way into the bedroom.

After laying out a plain navy suit (can't be too conservative) I went back into the bathroom, coffee in hand and began to blow my hair dry. Ten minutes later, hair back in place and make-up applied, I was back in the bedroom dressing.

Jack sat in a chair reading a copy of the *New York Times* and shouted out the odd interesting headline. The clock by the bed read 7:25 as I took one last look in the mirror at my plain blue suited reflection. I then grabbed my briefcase and made my way downstairs where I would catch a cab to the Hilton Hotel and Conference Centre. My talk was scheduled for 9:00 A.M. and there was plenty of time for me to review my slides, rehearse my speech and throw up as needed.

Let me say that I have always been a good public speaker. Perhaps it stems from the younger child syndrome of always being the family entertainer. The moments before I speak are plagued with uncertainty and dread, but then I stand up there in front of a hundred faces and something instantly clicks. My mouth may be dry and my bladder unstable but I'm hell-bent on winning each one of them with my words. Call it one woman's quest for self-approval.

The bellboy hailed a cab for me and I slipped him a few dollars. Let it be said, Jack would freak. He has a severe objection to tipping people for doing their job. Strangely, such acts make me feel elegant. I somehow transform into a diva the moment the money leaves my hand. All hail Princess Eve, she tipped me a flyer, she is God. Sometimes I am so shallow I shock myself.

7:45 A.M.

I never tire of this city. I have been here so many times, seen the same build-ings repeatedly, and each time I fall in love. The cab ride is short but it gives me a chance to take a deep breath before the madness will begin. The con-ference is a four-day affair, of which I plan to give my talk and spend the next three days anywhere but in a dark room surrounded by the great minds and egos of the twenty-first century.

I pay the cab driver and head for the doors of the Hilton. The street is its usual combination of the morning rush mixed with coffee. People fill the streets in their usual morning best. New York at this hour has its best on dis-play. Men look as though they were pressed in their suits, women born in their three-inch heels. My mind pauses to enjoy the urban glamour for a moment before facing the reality inside the conference center. I opened the door, took a deep breath, longed for a latte and entered the "hall of truth".

8:45 A.M.

It is always at these times that I fear I will be discovered. I will stand in front of these great minds on a pile of my own bullshit and the years of false self-importance will peel away one by one, leaving my audience faced with the truth. The truth is, I have created a facade which allows me to appear to be more than I really am. This is an arrogant and somewhat self-righteous con-fession, but it is true even in this very dialogue. I appear to be this all-togeth-er woman who has her control on all that it is important in 1ife, when the truth is I am only fooling those around me. The control has long been well beyond my reach. I, like many people in this world, am only treading water, struggling to survive while maintaining a smile and the appearance of some semblance of perfection.

In reality, my life is quite ordinary. When the initial luster passes, it is a rather regular existence clouded in an arrogance that would allow it to pre-sume to be more than it is. Who do I think I am? Here I stand staring at a laptop, waiting to give a talk on septic shock that I hardly understand myself. My job is less than satisfying, my family is dysfunctional, and I presume to think that to the outside world I appear to be a rather together person. I hate being wrong. I relish in the pain of evil people. I am shielded from my own bad thoughts by a veil of self-righteous indignation. I am a lazy person by nature who would rather sit on a couch in front of television than make a decent contribution to the world. Furthermore, I have fallen from grace long ago with no chance of reconciliation.

All this said, I place my computer on the podium, connect to the pro-jector and get ready to face the firing squad.

9:45 A.M.

The talk has gone well. The research has been well received and I was able to answer each question with enough knowledge and just enough bullshit to hold the truth-seekers at bay. I take one last sip of water as I pack up my computer and exchange appropriate nods at the audience.

Once out in the hallway, Dr. Leonard approaches me.

"Excellent talk, Dr. Solomon, you've done us proud." He shakes my hand sincerely.

"Thank you, sir. I'm very happy with the way the study has turned out." I continue trying to maintain some sense of professionalism when all I want to do run back to the hotel.

"Are you staying for the rest of the day?" he asked, grinning as though he's reading my mind.

"No," I confess, "my husband is back and the hotel and I promised to buy him breakfast." I smile, hoping he will understand.

"Good choice." He smiles, "Again, congratulations on today. Go enjoy your breakfast."

I return his friendly nod and, gripping my laptop case, head down the escalators to the front door where my cab and my freedom await.

I forgo the cab ride and decide to walk back to the hotel. With my bag and my suit I can convince myself that I belong on these streets amidst the glamorous and the powerful. With each step I can fool myself into thinking I too was born in Prada shoes with a Gucci bag. I stop on the street corner and finally get the coffee I feel I have well deserved. Three sweeteners go in and the hot cup goes to my lips. The drug spreads through me, putting a smile on my lips.

Here I am in the center of the world, glamorous and fabulous, intelligent and poised. I have my coffee and my computer. I am the picture of success. I continue walking on air with the full knowledge that in the past hour I have gone from self-loathing to megalomania in sixty minutes flat.

10:55 A.M.

I put the electronic key in the door and turn the handle. I am in the perfect mood. I love my life. I am going to spend $65 US dollars on breakfast, nay, brunch with the man I love.

"Hello," I call from the door.

"Hey, Eve. How was it?" Jack asks.

"Great. What's doing?" I answer.

"Well," and then I hear it in Jack's voice. There it is; the usual tension and stress that come with his next sentence. "Your mother called."

"Penny?"

"Hmm," he answers.

I've change and ordered another pot of coffee in preparation for the next hour. Jack has gone to the fitness center in the hopes of exercising the rest of the Valium out of his system. I get comfortable on the edge of the bed and dial my mother's number.

"Hi, Ma," I say after she picks up the phone on the second ring.

"Hi, sweetie." She exhales, "Let me just tell Phyllis I'll call her back." She clicks back to the other line. Moments later Phyllis has been dismissed and I now hold her full attention.

"So, how's New York?" she asks, feigning cheerfulness.

"Great, Mom. My talk went well."

"Oh, you gave a talk?" she asked, inhaling her cigarette slowly.

"Yes, on my research."

"What's it on?" she asked. God bless her for trying to understand.

"I'll tell you some other time, Mom? What's doing there? Jack tells me things aren't going well."

"It's Penny." Her tone changes.

"What's she done now?" I sound less than thrilled.

"She's having money problems," my mother begins.

I know there is more to this. Penny can't have money problems. My sister has declared bankruptcy three times in fifteen years and as such, hasn't any debt. Furthermore, my mother is Penny's personal financial advisor/counselor/guide. Penny's paycheck is directly deposited in my mother's account at the end of every month. As such, my mother then pays all of her eldest daughter's bills and gives her an allowance every two weeks. Penny remains financially responsible and my mother gets her mortgage payment. As such, Penny's only financial trouble could stem from some scam she has hidden from my mother.

"What has she done?" It's truth time, and I might as well get on with it.

"Well," Mom begin exhaling, "she's been making some extra money on the side." My mother's voice turns shaky.

"What's she doing, Ma?"

A pause then ensued and I spent the next few minutes listening to my mother chain smoke. "Oh, I might as well tell you," she said after forever. "She's doing phone sex," she blurted out.

"What, she's using phone sex?" I was confused. Penny had lost money by paying men to moan for her over the telephone?

"No, Eve, she's working." My mother's tears could be heard over the line as she tried her best to hold them back.

"Penny has a one-nine-hundred-number?" I clarified.

"Yes," Mom said solemnly.

This was it. Penny had been a professional deviant and fuck-up for most of her life and now she was following suit. Telephone prostitution was now the perfect addition to her life thus far.

"Hmm," was all I could muster as a response.

"Maybe you should talk to her," my mother suggested.

Long pause. Painful pause in fact. I played the scene in my mind. I would phone Penny and she would hang up on me. I would phone my mother back and let her know the reality of my relationship with my sister. This would break my mother's heart yet again and she may even confront Penny with this. If so Penny would burst into rage, claiming that Mom and Dad loved me more and the age-old argument would ensue. My parents would then be forbidden to see Ahava, Penny's daughter, ever again, and my sister's hate for me would grow deeper, if at all possible. One week later Penny would emerge from her madness and phone my parents to apologize, asking them to baby-sit and order, as it were, would be restored. Such was the wrath of Penny and such was her hold on my parents and her own sanity.

"Mom, Penny isn't speaking to me. I don't think it's a good idea."

"She'll talk to you." Denial is quite useful in a family such as ours.

"No," I sighed, "she's hung up on me every time I've called since the whole car incident." My parents bought Penny a car for her thirtieth birthday. Penny sold the damn thing the following year to pay off Elliot's drug dealer. She had often blamed Elliot for her deviant behavior. Now that he was no longer in the sickening picture she was running out of excuses. Without Elliot to absorb the brunt of the blame, Penny's own behavior was now being called into question. The truth was that Penny was as sick as her once *loving* and always fucked-up husband. After the car went up Elliot's nose, so to speak, I had a horrible fight with my prize sibling in which I let her know she could no longer live in Elliot's shadow. Thereafter began a yelling match where I was told I would never see my niece again. Incidentally, when I do visit my family, my offerings to baby-sit Ahava are never turned down. Make no mistake, Penny hates me, but if she needs something from me, I am momentarily her best friend.

"Oh," Mom said quietly.

"But," I couldn't bear it, "I'll try again," I resolved.

"Thank you, sweetie," Mom said, sucking on what must have been her forth cigarette in five minutes.

After a few inquiries about my father, whom I was told was at brunch with his buddies, and warm wishes from my mother to Jack, I hung up the phone. Calling my sister would be brief so I thought it best to get it done quickly.

I lifted the receiver again and dialed her number. After three rings Penny picked up the phone. Visions of her moaning for old men over the very same telephone flashed in my mind.

"Hello?" she answered. *What are you wearing big boy?* I half expected some sort of seedy greeting.

"Penny, it's Eve," I said, bracing for her name-calling.

"Eve," she paused, I almost expected her to be civil. I could hear her inhale and exhale at her cigarette, "go to hell." She yelled into the phone true to form and slammed down the receiver.

12:00 P.M.

Brunch would now officially be lunch as Jack returned from the gym and finished his shower. I was now on my second pot of coffee from room service and had since spoken to my mother twice since my phone call with Penny. The first time was to let her know my actions weren't very helpful. My mother resigned herself to my ill-fated effort and promised not to bring it up with Penny.

My second phone call was intended for my father.

"Ma, put Daddy on the phone," I asked her when she picked up.

"Here he is, just in from brunch with the boys," she said handing him the receiver. I heard her announce me to my Dad in her usual tone. For the first time that day she was not smoking.

My mother hated to smoke around my father. She thought it wasn't good for him, given that he had cancer. This was the irony that was my mother. She hated to smoke in front of a dying man, lest it contribute to the already rampant cancer in his system. My father often joked that it may speed up the process. His loving wife failed to see the humor in these statements.

"Hi, Daddy." I truly loved my father. He was the sanity amongst the madness in this family. The only animosity I harbored towards him was that he was dying and leaving me alone with these two lunatics.

"Sweetheart! How's New York?" I could tell he was smiling.

My father had one of those voices that always sounded like laughter.

"Wonderful, Daddy. How are things there?"

"The usual. Your mother is up to a pack a day and your sister is getting paid money to talk dirty to men." He was so matter of fact.

"So I hear."

"Let's not talk about her, Eve. She's crazy. I've been dealing with this all week, your mother isn't sleeping. Tell me, how's Jack?" My father had the uncanny way of changing the subject and being dramatic all in the same sentence

"Jack is great, Daddy. He's just in the shower. How are you feeling?"

"Same. I'm up to sixty milligrams a day on the morphine and Frank put me on a new medication called *Gabba-* something. He keeps telling me I'm a miracle." He started to laugh, "I don't know, Eve-ee, I don't feel like a miracle. What have you done in New York so far?" I could tell he didn't want to talk about his illness right now.

"I went for drinks with Nina and Theo last night," I told him.

"Oh, how's Nina?" My father loved Nina.

"She's great, Daddy. She's working hard and she loves her job." I smiled.

"And Theo?" he asked.

"He's great. He just got back from Europe. We had dinner last night at this amazing restaurant," I said.

"Good. Ask Jack how do I get my e-mail working again. I just put Microsoft Office 2000 on the computer and I can't open any of my e-mails."

"I'll let him know," I said. Jack was my father's computer therapist. Jack had built a basic computer for Daddy four years ago. With all of the upgrades and advancements in computers, my father's homemade hard-drive had become the technological equivalent a very large calculator. He was, however, still using it to download everything from movies to Frank Sinatra albums. After two months of constant computer crashes and thousands of phone calls to Jack for advice, I bought my father a new computer. I did, however, make the mistake of telling him of my impending purchase and he then spent the next week phoning me at all hours with new ideas about what kind of computer he wanted. After the third Sunday morning phone call before the hour of seven, I sent my father a check and wished him happy shopping. Now, after a series of phone calls to the online computer sales company, my father was blessed with the biggest, baddest piece of desktop technology that money could buy. The only problem was he couldn't figure out how to work the damn thing.

"Eve, I'm going to lie down. Call tomorrow, okay?" my father insisted.

"Sure, Daddy. Love you."

"Love you too, sweetheart." And with that, he was gone.

Chapter 24

Jack's perspective on the world continues to amaze me. My conversations with my mother had undeniably shaken me. I thought I had reached a point where anything Penny did was too typical to cause me mental disturbance. Unfortunately I was wrong. Penny continued to chip away at my emotional safety as she had done for the past twenty years. I was now at the point where there wasn't any love left. People would say, *"Well you love her because she's your sister, you just don't like her."*

I was well beyond that. I neither loved nor liked Penny. At times like these I had a twisted fantasy that she would disappear and leave me with custody of my niece, whom I would raise without the risk of Penny and Elliot's destructive clutches.

Regardless of what argument had transpired, Jack would always wash away the tears, so to speak. He had an uncanny way of making me laugh at the madness and move on. He did not in any way minimize these moments. Rather, he put them in their proper place. Penny was a mad woman. To succumb to her insanity was to let her affect your world. To triumph was to continue life as planned.

And so, on Jack's insistence we went to lunch as planned. Lunch was followed by a visit to the Guggenheim museum. Walking up the beehive, eyes upward, mouth open, restored my soul. If there was any shred of evil left in me it was banished with a trip down Fifth Avenue, where I convinced my husband he needed to buy me a silver Tiffany's charm bracelet.

Jack, like many men, had no idea about gifts. I often thought there should be a manual for men called *Standard Procedure*. In it should be a list of occasions that can't be forgotten. Birthdays, anniversaries, first days at work, special achievements and certain moments in a woman's menstrual cycle all warrant special gifts. Be it flowers, jewelry, or god-forbid appliances, men need a guide to the "standard procedures" in a relationship. Jack was a prince but he was oblivious to the gift giving process. I usually bought my own birthday presents or he took me along when shopping. I had once made him a list of foolproof gifts and he worked off that for a while. Now in desperate need of a new list, he was easily persuaded into buying me the charm bracelet as a Happy-Your-Sister-Is-Really-Fucked-Up-Day present.

After walking for the rest of the day, in the true spirit of a New York tourist we headed back to the hotel. We were having dinner with Nina as guests at her restaurant and then going dancing with her, Theo, and Jennifer. Having Jennifer join us somehow brought me comfort. It somehow legitimized Theo in front of Jack. It was as though I was showing my husband that Theo was a normal loving man in a normal relationship and worthy of Jack's approval. I had met Jennifer twice before on trips to New York. Her relationship with Theo was far from loving. She was miserable and she made him miserable. However, considering this was likely to be Theo's next bride, I was hell-bent on forming an alternate opinion. Perhaps with other people around I may see a side of Jennifer that had escaped me thus far.

Back at the hotel I poured myself a bath and spent ten minutes lying in the apricot scented bubbles before shaving my legs and joining Jack for a nap. Vacations and weekends were always occasions for mid-day napping. No matter what we had done during the day, a vacation prompted an hour or two of sleeping in the middle of the day. Our daily lives never permitted this kind of behavior but we took full advantage of the opportunity to stray from a normal routine. I snuggled up to Jack, smelling clean and fruity and wrapped in a plush white robe.

"Good day?" Jack asked.

"Hmmm," I said smiling into sleep.

7:30 P.M.

The bedside table alarm went off letting us know we had half an hour to get ready before we had to be at Nina's restaurant. We rushed, knowing full well we'd be late. Nina had known me long enough to expect me to arrive fifteen minutes after a given time. I helped Jack pick out an outfit and slipped into my usual little black dress. Makeup in place, hair in a ponytail and husband in check we headed downstairs to fetch a cab to the restaurant.

"Dance with me later?" Jack asked in the elevator.

"Sure thing, baby." I smiled at him.

The elevator doors opened and we were on our way.

Nina greeted us at the door to Les Villages. From her dress I knew she would not be working tonight. Nina was one of the most striking women I had ever seen. She was statuesque almost to a fault. Her massive mane of hair was tied back into a knot hiding its true form. Nina had a great figure. This was pure genetics at work. She was a pastry chef, for god's sake. She smoked a pack a day and thought a treadmill was a torture device. I had seen Nina do aerobics once and it was not pretty. As such she was left with a size eight frame on a six-foot tall body and legs that went up to her neck. Garbage bags looked good on this woman. It would have been infuriating but I loved her too much to care. Tonight Nina was wearing a black sheath dress with a ragged hem and a strategic hole cut just below the neckline. It was punk meets pretty and had the desired effect. Her long legs were further accentuated by a pair of black stiletto boots. Nina's style was all her own.

Jack and Nina exchanged their usual friendly embrace. I loved watching them together. Nina towered over him and they communicated in a way that made them more like loving siblings and less like friends by marriage.

"I'm going to eat with you," she said, kissing both my cheeks.

"Perfect." Jack smiled as Nina looped her arm in his and showed us to our table.

"Great restaurant, Nina," Jack said looking around the room. Our table was a corner booth covered in red velvet. Nina slid in first, adjusting her outfit and Jack and I followed suit.

"So," Jack smiled once we were all in place, "how's life? Tell me about this amazing new job. Eve tells me you are on your way to becoming famous."

Nina shot me a look before she began to hail us with tales of the culinary world. She had worked for a few smaller restaurants on the upper west side and had always been unfulfilled. This was followed by several jobs in catering before she met Antoine, the owner and head chef of Les Village. Antoine was really Tony Marconi, an Italian-Irish Catholic from the Bronx who fled his split heritage for the French countryside where he trained for five years to be a chef. Tony returned to Manhattan as Antoine Marcone, a celebrated French Chef with serious financial backing. He opened Les Village eight years ago. Having survived that long in the food world in New York allowed him to not only be a celebrity, but also to get what he wanted. Antoine's last pastry chef was substandard as Nina explained. Really good pastry chefs were difficult to find. It was as though many felt that dessert was an afterthought and not a real part of the meal. Antoine Marcone was a victim of this plague in the culinary world. He was unhappy with the standard of crème Brule at his flourishing Les Villages and was constantly looking for a solution. Two years ago it came in the form of a charity auction for breast cancer catered by A La Carte, Nina's fourth place of employment after she left the restaurant world. One taste of Nina's Ganache and homemade ice cream and Tony Marconi was in love. He hired Nina on the spot. After three months of phone calls and negotiation, she took the job.

Now she ran the pastry department and was developing a reputation for being a goddess with ice cream. Nina was achieving recognition in the most difficult of positions, as a woman in a man's world.

As our chef's tasting dinner began to arrive, Nina kept us laughing with stories from the kitchen. The lobster bisque was accompanied by Nina's stories of life at the Culinary Institute. She kept us intrigued and laughing well into the main course. As the rosemary and almond encrusted rack of lamb arrived, Nina turned her attentions to Jack.

"So, geek boy, Eve tells me you are taking the computer world by storm."

"Work is going well, Nina," Jack said humbly. "This lamb is amazing," he said in an attempt to change the subject. Jack was very private, even with those close to him.

"Yeah, yeah." Nina wasn't being fooled. "Tell me what you do," she demanded.

Jack spent the rest of the main course talking about his current contract to do the special effects for a BMW commercial. His face and voice came alive as he talked about the work he was doing. He had us focused on his stories of different commercials and movie sequences his firm had done. Jack's dream was to work on a movie in a significant way. He could see himself creating animation sequences for the big screen.

We spent the rest of the meal talking about New York and all there was to see and do. Nina left the table briefly after the main course was taken away to check on her dessert creations waiting in the back. She emerged a few moments later with a bottle of champagne and three glasses. Behind her was a waiter carrying a tray of Nina's specialties. The tray was a work of art. Each pastry was perfectly displayed as though hours of deliberation went into the placement of each piece.

Nina opened the bottle of bubbly with ceremonial ease. She poured equal amounts into each glass and placed the bottle into an ice bucket before returning to her place in the velvet booth. She began to explain the name and contents of each pastry on the tray when Antoine himself emerged from the kitchen. He stopped the waiter on the way, motioning him to bring a glass and a chair to our table. Nina introduced us to the famous chef and he went so far as to kiss my hand. I couldn't help but chuckle, thinking that Tony had come a long way from his home across the bridge.

Antoine sat at the head of our table, glass of champagne in hand and raised his glass in a toast to Nina. We all joined in and Jack began the conversation by complimenting our host on his wonderful meal.

"You like?" Antoine asked. I thought I even sensed a hint of a French accent.

"It was wonderful," I gushed, the wine and the food now taking their full effect. Good food, like good wine, always made me lose my head just enough to give me a delightful buzz.

Nina's dessert tray was outstanding. She had a way of making each pastry take you through a journey of tastes. It was an experience I hadn't ever had. I loved the whole scene. There I was with the famous of New York's culinary world sharing in the delights of my best friend's creation. I was drunk on wine and high on life. It was magical.

11:45 P.M.

We thanked Antoine one last time and headed to the street to hail a cab. Nina called Theo's cell phone and told him to meet us at the Iguana, a chic dance bar in midtown. As Nina had done an amazing six-tiered cake for the club's opening, we were assured a VIP treatment. The cab stopped in front of the restaurant's blue-green facade. Hanging from the roof above the doorway was a massive glass iguana, which I was told was imported from Italy and worth an extraordinary amount of money.

Midnight

The club was alive with the "beautiful people". This was New York's glamorous playground. Women towering in stilettos and strapped sandals on long perfect legs made smoking look good. Men smelling of good cologne, sex, and money stood confidently throughout the place drinking vodka straight and surveying the territory. Nina kissed the man at the door on both cheeks as though he were president of her fan club. He called for Tina, a tall, beautiful aspiring actress, to show us into the VIP room. She took our drink orders with vacant eyes and told us she would send Theo and Jennifer in when they arrived.

Moments later Tina reappeared with Jennifer and Theo behind her. I stood up to greet Jennifer and she kissed the air around both my cheeks. *Mistake number one.* After introducing her to both Jack and Nina, she repeated the air kissing on both of them. *Mistakes two and three.* Clearly I was not Jennifer's biggest fan. She was, as Theo had insisted, a beautiful and intelligent woman. But she was also closed minded and affected. My previous meetings with Jennifer had been spent with her pumping me for information on Theo and insisting that she wasn't threatened by my friendship with *her man.* In retrospect her position was laughable and I shouldn't be angered. After all she was one of Theo's transitory companions. It would only be a matter of time before he married her, fell out of love with her, and started looking around. I should have just been happy for Theo that he had companionship. But sitting in front of Jennifer in her Versace knock off dress with her air kissing my husband when she didn't know him from Adam and I was about to lose my supper. Theo's twisted sense of monogamous relationships was quickly growing stale.

"This place is interesting," Jennifer said, looking around.

"Hmmm," Jack responded smiling.

Theo looked over in my direction and raised an eyebrow. I smiled back at him as the source of my new vocabulary had been revealed.

"So that's where you got that from?" he confirmed.

"Hmmm," I smiled.

"May I dance with your wife?" Theo asked Jack after our drinks had arrived.

"You'll have to clear that with her." He smiled over in my direction.

"Well, doc?" He motioned to me.

I stood up and walked him over to the dance floor. The music was a mixture of acid jazz with a bit of blues beat. Theo was a good dancer and I was able to keep up with him and the music, despite my slightly impaired state.

"Hey," Theo yelled over the music, "how was dinner?"

"Amazing," I responded, "Nina is a celebrity!" I laughed.

"So, what do think of Jennifer?" he asked.

"Theo, I've met her before," I said over the music.

"I know, but it's been a while."

"Well, I promise to talk to her tonight and get to know her better," I pledged.

We continued dancing and Theo pulled me close.

"Be nice, Eve," he whispered in my ear.

"Aren't I always?" I said, pulling away from him looking into his eyes. He kissed my cheek and we returned to the table where I could see we had arrived midway through the *get to know you* session that was playing out between Jack, Jennifer, and Nina.

"I'm a pastry chef," Nina was saying as I sat back down in my seat.

"Sounds interesting," Jennifer said. In fact she sounded bored.

"How's work?" I asked Jennifer.

"Busy," she replied, taking a sip of her white wine.

"What is it you do?" Jack asked her.

"I'm an investment banker. I work in the same building as Theo," she informed us.

"That sounds pretty intense," Nina said lighting a cigarette.

"It is. But I can handle it. Oh," she said looking over at Nina, "would you mind smoking over by the bar? I'm allergic."

Nina smiled and politely picked up her cigarettes and made her way over to the bar. She took a deep puff of the current cigarette and asked me to join her in her exile. Nina was the picture of grace, but I could tell it was only her love for me that prevented her from "decking the scrawny bitch". I looked over at Theo who was visibly embarrassed and Jennifer who was visibly victorious. My husband smiled at me almost enjoying the scene.

"I'll hold down the fort here, love." Jack winked.

I maintained my drunken smile long enough to make it over to the bar, where, out of sight and sound of Jennifer and the rest, Nina unleashed the wrath of hell.

"Why would a man that nice choose to spend time with such a skanky bitch?" she was being relatively passive.

"He's lonely," I said, repeating Theo' s own defense.

"Lonely my ass. She makes me ashamed to be a woman. *I'm allergic?*" she mimicked Jennifer. "For fuck's sake we're in a bar!" Nina said inhaling deeply.

I ordered each of us another drink and Nina smoked away.

"She's evil," Nina resolved after a long pause.

"Not evil," I corrected, "self-centered and shallow, yes, but evil is beyond her.

"Oh…," said Nina turning towards me, "so we don't like Theo's choice of mate?" Nina confirmed.

"No," I confessed.

"And why not?" she was being coy.

"She's his coaster."

"His what?" she cringed her nose and exhaled before looking straight at me.

"His coaster," I repeated. "He's coasting and she's there right along with him. She's not the love of his life, she's not even the like of his life. He's bored and she's here and it's easy." I continued, "Come on Nina, it's the teenage love mentality. Don't you remember high school? Didn't you just want someone in your life and it didn't really matter if you really liked them or not? Well this is that feeling in a thirty something man." I had summed it up in a few sentences.

Our drinks arrived and Nina clinked her martini glass to mine. She smiled at me and took another drag of her cigarette.

"Sure love you, Eve," she said looking straight into my face.

"Sure love you," I replied.

There we sat, two women in solidarity against the less fortunate of our species. There on those barstools, amidst the Italian glassware and outrageous design, we drank martinis with the beautiful people. Nina smoked her second cigarette in exile in defiance of the Jennifers of the world. I sat next to her, alcohol and love oozing from every pore. I not only adored this woman, I admired her, not in spite of her smoking and her temper and her very long legs. No, in the true spirit of sisterhood, I loved her so deeply because of all of those things.

1:30 A.M.

We returned to the table after Nina's third and final cigarette, Theo and Jack were talking computers and Jennifer was watching people dance.

"Hey," I said as we returned to the table, "miss us?"

Jack smiled and kissed me on the cheek as I sat down next to him. He and Theo returned to their conversation which left me to "be nice" to Jennifer.

"So, Jennifer," I began, "are you planning on taking a holiday soon?" I asked. Nina looked at me as though I'd asked the stupidest of questions and I returned her a glance to reveal my helplessness in the situation.

She turned to me and smiled, "We may go to visit my folks for Thanksgiving next month."

"Where do they live?" this was painful.

"Connecticut."

"I've never been," I said. "What's it like?"

"Well it's a whole state you know, so each part of it is very different." *Thanks for the geography lesson, sweetheart.*

I just smiled and nodded my head. Nina got up invariably for another cigarette. I was beginning to think she was quite happy to have to smoke at the bar.

"Theo says you're a doctor," she began.

"Yes," I replied.

"What exactly do you do?" there was almost a hint of vinegar in her voice. Perhaps I was imagining it because I didn't really like her. It's funny how when you don't like someone, everything they do has a toast of distaste. They could cure world hunger and you would fault them for paying far too much attention to one particular cause.

"Well I'm in my last year of an Intensive Care fellowship," I said.

"What's a fellowship?" a common question.

"After Medical School I did a residency in Internal Medicine for three years. The ICU fellowship is a two year subspecialty training program."

"What are you going to do when you're done?" she asked.

"Hopefully practice."

"Where?" she asked.

"I'm not sure. I'll apply both in Canada and the United States and see what happens," I confessed.

Yes the *brain drain* from Canada to the United States had lured me as well. It was shameful to admit one's intentions to move southward. The move always implied that money was the only important thing. Canada's medical system had done too good a job at convincing all of us that socialized medicine was the only place to practice. Below the border we would be plagued with HMO's and insurance companies. We would be paralyzed in our medical practices by administrative nightmares and cost efficiency experts. Here in Canada, we were better trained, or so we were told, and would be free to order an MRI whenever we wanted one. We just had to wait six months for it. It was in the America where diagnostic tests flowed freely, where hospitals were hotels and patients sued their doctors. These tales were told like bedtime stories in the hopes of keeping us here. Don't get me wrong, I would love to stay in Canada; it was my home. I may move south for a time but I always knew I'd come back north to live out the rest of my life. It wasn't because I fear the American medical system as I had been taught to fear. No it was simple, I liked Canada. I knew what to expect there and for all of its vice and virtue, I couldn't see my life carrying on elsewhere. The problem was that in a country so hungry for physicians, I needed to be an academic in order to work in a major hospital. All large cities had university-affiliated hospitals. In order to work in such a place I had to have an academic background. This meant being more educated than the people hiring me. This meant that now twelve years of medical training needed 'an edge'. This meant I needed a masters degree in epidemiology or medical education or biostatistics. They wanted research in addition to my years of study. I was thirty and tired of being in school. I'd rather move to a smaller center in Canada or even, God forbid, the United States, than spend a further two years in academic pursuits.

I trained with several people who took their brass ring and went south for money, work, and freedom. I also knew many who stayed above the border and went into private practice or continued in academics. The former was frightening, but I couldn't deny its intrigue. The money southward was three times that in Canada. There was a multitude of work for Canadian trained doctors and I need not think about any more school. But, true to the stories of my training, I feared the HMO's like a child fears the boogey man. And so the *brain drain* as it has been called from Canada to the United States raged on and I would likely follow suit.

I tried to explain some of this to Jennifer. Theo and Jack broke away from their conversation and began to listen to me. Jennifer looked bored.

"So are you two going to move south?" Theo looked excited.

"We don't know," I answered, "but it would be an opportunity for both of us."

"We probably will. We'll see what happens after Eve finishes her fellowship," Jack volunteered.

Jennifer looked around one last time and turned to Theo.

"We should be going." She smiled, "I have an early day tomorrow." It was Friday night. Unless she was working on a Saturday she was making excuses to get the hell out of here.

Nina returned from her cigarettes to see Jennifer stand up and Theo follow. "Leaving?" Nina asked.

"I have an early day tomorrow," Jennifer said.

"Tomorrow's Saturday," Nina piped in. God love that bitch

"It's a full day for me," she said, looking down at us.

"Well it was nice meeting you, Jennifer." Nina walked over and put out her hand.

Jennifer returned the sentiment. Nina then sat down at the table, pulled out her cigarettes and lit up victoriously.

Jack and I stood up to say our goodbyes. Jack and Theo exchanged niceties while Jennifer kissed the air around both my cheeks. She did the same to Jack and then turned to Theo to let him know she'd wait outside while we said our goodbyes. Once Jennifer was out of earshot I turned to Theo.

"I don't think she likes us," I said.

"We had a fight. She's pissed at me and she's taking it out on you."

"Good to know," I said.

"Sorry about the smoking thing, Nina," Theo said apologetically in her direction.

"No big deal, Theo." Nina smiled, puffing away.

Theo put his arms around me in a moment of affection touched with sorrow. I could hear him sigh as his body relaxed in my embrace.

"I'll call you in the morning," was all he said.

"Thanks for the visit," I said.

He shook Jacks hand sincerely and let him know how nice it was to spend time together. And then he did something that was so very "Theo". He turned back to me, grabbed me by the shoulders and mockingly kissed the air around both my cheeks. Then winking at me as I fell into laughter, he turned and headed for the door.

Chapter 25

Sunday, 3:26 PM

Jack lay unconscious in the seat next to me. I had given him a Valium the minute the plane had begun to move. He was now snoring soundly, oblivious to any future turbulence. I sat next to him with a *Wallpaper* magazine in my lap, passing the time until the in flight movie began. Unlike Jack, I loved plane rides. I love the whole ceremony that is associated with them. They force me to take time. I sit in an enclosed box with whatever is before me and I must either relax or work or sleep as the hours play out at 30,000 feet above the earth.

We spent our last days in New York walking its streets and falling in love; both with the city and with one another. Theo took us on a walking tour of the Lower East Side sans Jennifer. Theo is great on walking tours. He comes alive amidst the history and the commotion. He has taken official tours hundreds of times and now goes on his own. I've been a guest on several of them in the past. They only serve to remind me why I love him. He has his faults as we all do. He will berate himself in an instant to the point where you want to smack him, but get him on a walking tour and he's confidant as hell. His selfishness vanishes there in the streets and he comes alive with wonder. I see Theo in these moments and he the man, no, the boy of his youth. He lacks the practicality and the chains of logic that have pushed him into adulthood. I'm not sure if it was real or a figment of my interpretation but I recall Theo being so much more hopeful when we were younger. Youth by its very nature breeds optimism but I am quite sure he saw the world differently then. Years later there is a sadness about him that is more than just a function of years passed by. There is a sense of sorrow within him. Although I cannot completely identify the nature of this sadness, it is as constant a fixture as the grey in his hair. Theo is the man I have adored since my youth. He is the keeper of my first crush and now the brother I have adopted. But he is also the man who has somehow stolen a part of the self he once was and locked it away. Perhaps this upsets me more than I will let on. Perhaps this is my own arrogance for wanting the world to exist on my terms. I don't know.

I do know that when this man takes me through the streets of the city he himself adores, he becomes whole again. It's as though he reaches deep within himself and for several hours repairs a lost and wounded soul. It was the perfect way to spend the day.

And now reality sets in and I realize that I have to be back at work tomorrow morning. Gone will be the glamour and the sense of freedom and I miss it already. Perhaps that is why Medicine is so unrelenting. In the face of the days before me I will long for the play of the past few days. Maybe I need to "work hard in order to play hard." Really, I think that philosophy is bullshit. Life should be a balance and not a mixture of extremes. One can't be happy with a life of so many luxuries mixed with sorrow and longing. That is depression mentality and it only goes so far before madness and greed set in.

No, life should be filled with love and loss, respect and self-loathing, needs, and wants. Each should have and know its own place. Each should bring balance to one's overall world.

As I sit on this plane, bound for a world I am not so sure I want anymore, I realize my life is far from balanced. My work serves as my great source of disdain. I have such rage and bitterness inside for a world which always seems to leave me cold. Yet my life outside of this seems so full. It spills over with people and places who never fail to love me with a passion that one day may banish away all the demons.

I don't know what I will do with all of this. It may, like so many before me, leave me unfulfilled in a cold bed someday having abandoned all that was once sacred to me. I hope not.

It may cause me to one day throw off the conventions of the work laid out before me and find something else to do with my life. This is so much more difficult than it sounds. I may never leave Medicine. Why should I? I am good at what I do. I may be different from those before me but that's no reason to let them drive me out. Besides I have invested so much in these past few years that to walk away may very well break my heart. In some ways you might say that I'm stuck. I'm caught between the life I want and the life I see for myself and I am as yet so powerless to make something happen. I am so fearful it will happen for me.

But amidst the heartbreak and the fear of uncertainty lies a life that for all of its faults and misgivings is better than one might hope for. There is the unknown and the lack of fulfillment but there is also hope. There is hope that one day the sorrows of yesterday will drift further into the past and be forgotten. One day this life will have meaning. One day I will throw off these chains and be the person I was destined to be. With some soul commitment, this life will be better than it ever was meant to be. It will be more than before.

But despite my complaints and my feelings of failure I must remind myself daily that, yes, above all, life is good.